J 741.5 BET

Betty and Veronica in The last word.

the Archie® DIGEST LIBRARY

Betty AND Veronica®

– in –

The Last Word

Spotlight

visit us at
www.abdopublishing.com

Exclusive Spotlight library bound edition published in 2007 by Spotlight, a division of ABDO Publishing Group, Edina, Minnesota. Spotlight produces high quality reinforced library bound editions for schools and libraries. Published by agreement with Archie Comic Publications, Inc.

Library of Congress Cataloging-in-Publication Data

Betty and Veronica in The last word / edited by Nelson Ribeiro & Victor Gorelick. -- Library bound ed.
p. cm. -- (The Archie digest library)
Revision of issue 122 (Sept. 2001) of Betty and Veronica digest magazine.
ISBN-13: 978-1-59961-266-9
ISBN-10: 1-59961-266-6
1. Graphic novels. I. Ribeiro, Nelson. II. Gorelick, Victor. III. Betty and Veronica digest magazine. 122. IV. Title: Last word.

PN6728.A72B487 2007
741.5'973--dc22

2006050275

Spotlight

All Spotlight books are reinforced library binding
and manufactured in the United States of America.

Contents

Betty and Veronica®

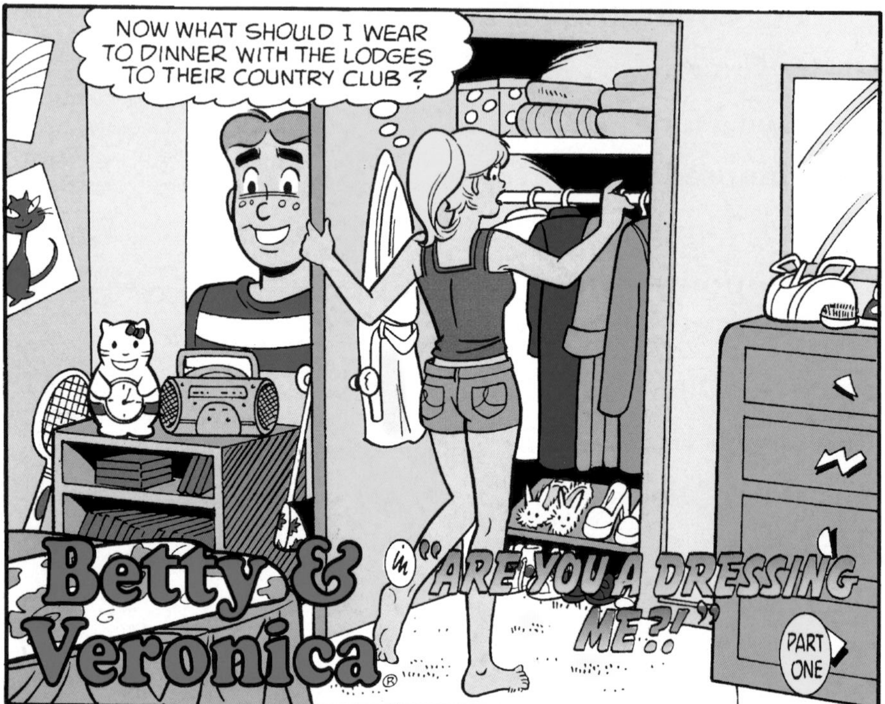
NOW WHAT SHOULD I WEAR TO DINNER WITH THE LODGES TO THEIR COUNTRY CLUB?
Betty & Veronica®
in "ARE YOU A DRESSING ME?!"
PART ONE

SCRIPT & PENCILS: HOLLY G! INKS: JOHN COSTANZA
COLORS: BARRY GROSSMAN LETTERS: BILL YOSHIDA
EDITORS: NELSON RIBEIRO & VICTOR GORELICK EDITOR-IN-CHIEF: RICHARD GOLDWATER

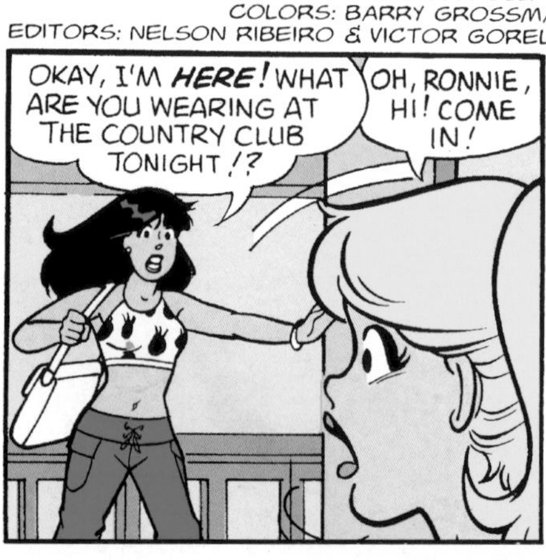
OKAY, I'M ***HERE***! WHAT ARE YOU WEARING AT THE COUNTRY CLUB TONIGHT!?
OH, RONNIE, HI! COME IN!

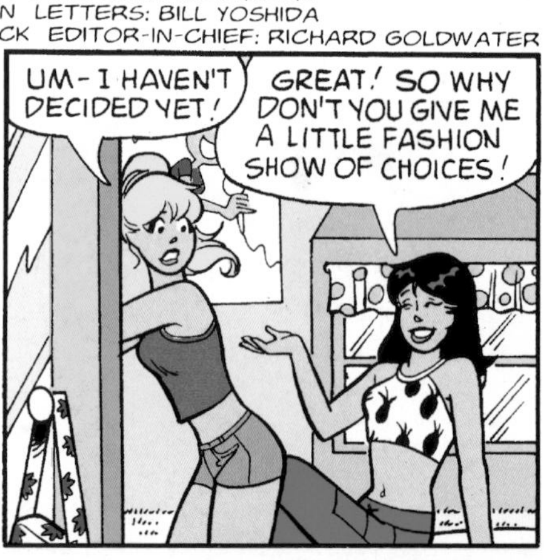
UM- I HAVEN'T DECIDED YET!
GREAT! SO WHY DON'T YOU GIVE ME A LITTLE FASHION SHOW OF CHOICES!

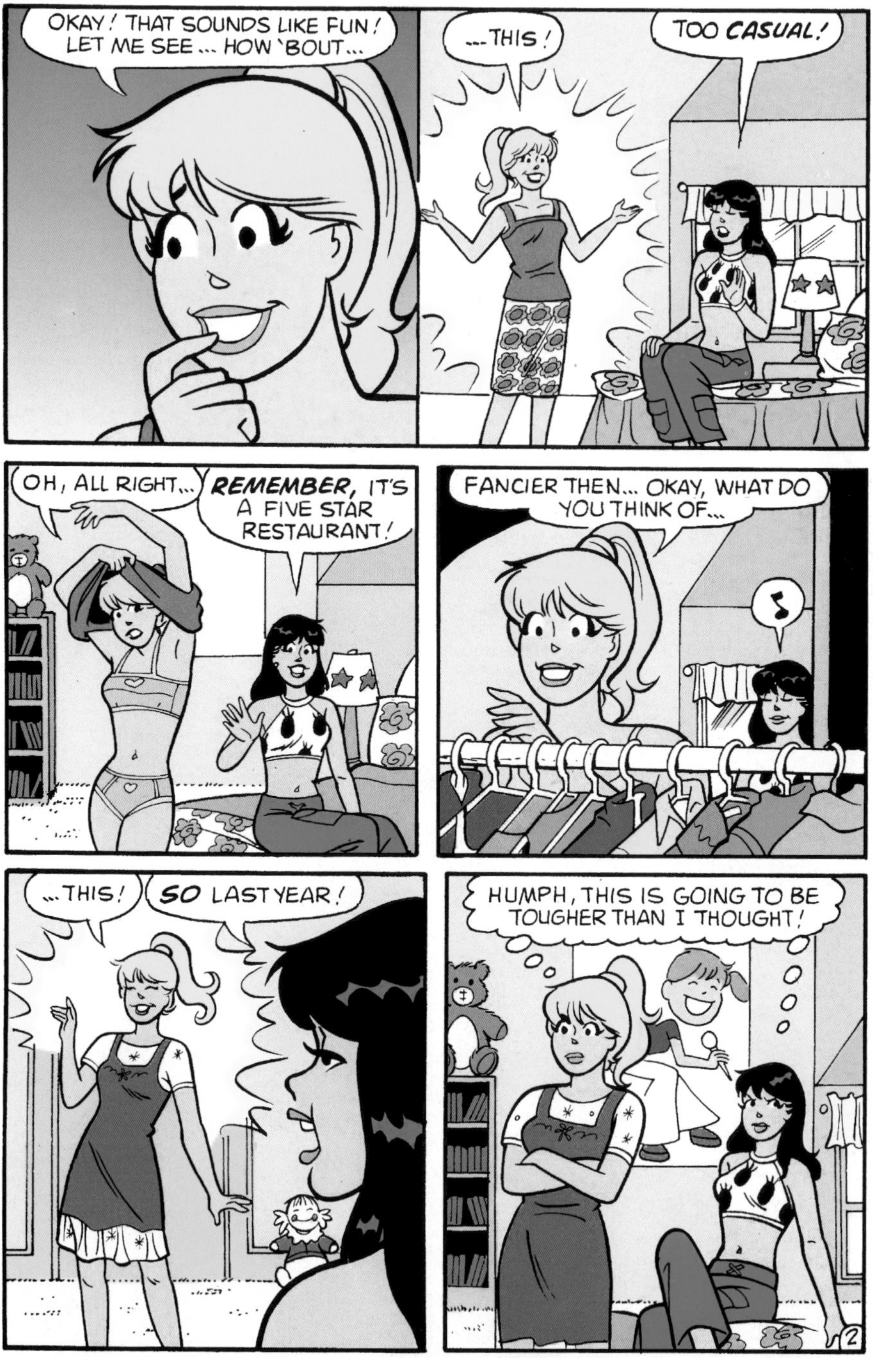
OKAY! THAT SOUNDS LIKE FUN! LET ME SEE... HOW 'BOUT...
...THIS!
TOO *CASUAL*!
OH, ALL RIGHT...
REMEMBER, IT'S A FIVE STAR RESTAURANT!
FANCIER THEN... OKAY, WHAT DO YOU THINK OF...
...THIS!
SO LAST YEAR!
HUMPH, THIS IS GOING TO BE TOUGHER THAN I THOUGHT!
2

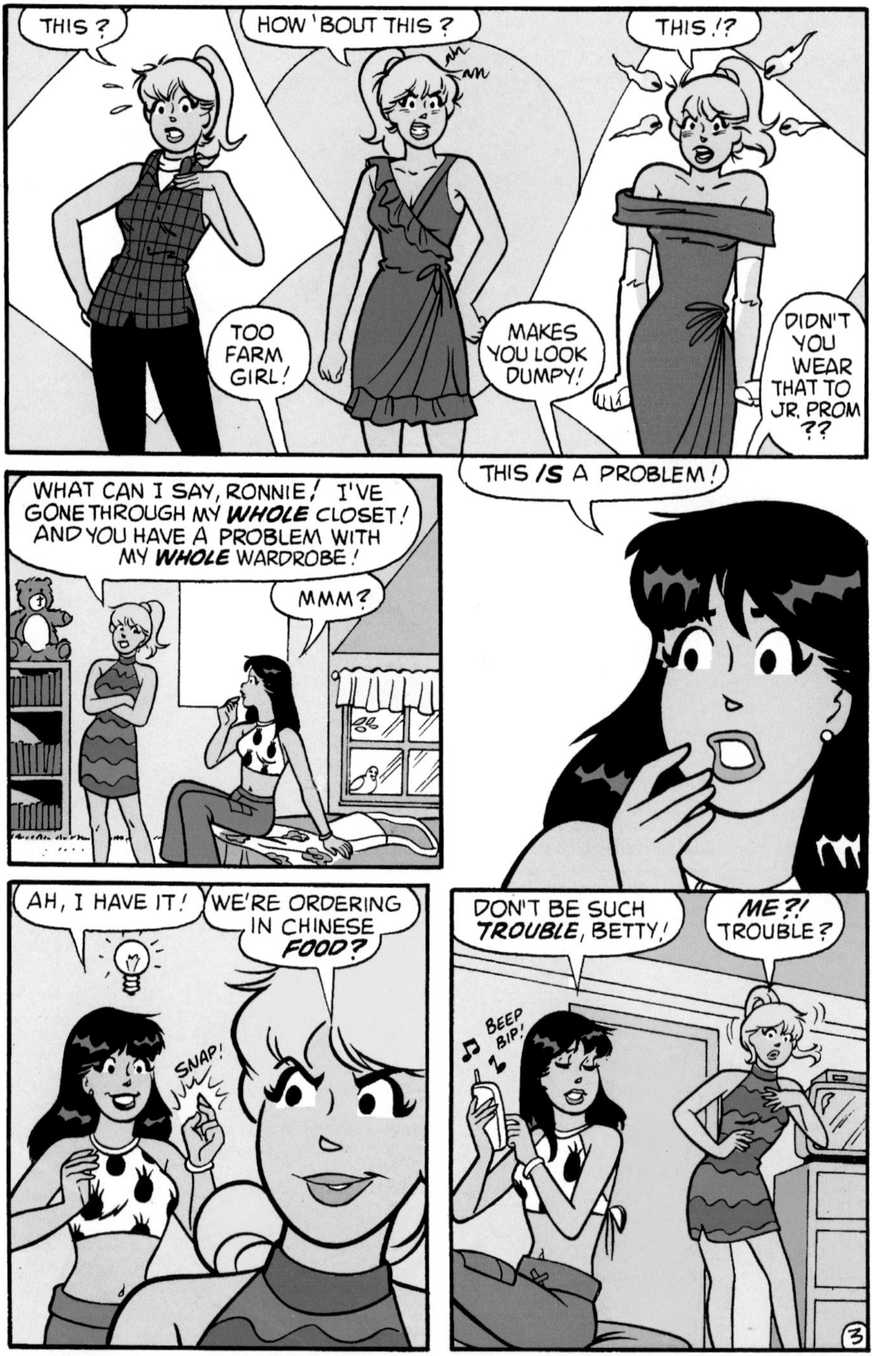
THIS ?
TOO FARM GIRL!
HOW 'BOUT THIS ?
MAKES YOU LOOK DUMPY!
THIS !?
DIDN'T YOU WEAR THAT TO JR. PROM ??
WHAT CAN I SAY, RONNIE! I'VE GONE THROUGH MY WHOLE CLOSET! AND YOU HAVE A PROBLEM WITH MY WHOLE WARDROBE!
MMM?
THIS IS A PROBLEM!
AH, I HAVE IT!
SNAP!
WE'RE ORDERING IN CHINESE FOOD?
DON'T BE SUCH TROUBLE, BETTY!
BEEP BIP!
ME?! TROUBLE?
3

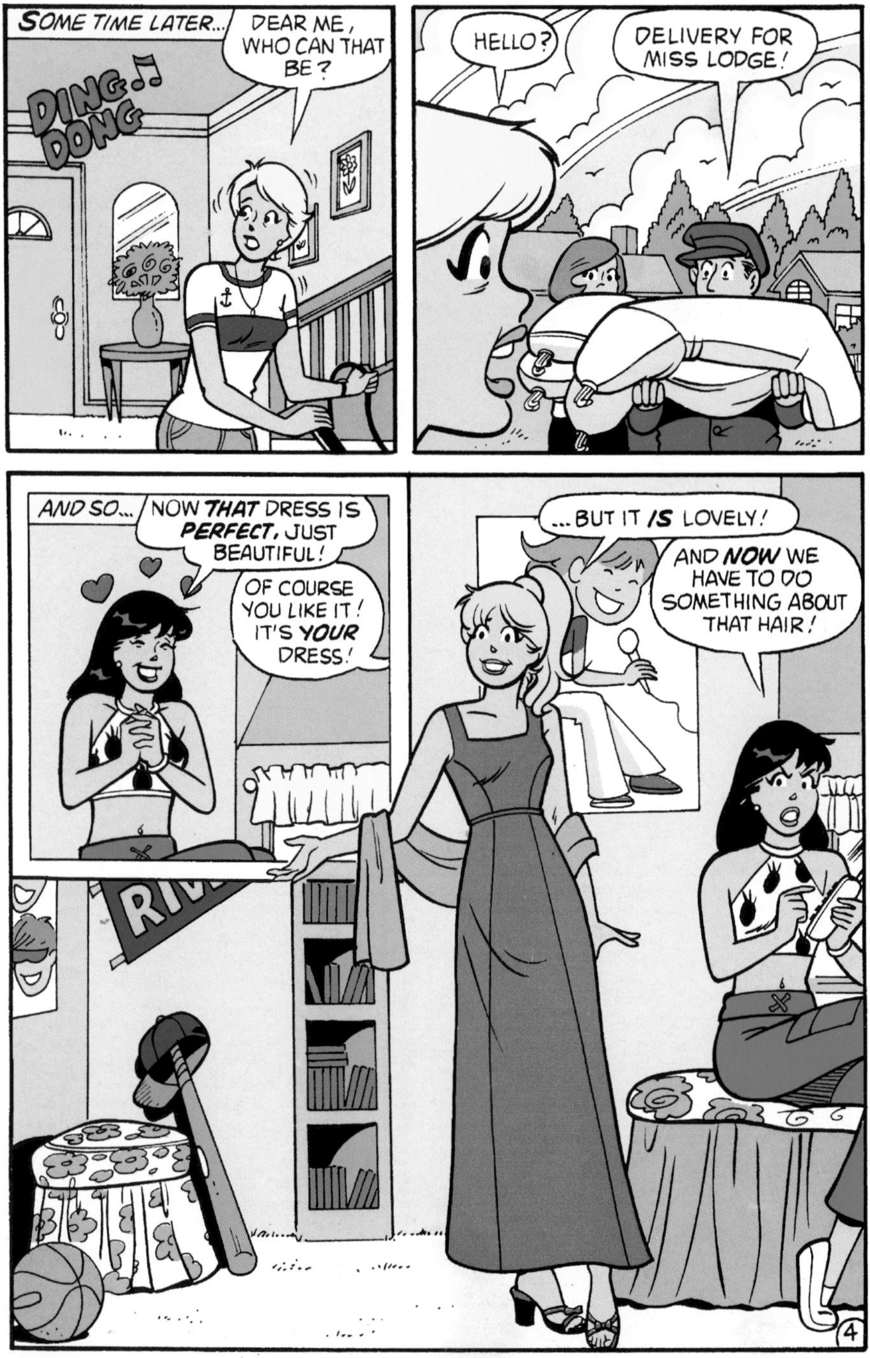
SOME TIME LATER...
DEAR ME, WHO CAN THAT BE?
DING DONG
HELLO?
DELIVERY FOR MISS LODGE!
AND SO...
NOW THAT DRESS IS PERFECT, JUST BEAUTIFUL!
OF COURSE YOU LIKE IT! IT'S YOUR DRESS!
...BUT IT IS LOVELY!
AND NOW WE HAVE TO DO SOMETHING ABOUT THAT HAIR!
4

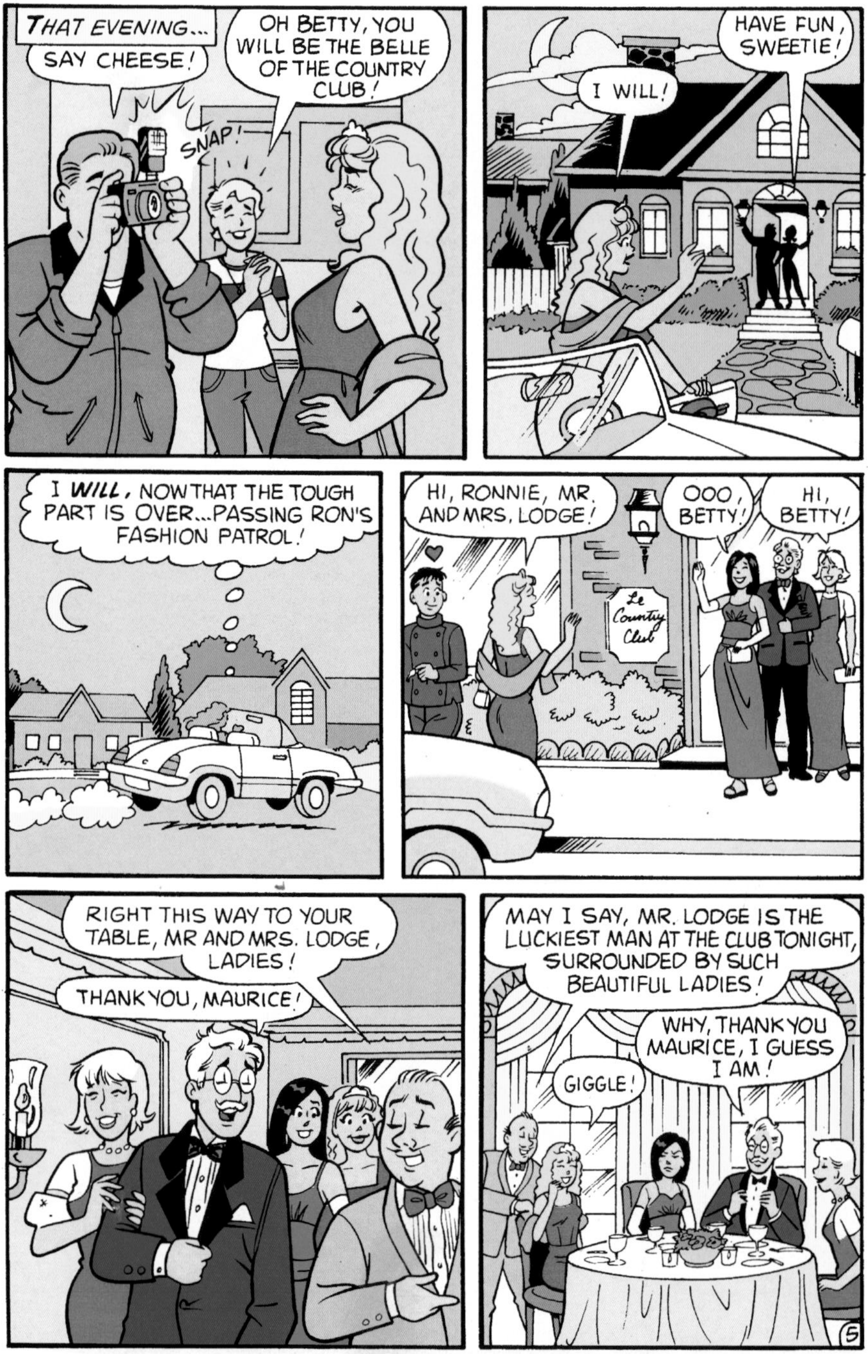
THAT EVENING...
SAY CHEESE!
OH BETTY, YOU WILL BE THE BELLE OF THE COUNTRY CLUB!
SNAP!
HAVE FUN, SWEETIE!
I WILL!
I WILL, NOW THAT THE TOUGH PART IS OVER...PASSING RON'S FASHION PATROL!
HI, RONNIE, MR. AND MRS. LODGE!
OOO, BETTY!
HI, BETTY!
Le Country Club
RIGHT THIS WAY TO YOUR TABLE, MR AND MRS. LODGE, LADIES!
THANK YOU, MAURICE!
MAY I SAY, MR. LODGE IS THE LUCKIEST MAN AT THE CLUB TONIGHT, SURROUNDED BY SUCH BEAUTIFUL LADIES!
WHY, THANK YOU MAURICE, I GUESS I AM!
GIGGLE!
5

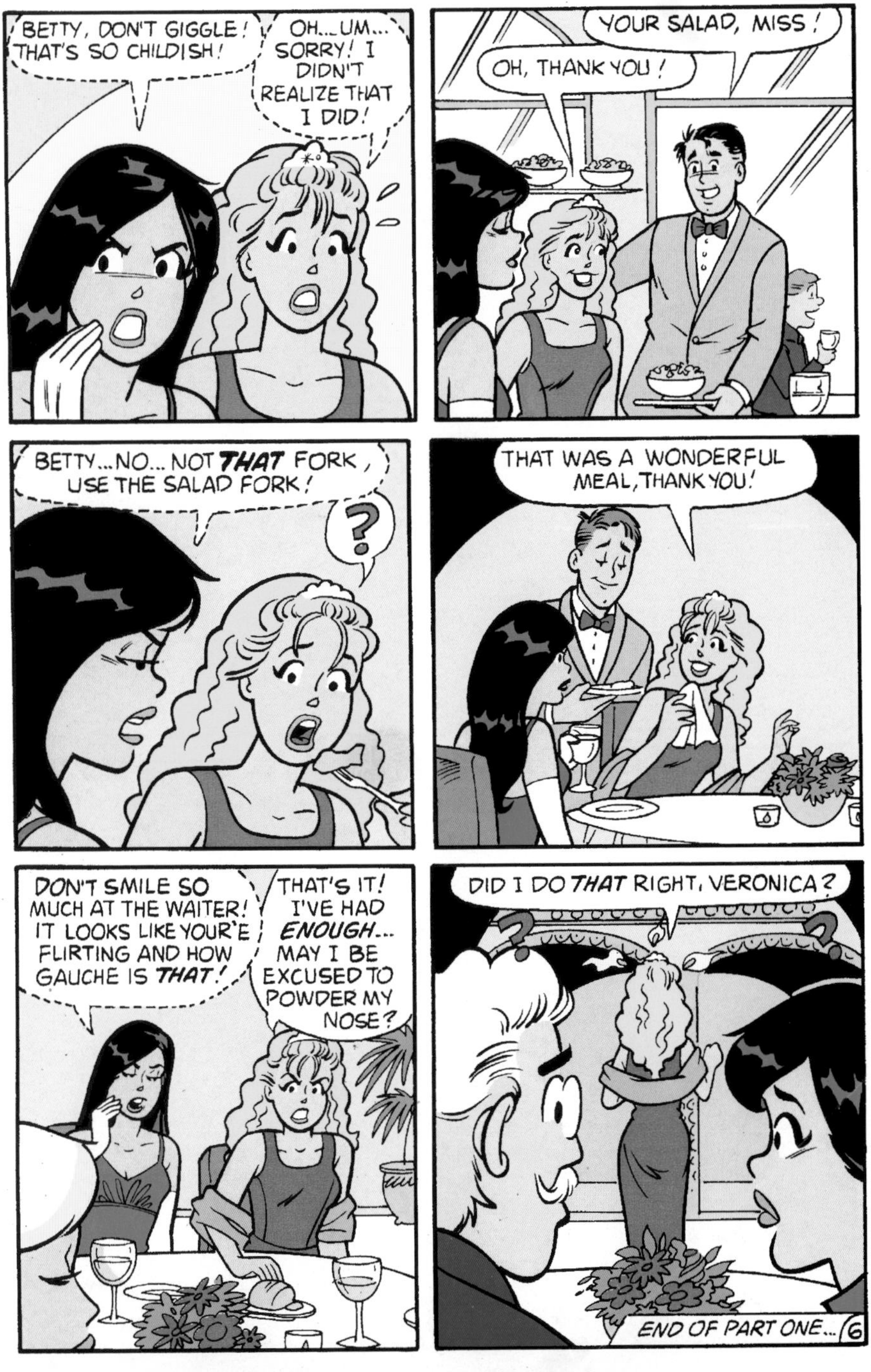
BETTY, DON'T GIGGLE! THAT'S SO CHILDISH!
OH...UM... SORRY! I DIDN'T REALIZE THAT I DID!
YOUR SALAD, MISS!
OH, THANK YOU!
BETTY...NO... NOT THAT FORK, USE THE SALAD FORK!
?
THAT WAS A WONDERFUL MEAL, THANK YOU!
DON'T SMILE SO MUCH AT THE WAITER! IT LOOKS LIKE YOUR'E FLIRTING AND HOW GAUCHE IS THAT!
THAT'S IT! I'VE HAD ENOUGH... MAY I BE EXCUSED TO POWDER MY NOSE?
DID I DO THAT RIGHT, VERONICA?
END OF PART ONE...
6

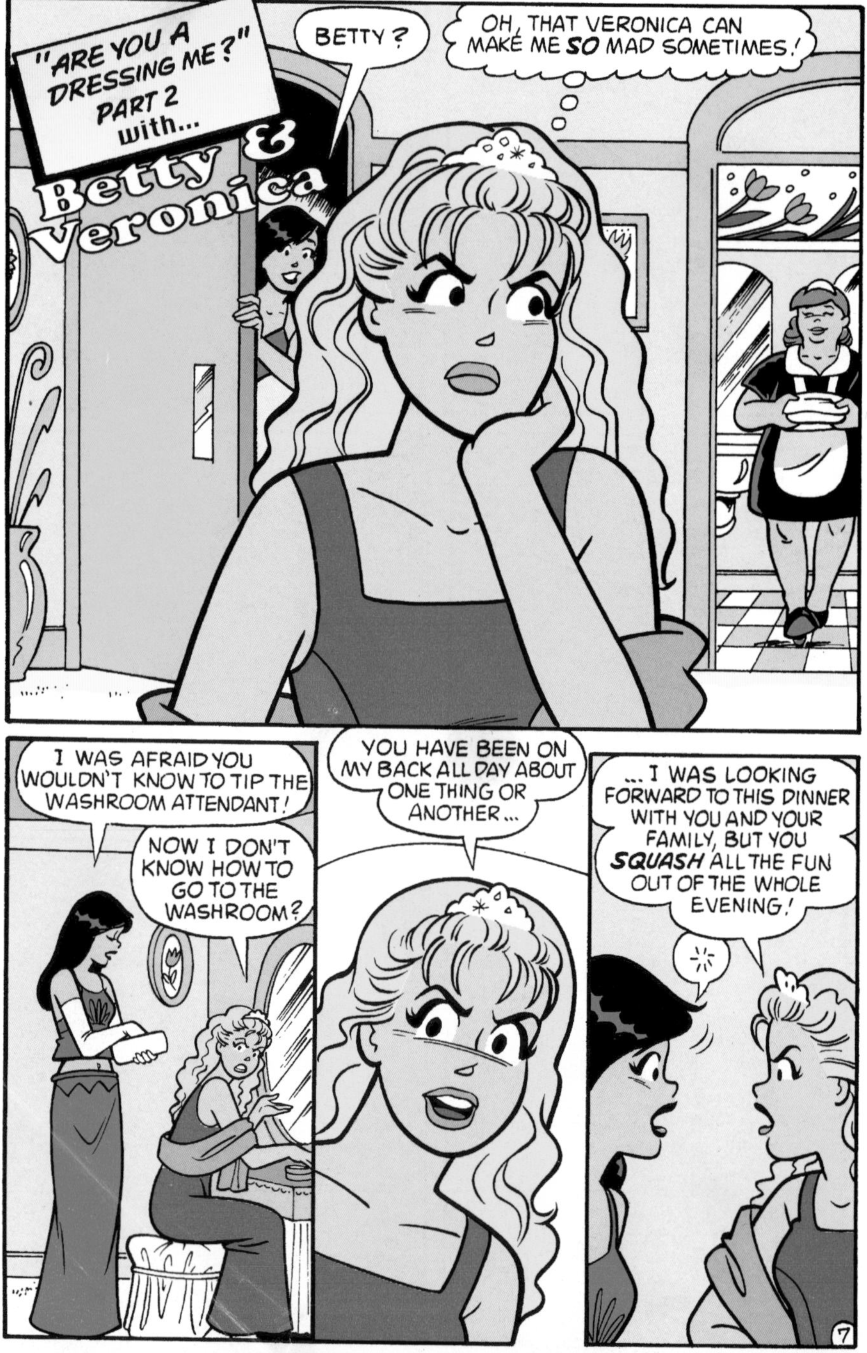

"ARE YOU A DRESSING ME?" PART 2 with...
Betty & Veronica
BETTY?
OH, THAT VERONICA CAN MAKE ME SO MAD SOMETIMES!
I WAS AFRAID YOU WOULDN'T KNOW TO TIP THE WASHROOM ATTENDANT!
NOW I DON'T KNOW HOW TO GO TO THE WASHROOM?
YOU HAVE BEEN ON MY BACK ALL DAY ABOUT ONE THING OR ANOTHER...
...I WAS LOOKING FORWARD TO THIS DINNER WITH YOU AND YOUR FAMILY, BUT YOU SQUASH ALL THE FUN OUT OF THE WHOLE EVENING!
7

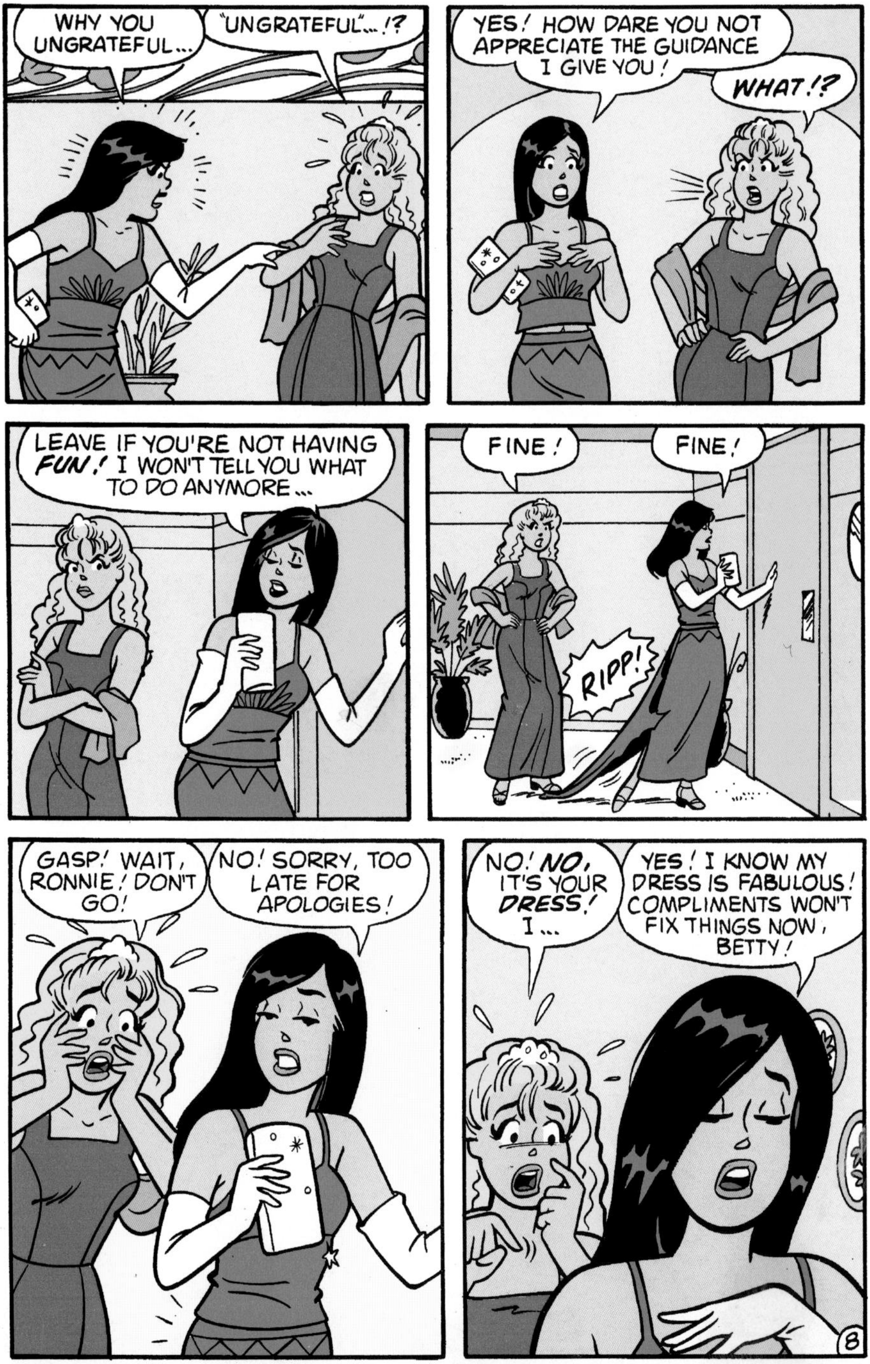
WHY YOU UNGRATEFUL...
"UNGRATEFUL"...!?
YES! HOW DARE YOU NOT APPRECIATE THE GUIDANCE I GIVE YOU!
WHAT!?
LEAVE IF YOU'RE NOT HAVING FUN! I WON'T TELL YOU WHAT TO DO ANYMORE...
FINE!
FINE!
RIPP!
GASP! WAIT, RONNIE! DON'T GO!
NO! SORRY, TOO LATE FOR APOLOGIES!
NO! NO, IT'S YOUR DRESS! I...
YES! I KNOW MY DRESS IS FABULOUS! COMPLIMENTS WON'T FIX THINGS NOW, BETTY!
8

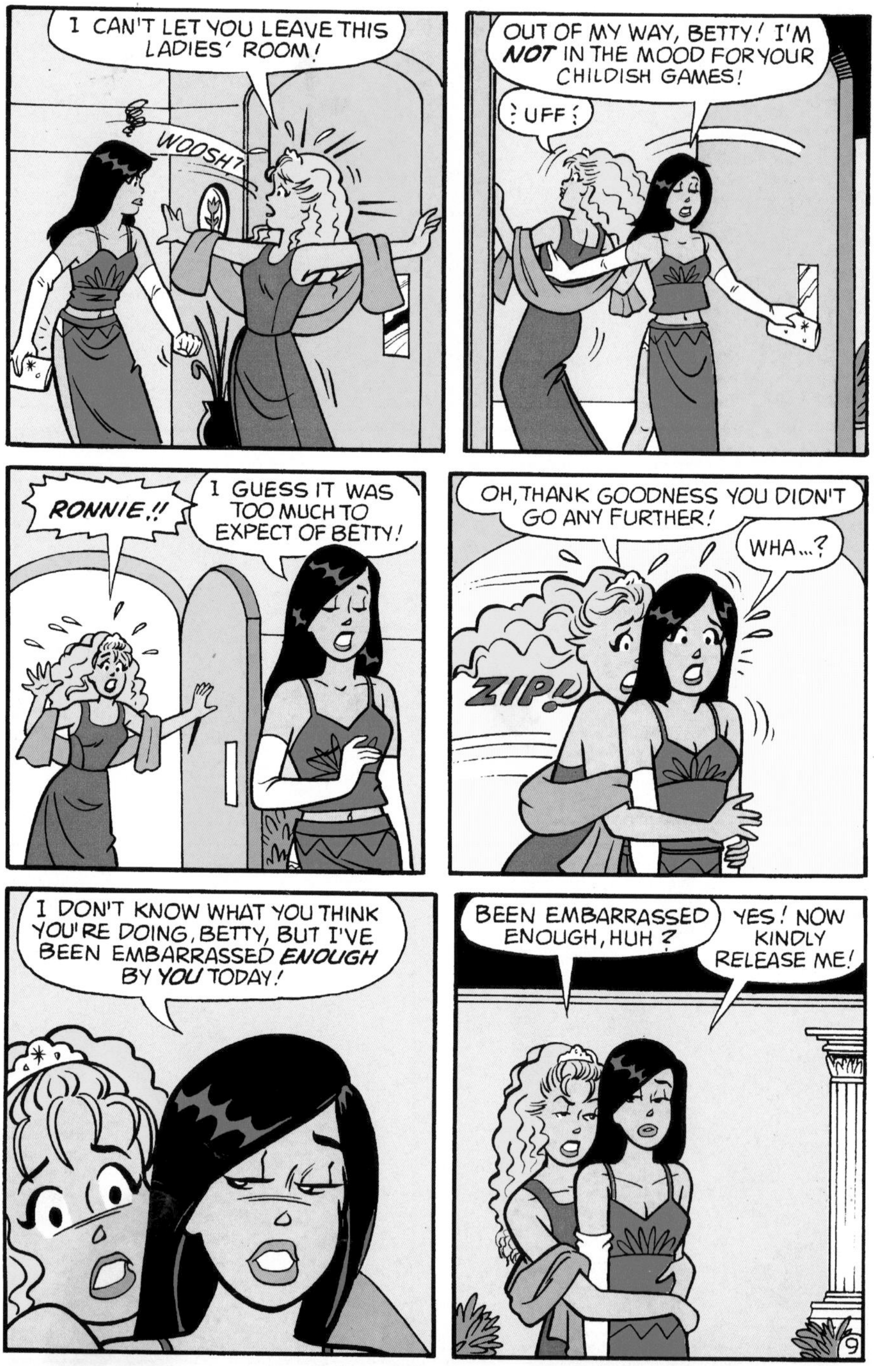

I CAN'T LET YOU LEAVE THIS LADIES' ROOM!
WOOSH!
OUT OF MY WAY, BETTY! I'M NOT IN THE MOOD FOR YOUR CHILDISH GAMES!
UFF
RONNIE!!
I GUESS IT WAS TOO MUCH TO EXPECT OF BETTY!
OH, THANK GOODNESS YOU DIDN'T GO ANY FURTHER!
WHA...?
ZIP!
I DON'T KNOW WHAT YOU THINK YOU'RE DOING, BETTY, BUT I'VE BEEN EMBARRASSED ENOUGH BY YOU TODAY!
BEEN EMBARRASSED ENOUGH, HUH?
YES! NOW KINDLY RELEASE ME!
9

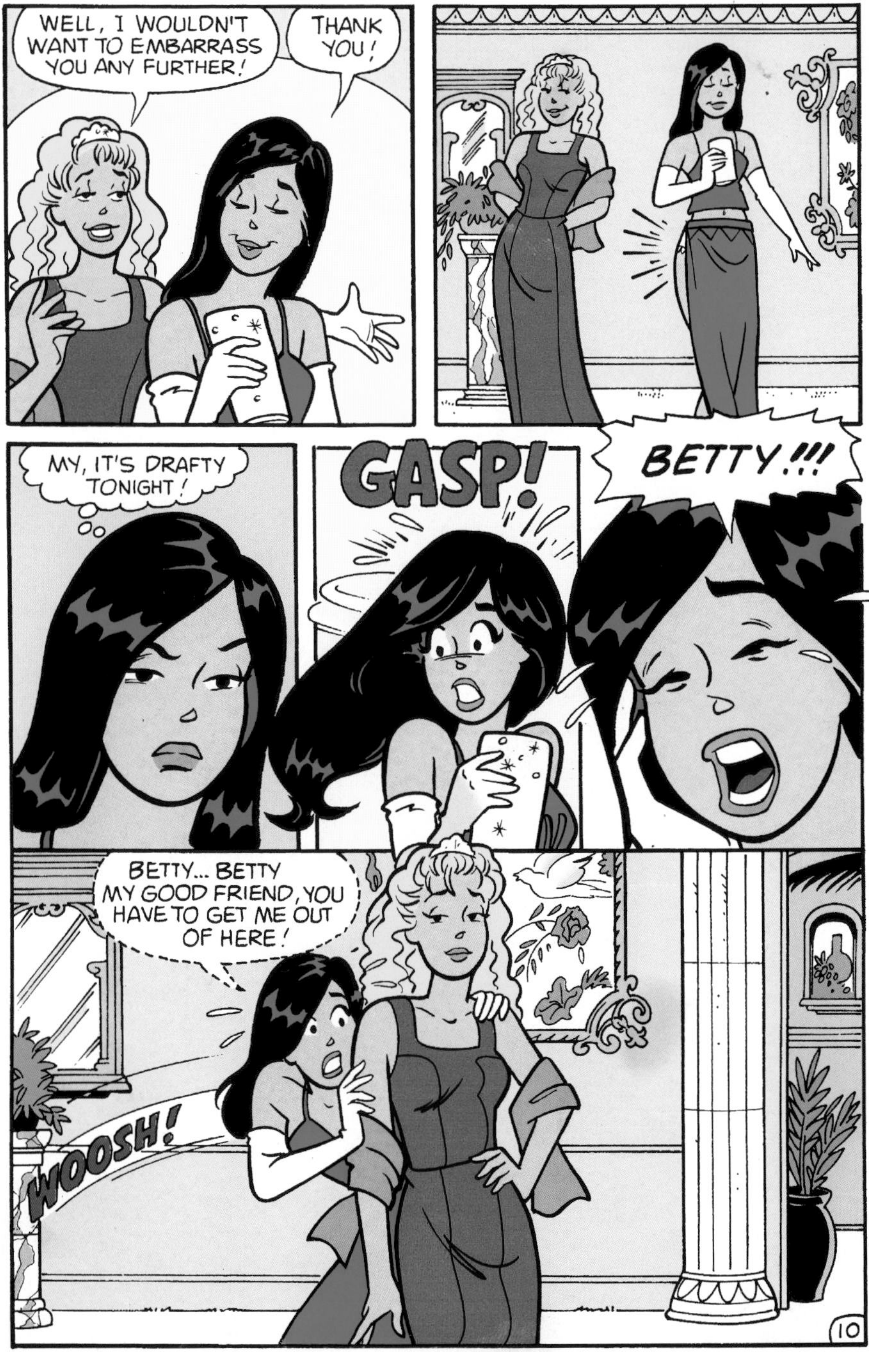
WELL, I WOULDN'T WANT TO EMBARRASS YOU ANY FURTHER!
THANK YOU!
MY, IT'S DRAFTY TONIGHT!
GASP!
BETTY!!!
BETTY... BETTY MY GOOD FRIEND, YOU HAVE TO GET ME OUT OF HERE!
WOOSH!
10

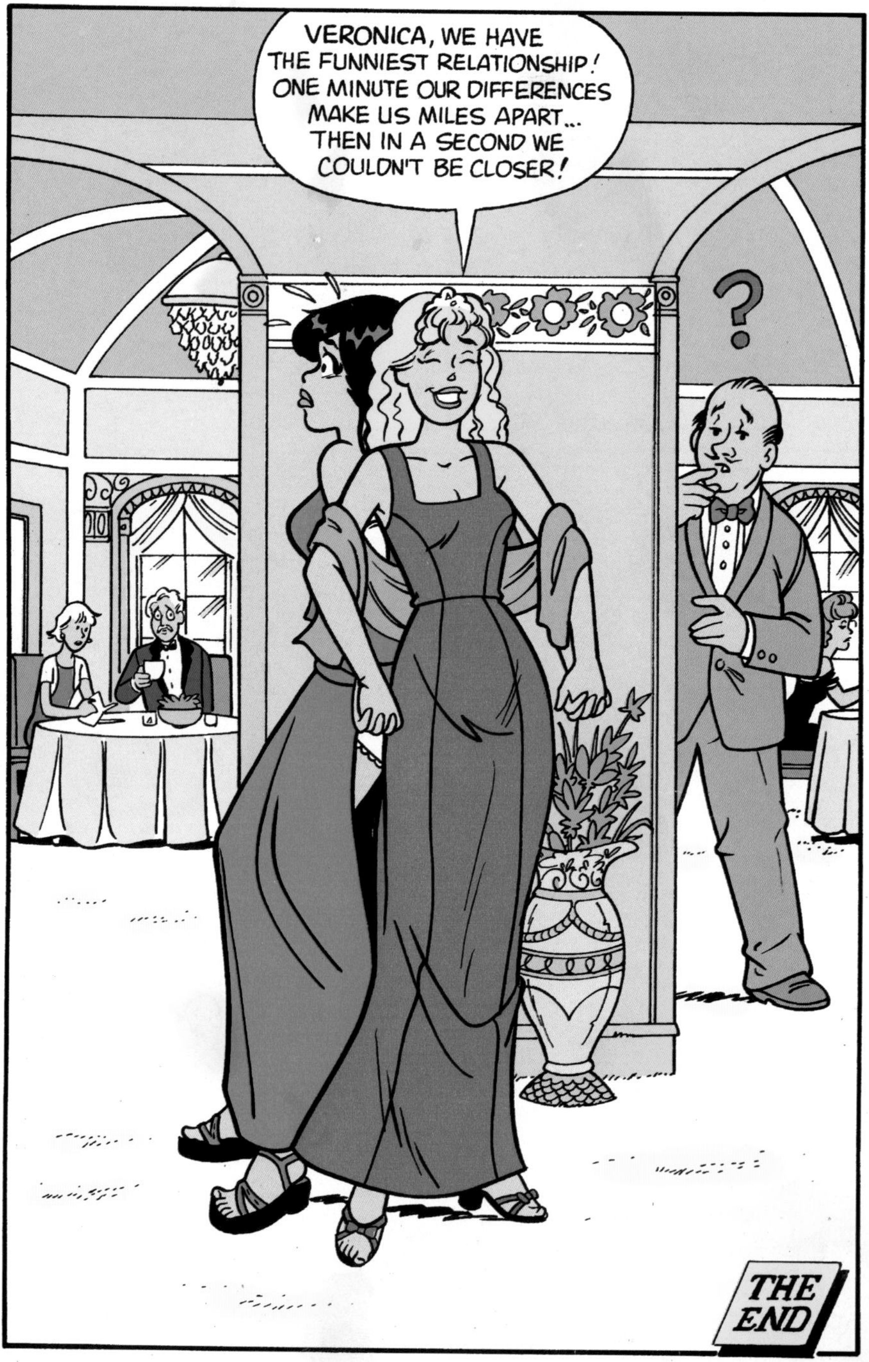
VERONICA, WE HAVE THE FUNNIEST RELATIONSHIP! ONE MINUTE OUR DIFFERENCES MAKE US MILES APART... THEN IN A SECOND WE COULDN'T BE CLOSER!
?
THE END

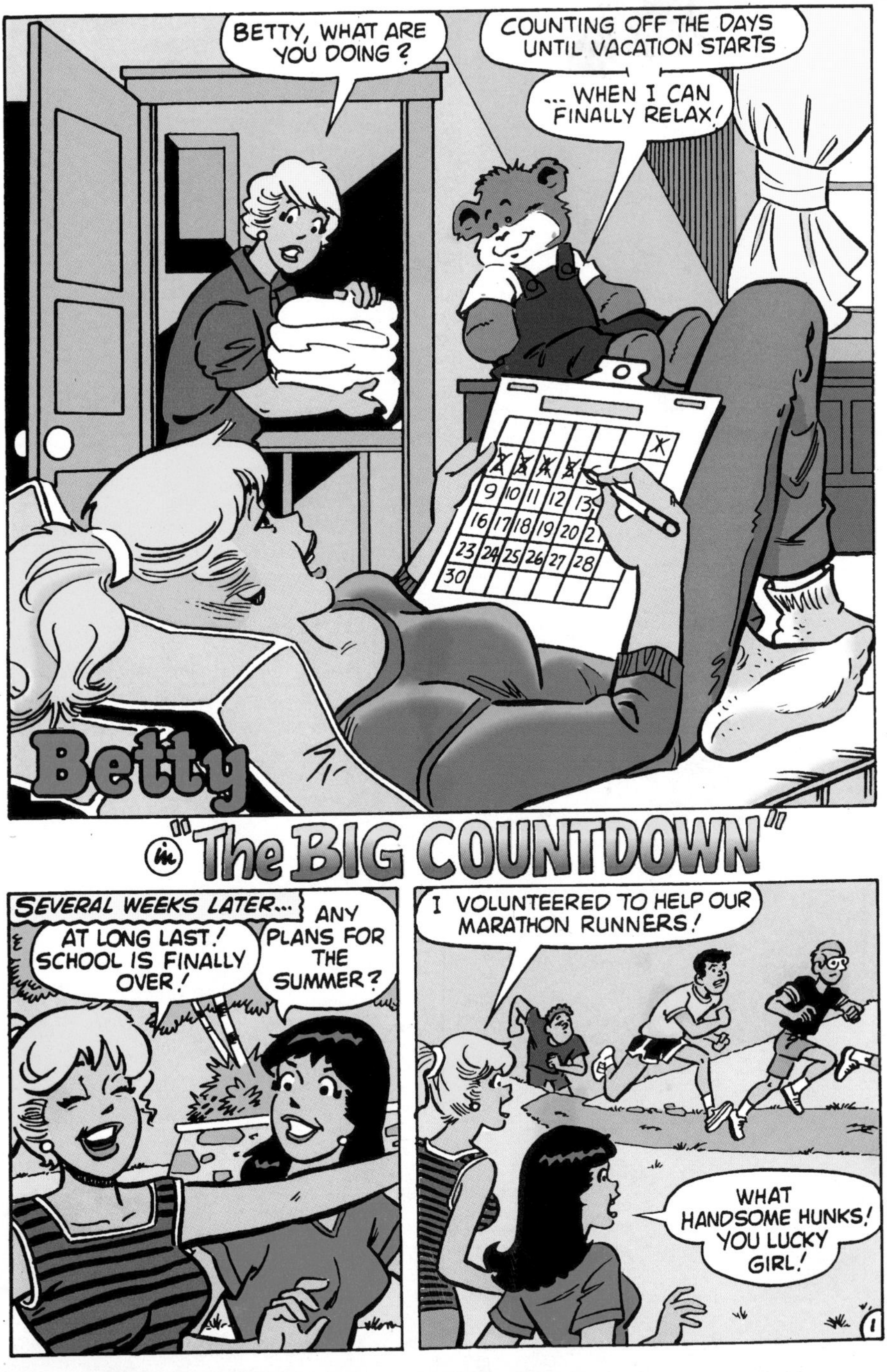
BETTY, WHAT ARE YOU DOING ?
COUNTING OFF THE DAYS UNTIL VACATION STARTS
... WHEN I CAN FINALLY RELAX!
Betty
in "The BIG COUNTDOWN"
SEVERAL WEEKS LATER...
AT LONG LAST! SCHOOL IS FINALLY OVER!
ANY PLANS FOR THE SUMMER?
I VOLUNTEERED TO HELP OUR MARATHON RUNNERS!
WHAT HANDSOME HUNKS! YOU LUCKY GIRL!

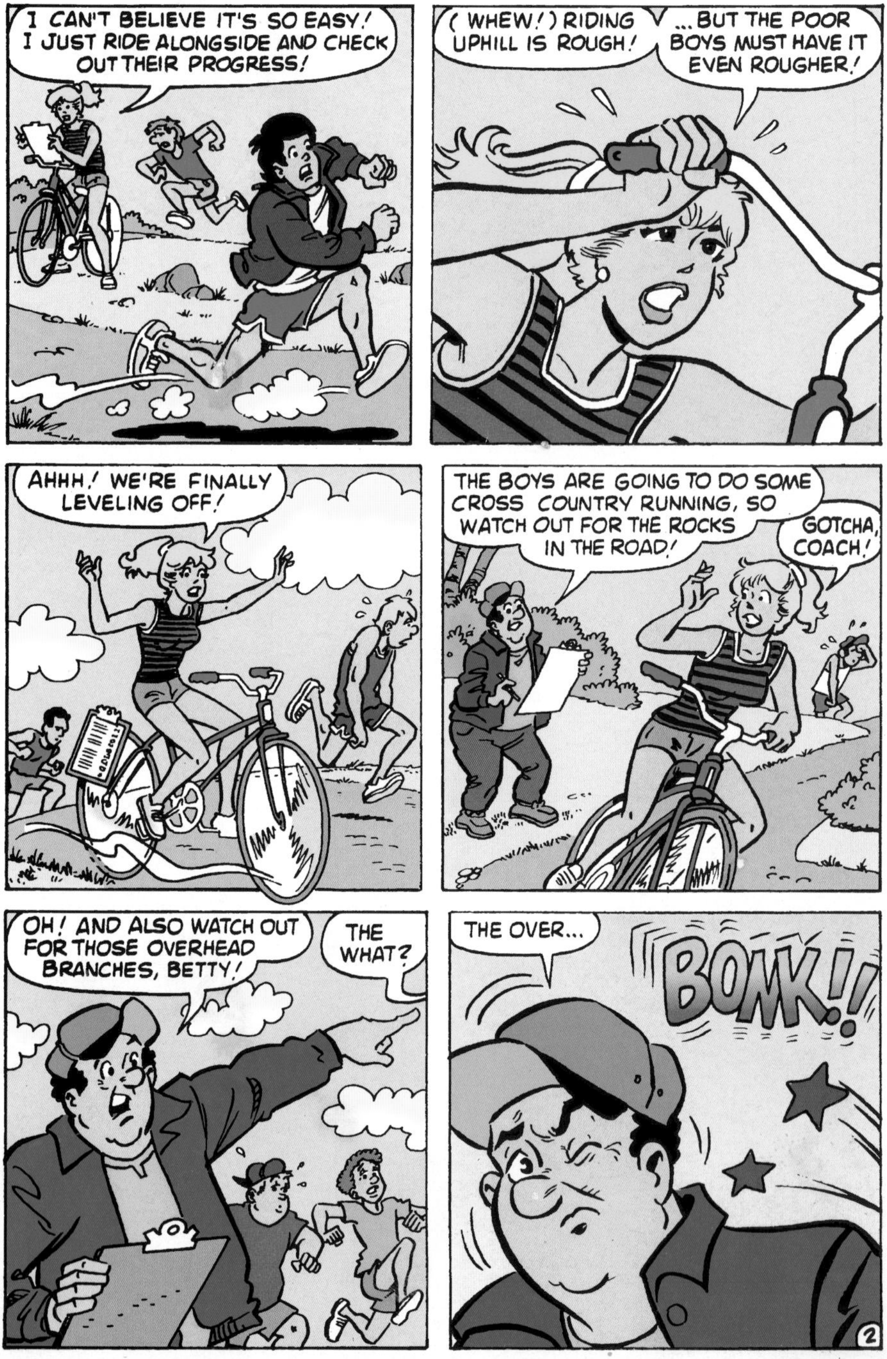
I CAN'T BELIEVE IT'S SO EASY! I JUST RIDE ALONGSIDE AND CHECK OUT THEIR PROGRESS!
(WHEW!) RIDING UPHILL IS ROUGH!
...BUT THE POOR BOYS MUST HAVE IT EVEN ROUGHER!
AHHH! WE'RE FINALLY LEVELING OFF!
THE BOYS ARE GOING TO DO SOME CROSS COUNTRY RUNNING, SO WATCH OUT FOR THE ROCKS IN THE ROAD!
GOTCHA, COACH!
OH! AND ALSO WATCH OUT FOR THOSE OVERHEAD BRANCHES, BETTY!
THE WHAT?
THE OVER...
BONK!!
2

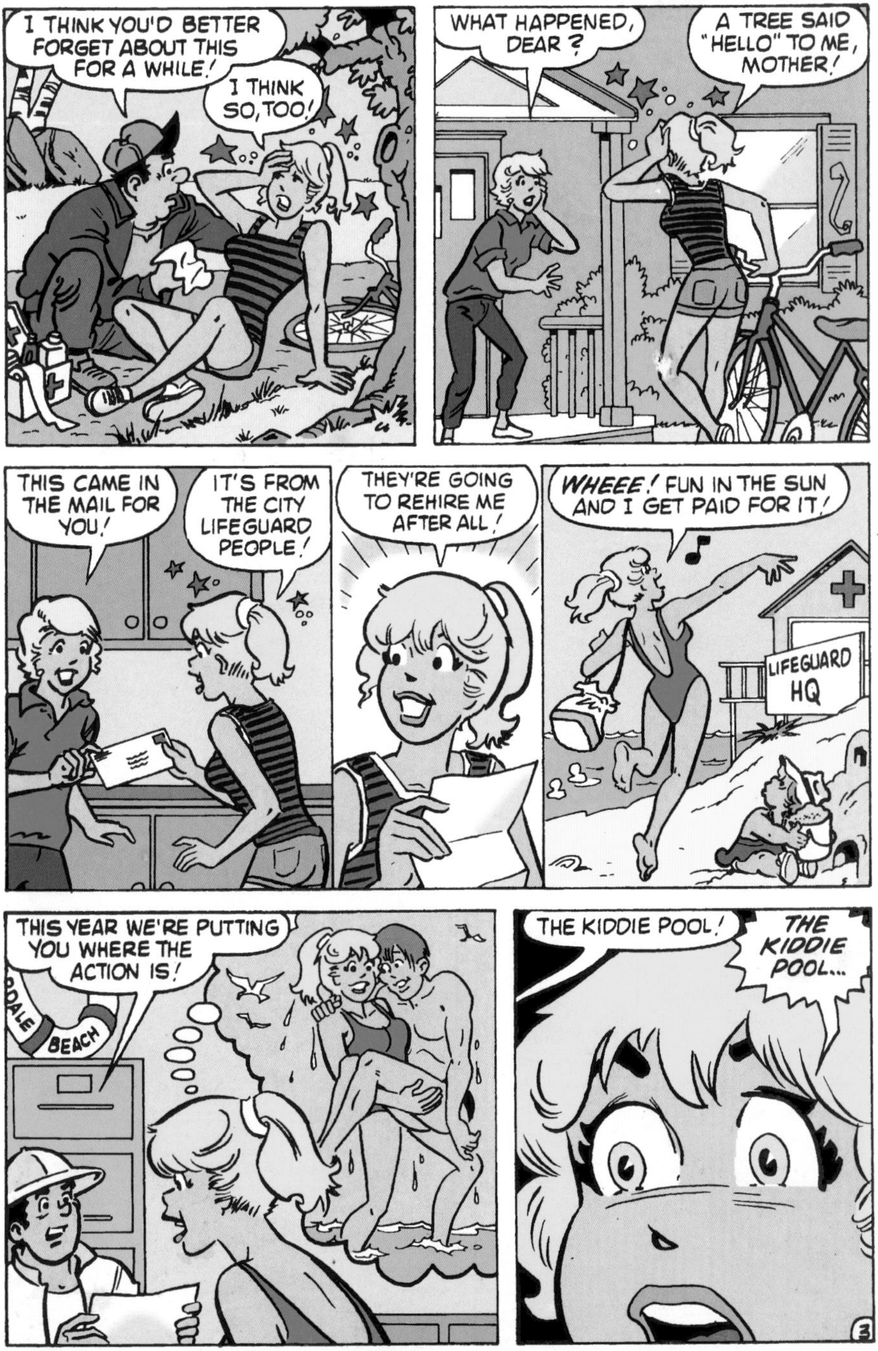
I THINK YOU'D BETTER FORGET ABOUT THIS FOR A WHILE!
I THINK SO, TOO!
WHAT HAPPENED, DEAR?
A TREE SAID "HELLO" TO ME, MOTHER!
THIS CAME IN THE MAIL FOR YOU!
IT'S FROM THE CITY LIFEGUARD PEOPLE!
THEY'RE GOING TO REHIRE ME AFTER ALL!
WHEEE! FUN IN THE SUN AND I GET PAID FOR IT!
LIFEGUARD HQ
THIS YEAR WE'RE PUTTING YOU WHERE THE ACTION IS!
BEACH
THE KIDDIE POOL!
THE KIDDIE POOL...
3

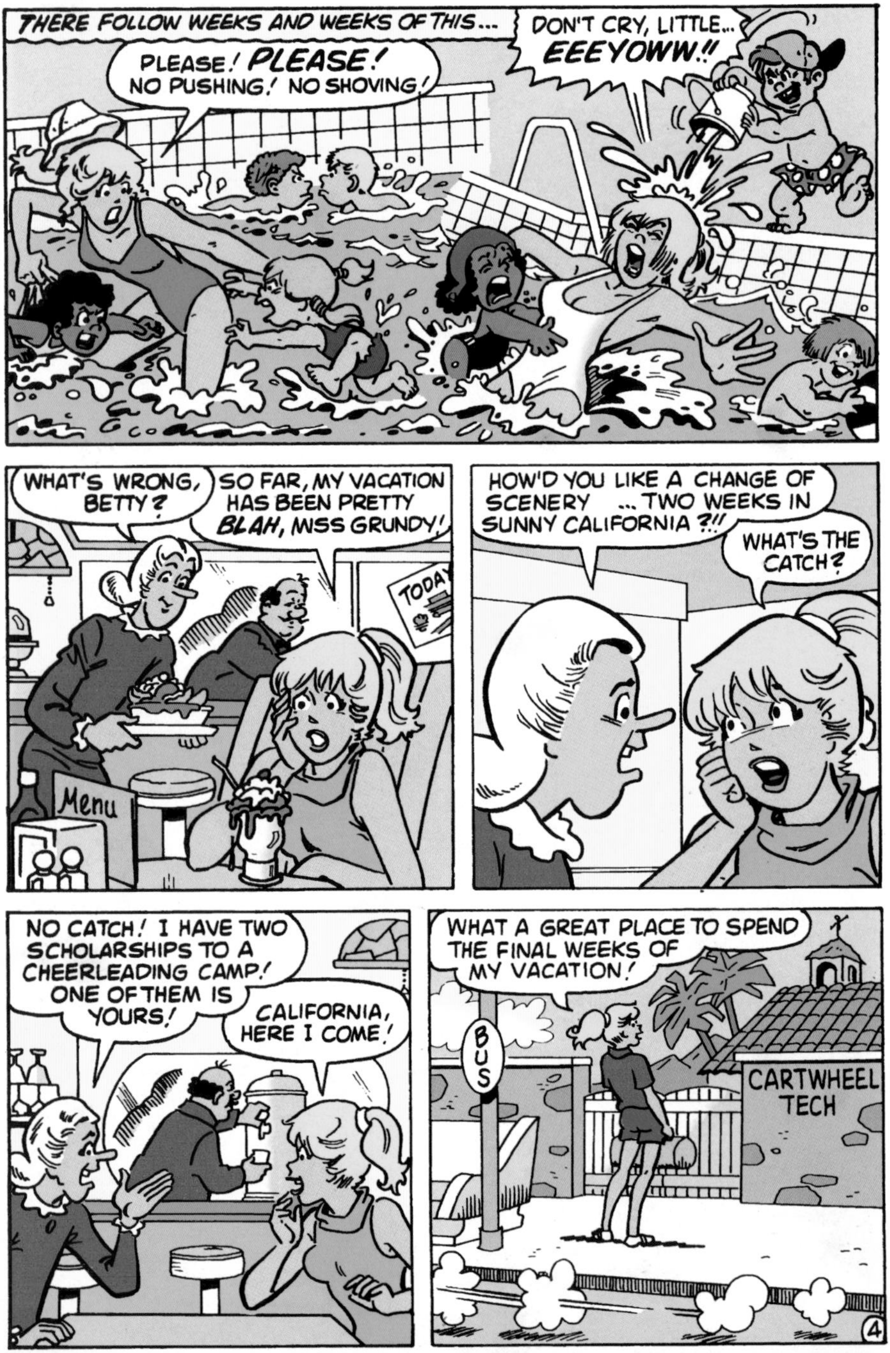
THERE FOLLOW WEEKS AND WEEKS OF THIS...
PLEASE! PLEASE! NO PUSHING! NO SHOVING!
DON'T CRY, LITTLE... EEEYOWW!!
WHAT'S WRONG, BETTY?
SO FAR, MY VACATION HAS BEEN PRETTY BLAH, MISS GRUNDY!
TODAY
Menu
HOW'D YOU LIKE A CHANGE OF SCENERY ... TWO WEEKS IN SUNNY CALIFORNIA ?!!
WHAT'S THE CATCH?
NO CATCH! I HAVE TWO SCHOLARSHIPS TO A CHEERLEADING CAMP! ONE OF THEM IS YOURS!
CALIFORNIA, HERE I COME!
WHAT A GREAT PLACE TO SPEND THE FINAL WEEKS OF MY VACATION!
BUS
CARTWHEEL TECH
4

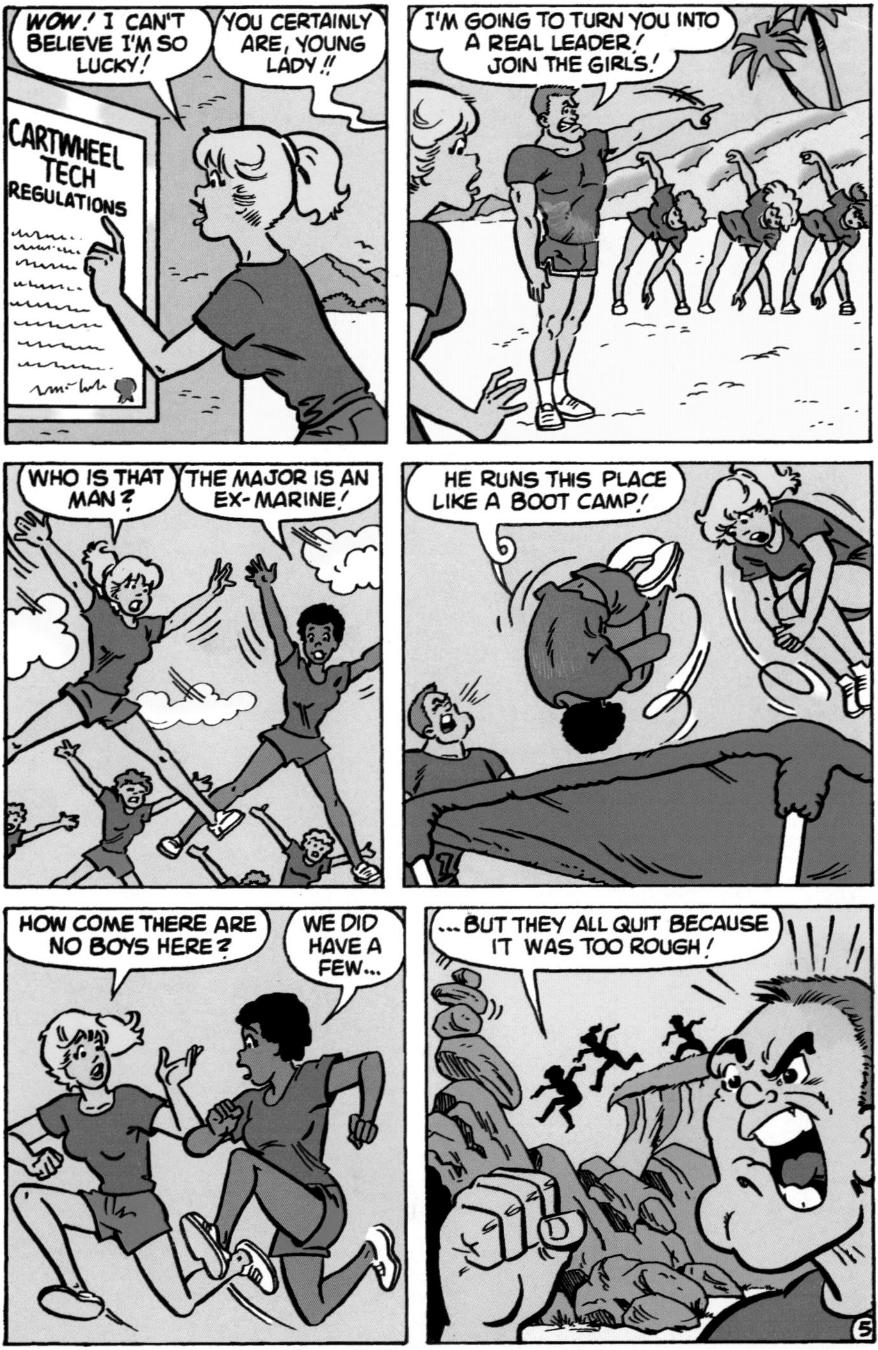
WOW! I CAN'T BELIEVE I'M SO LUCKY!
YOU CERTAINLY ARE, YOUNG LADY!!
CARTWHEEL TECH REGULATIONS
I'M GOING TO TURN YOU INTO A REAL LEADER! JOIN THE GIRLS!
WHO IS THAT MAN?
THE MAJOR IS AN EX-MARINE!
HE RUNS THIS PLACE LIKE A BOOT CAMP!
HOW COME THERE ARE NO BOYS HERE?
WE DID HAVE A FEW...
...BUT THEY ALL QUIT BECAUSE IT WAS TOO ROUGH!
5

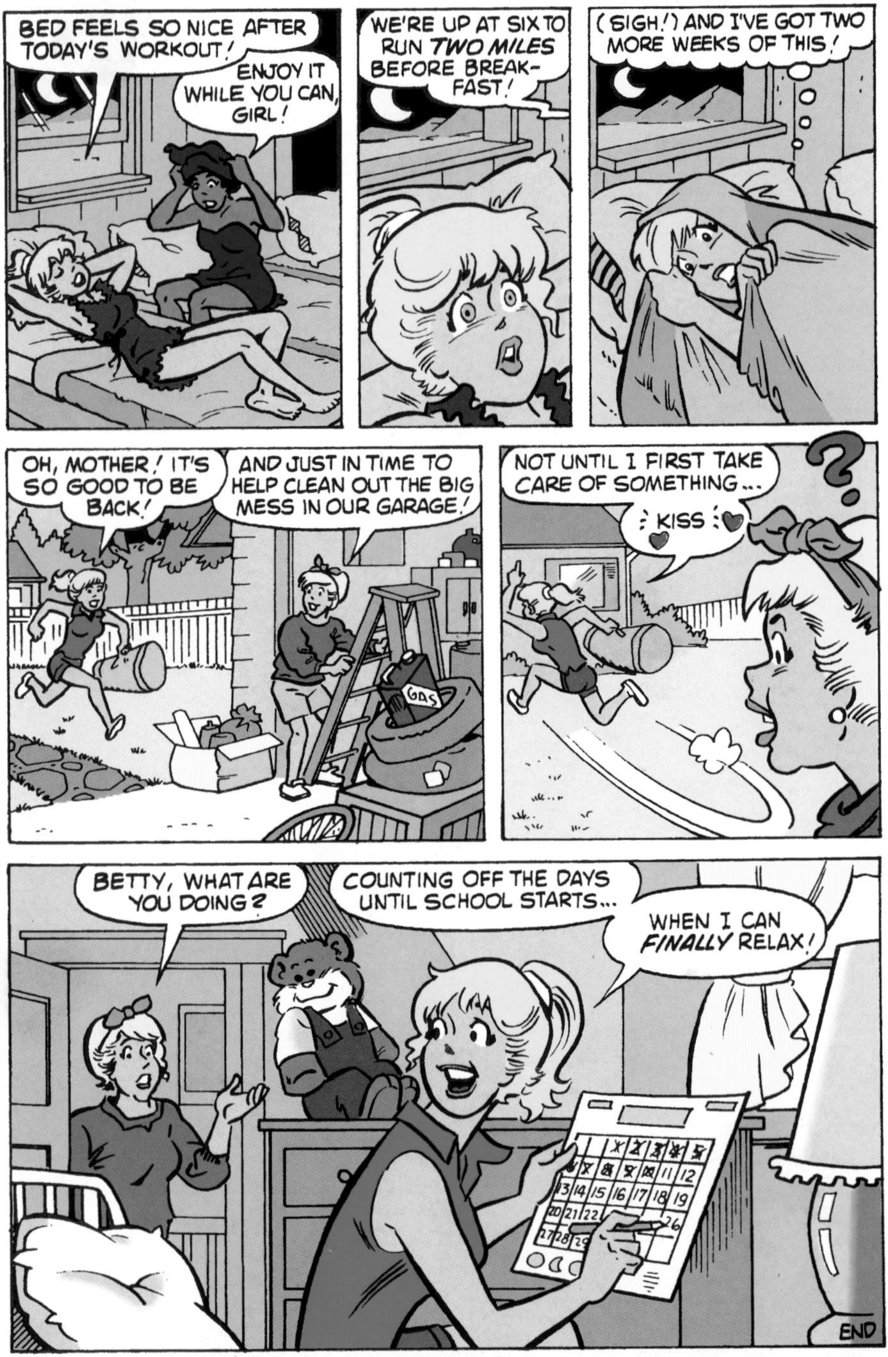
BED FEELS SO NICE AFTER TODAY'S WORKOUT!
ENJOY IT WHILE YOU CAN, GIRL!
WE'RE UP AT SIX TO RUN TWO MILES BEFORE BREAK-FAST!
(SIGH!) AND I'VE GOT TWO MORE WEEKS OF THIS!
OH, MOTHER! IT'S SO GOOD TO BE BACK!
AND JUST IN TIME TO HELP CLEAN OUT THE BIG MESS IN OUR GARAGE!
GAS
NOT UNTIL I FIRST TAKE CARE OF SOMETHING...
KISS
BETTY, WHAT ARE YOU DOING?
COUNTING OFF THE DAYS UNTIL SCHOOL STARTS...
WHEN I CAN FINALLY RELAX!
END

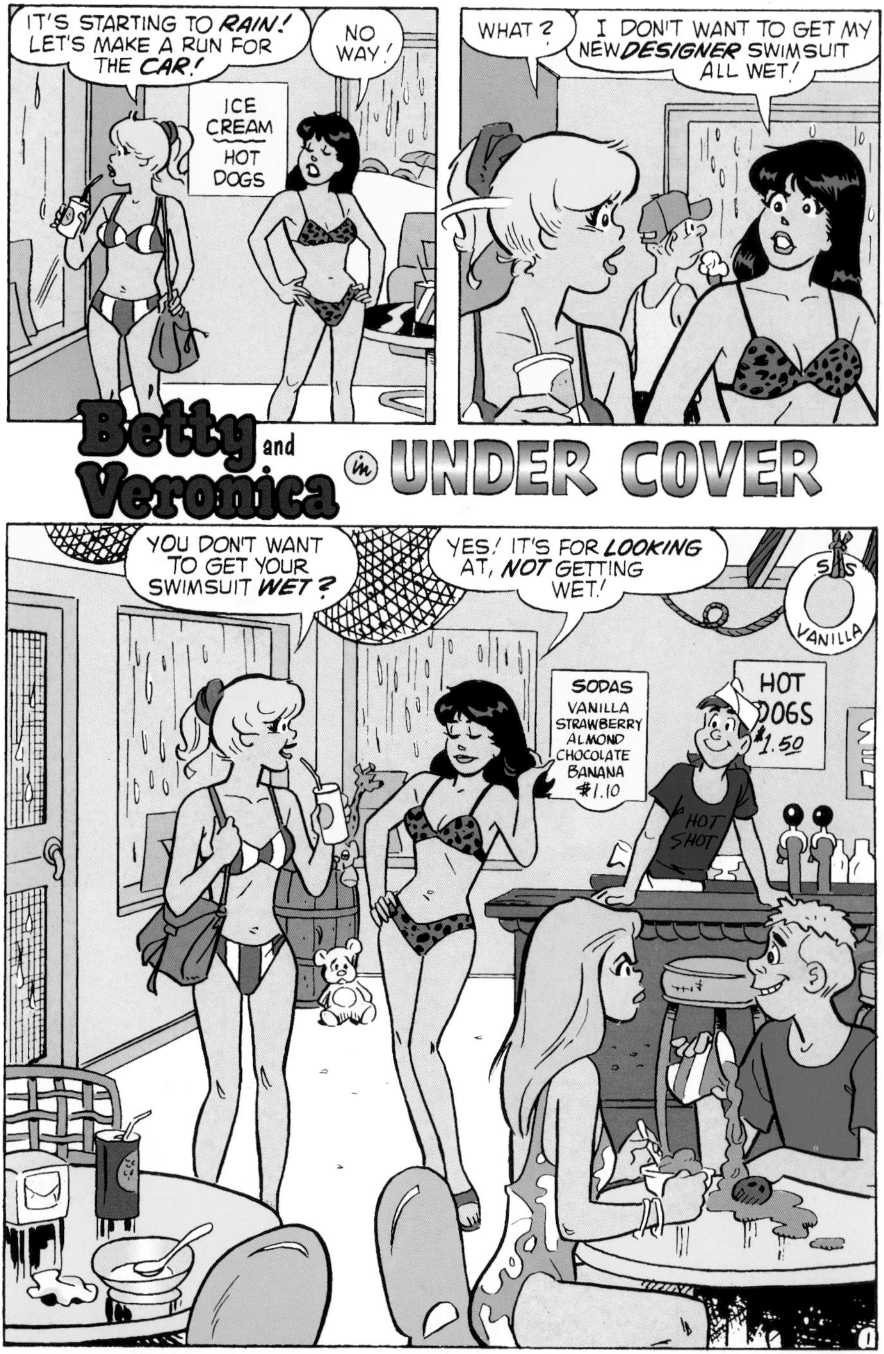
IT'S STARTING TO RAIN! LET'S MAKE A RUN FOR THE CAR!
NO WAY!
ICE CREAM HOT DOGS
WHAT?
I DON'T WANT TO GET MY NEW DESIGNER SWIMSUIT ALL WET!
Betty and Veronica in UNDER COVER
YOU DON'T WANT TO GET YOUR SWIMSUIT WET?
YES! IT'S FOR LOOKING AT, NOT GETTING WET!
VANILLA
SODAS VANILLA STRAWBERRY ALMOND CHOCOLATE BANANA $1.10
HOT DOGS $1.50
HOT SHOT

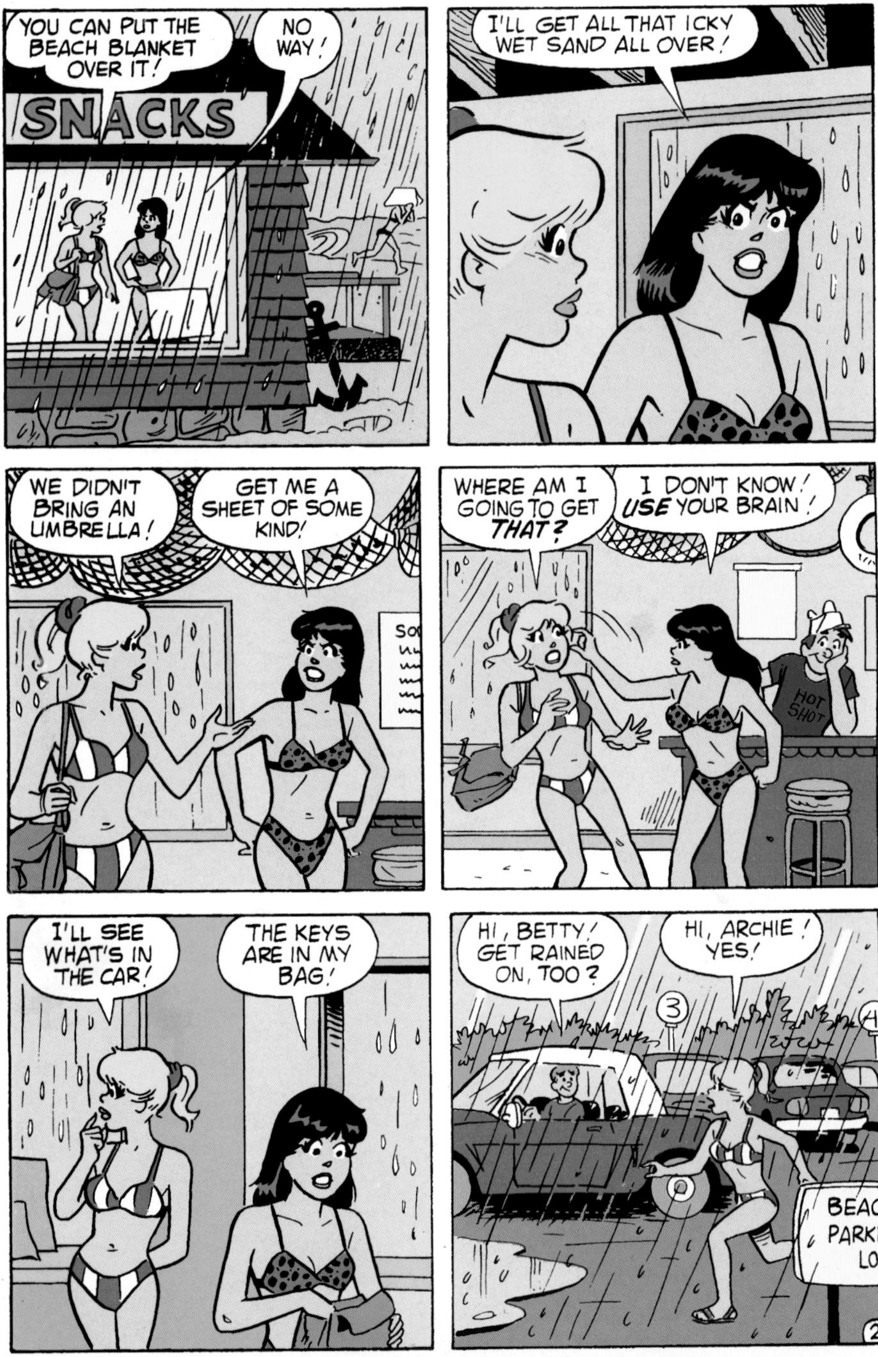
YOU CAN PUT THE BEACH BLANKET OVER IT!
NO WAY!
SNACKS
I'LL GET ALL THAT ICKY WET SAND ALL OVER!
WE DIDN'T BRING AN UMBRELLA!
GET ME A SHEET OF SOME KIND!
WHERE AM I GOING TO GET THAT?
I DON'T KNOW! USE YOUR BRAIN!
HOT SHOT
I'LL SEE WHAT'S IN THE CAR!
THE KEYS ARE IN MY BAG!
HI, BETTY! GET RAINED ON, TOO?
HI, ARCHIE! YES!
3
BEAC
PARKI
LOT
2

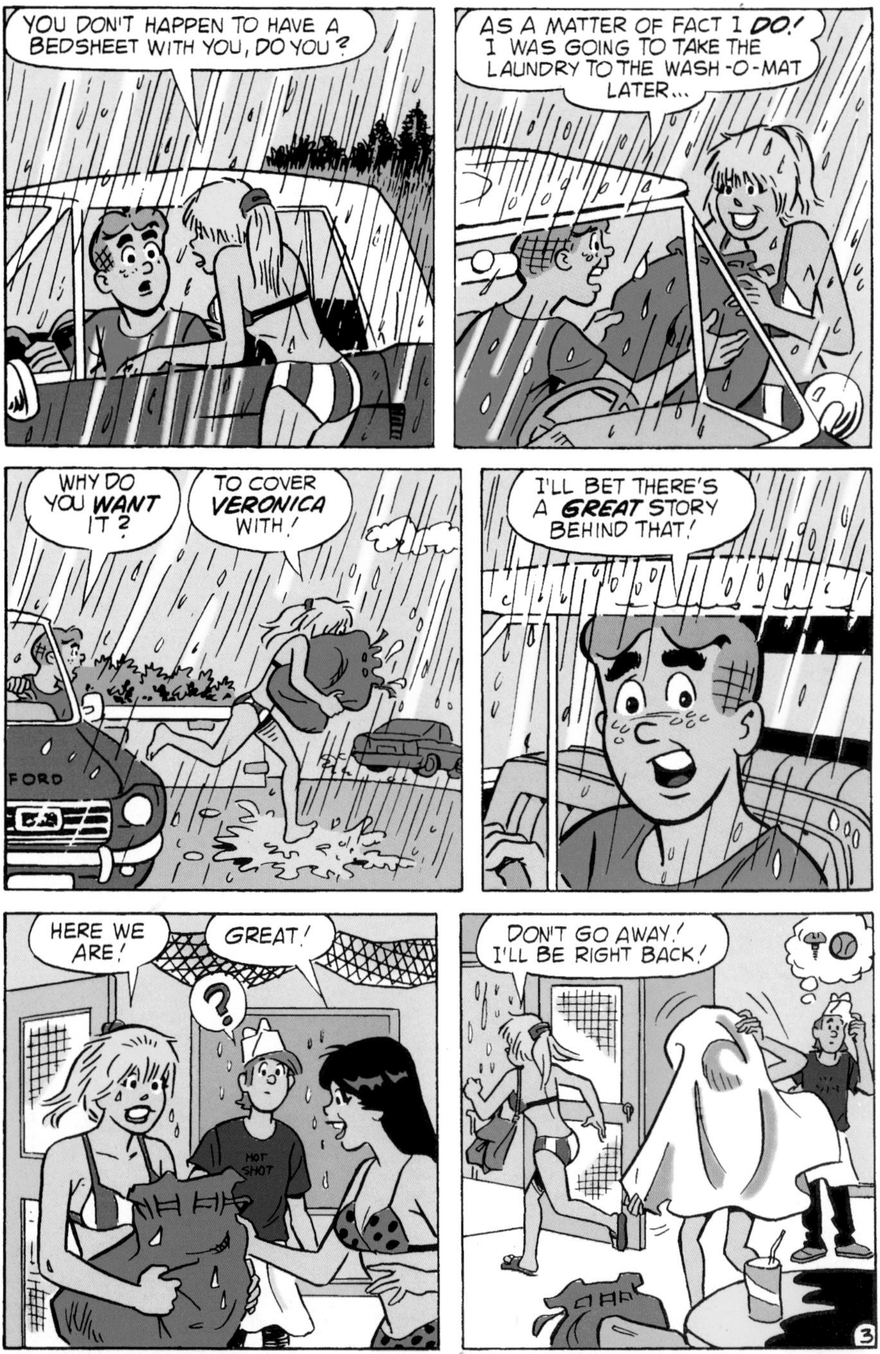
YOU DON'T HAPPEN TO HAVE A BEDSHEET WITH YOU, DO YOU?
AS A MATTER OF FACT I DO! I WAS GOING TO TAKE THE LAUNDRY TO THE WASH-O-MAT LATER...
WHY DO YOU WANT IT?
TO COVER VERONICA WITH!
FORD
I'LL BET THERE'S A GREAT STORY BEHIND THAT!
HERE WE ARE!
GREAT!
HOT SHOT
DON'T GO AWAY! I'LL BE RIGHT BACK!
3

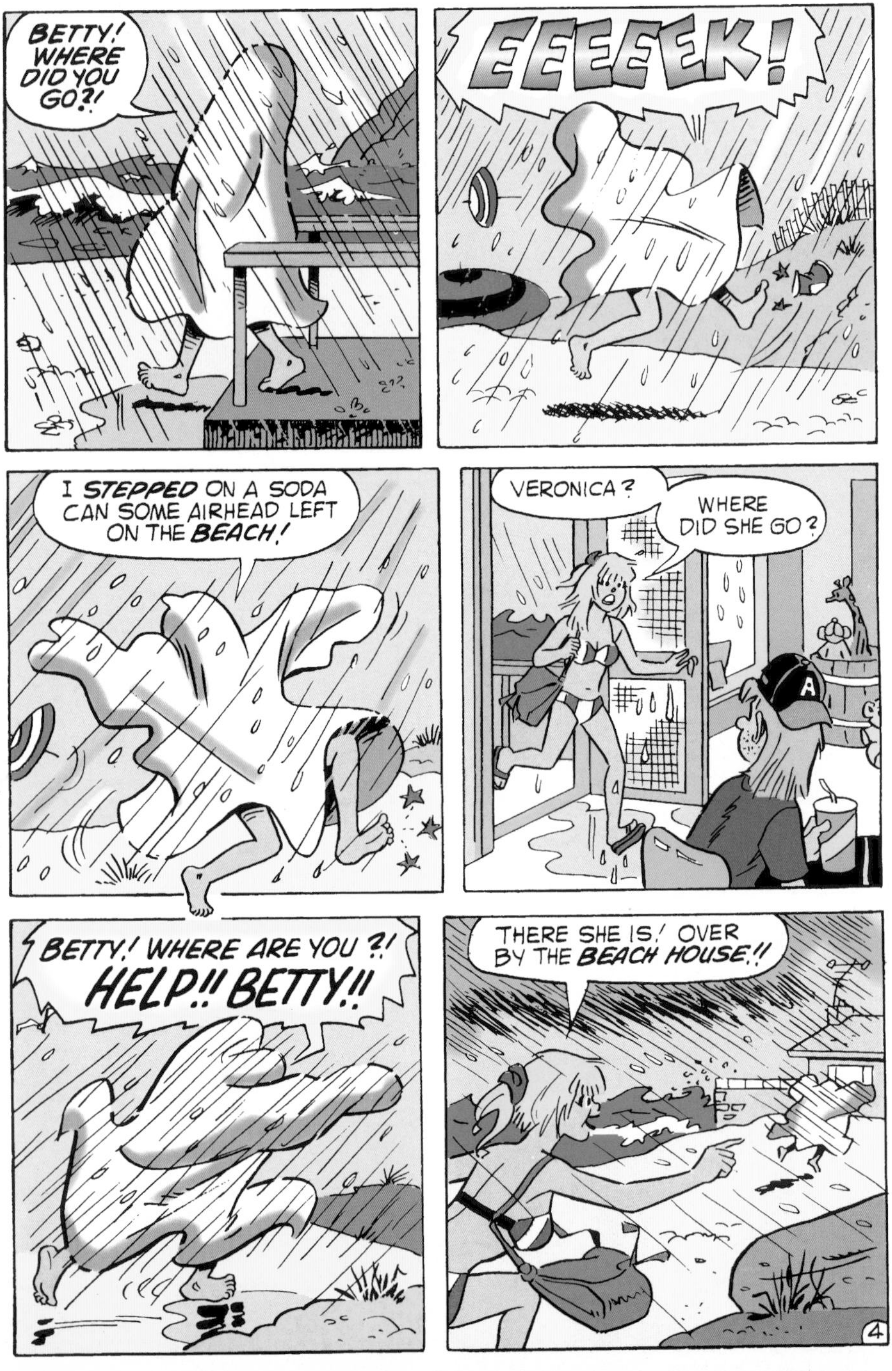
BETTY! WHERE DID YOU GO?!
EEEEEK!
I STEPPED ON A SODA CAN SOME AIRHEAD LEFT ON THE BEACH!
VERONICA?
WHERE DID SHE GO?
BETTY! WHERE ARE YOU ?!
HELP!! BETTY!!
THERE SHE IS! OVER BY THE BEACH HOUSE!!
4

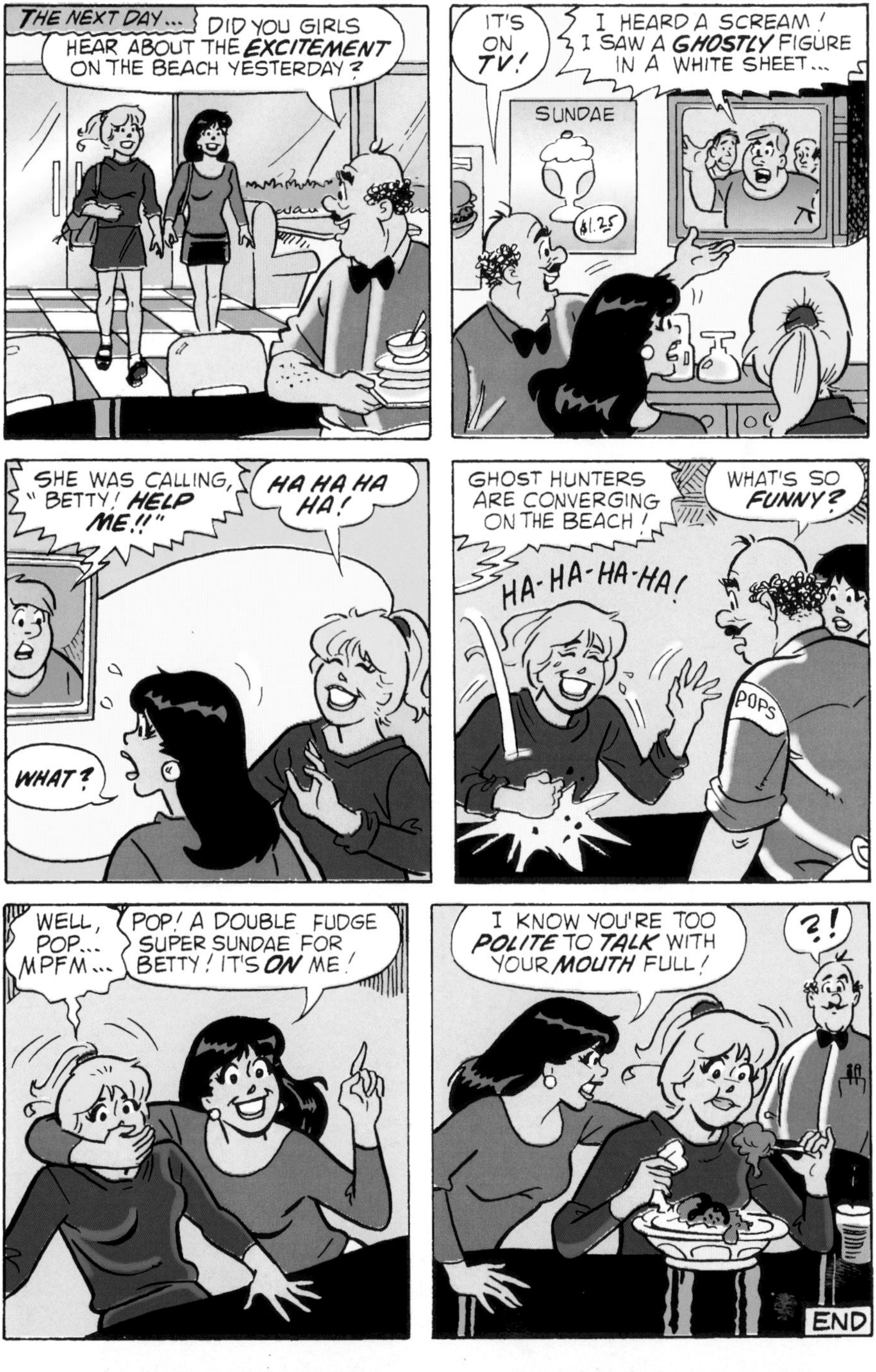
THE NEXT DAY...
DID YOU GIRLS HEAR ABOUT THE EXCITEMENT ON THE BEACH YESTERDAY?
IT'S ON TV!
I HEARD A SCREAM! I SAW A GHOSTLY FIGURE IN A WHITE SHEET...
SUNDAE
$1.25
SHE WAS CALLING, "BETTY! HELP ME!!"
HA HA HA HA!
WHAT?
GHOST HUNTERS ARE CONVERGING ON THE BEACH!
WHAT'S SO FUNNY?
HA-HA-HA-HA!
POPS
WELL, POP... MPFM...
POP! A DOUBLE FUDGE SUPER SUNDAE FOR BETTY! IT'S ON ME!
I KNOW YOU'RE TOO POLITE TO TALK WITH YOUR MOUTH FULL!
?!
END

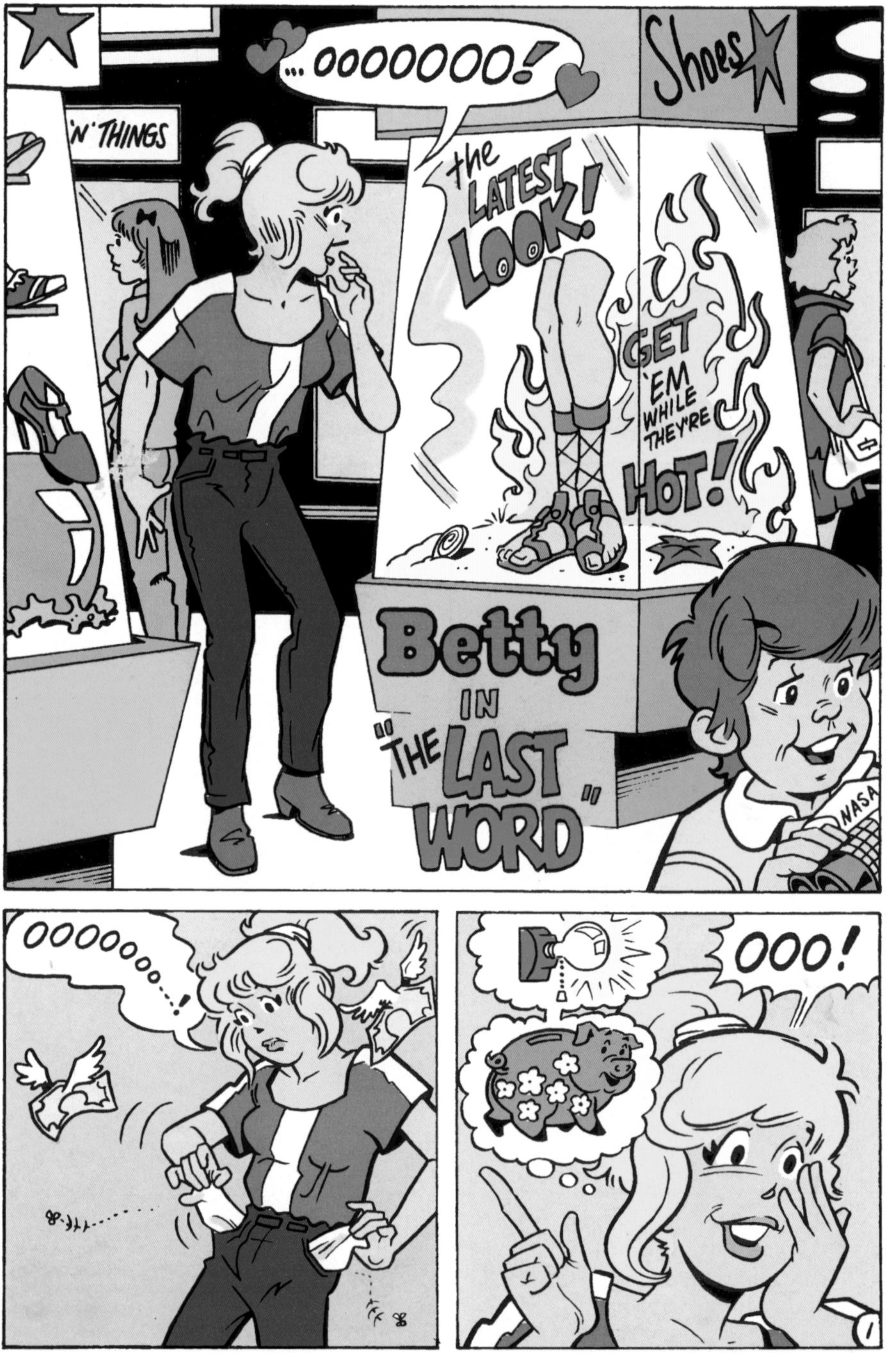
...OOOOOOO!
Shoes
'N' THINGS
the LATEST LOOK!
GET 'EM WHILE THEY'RE HOT!
Betty
IN
"THE LAST WORD"
NASA
OOOOOOO...!
OOO!

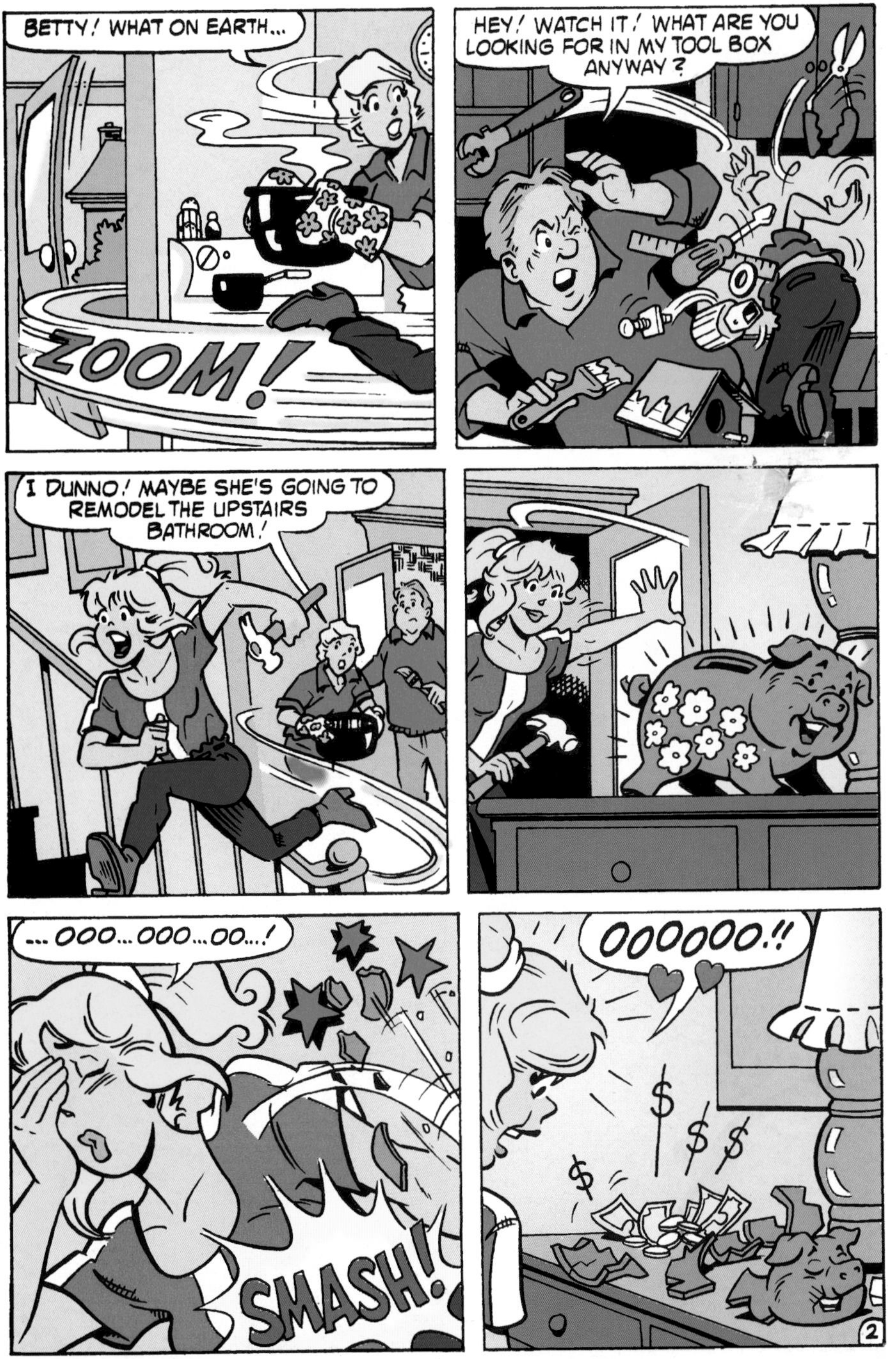
BETTY! WHAT ON EARTH...
ZOOM!
HEY! WATCH IT! WHAT ARE YOU LOOKING FOR IN MY TOOL BOX ANYWAY?
I DUNNO! MAYBE SHE'S GOING TO REMODEL THE UPSTAIRS BATHROOM!
...OOO...OOO...OO...!
SMASH!
OOOOOO.!!
2

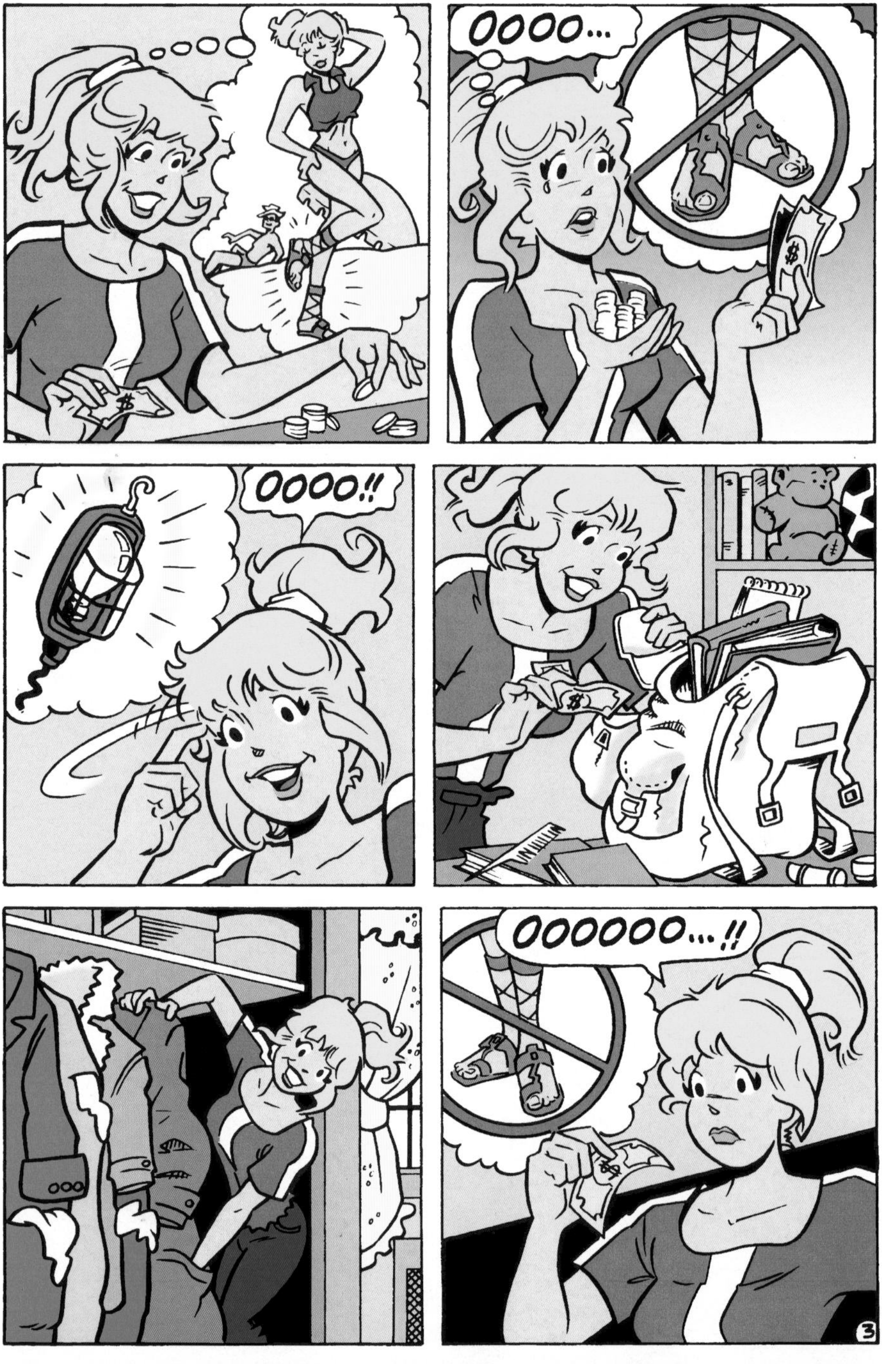
OOOO...
OOOO!!
OOOOOO...!!
3

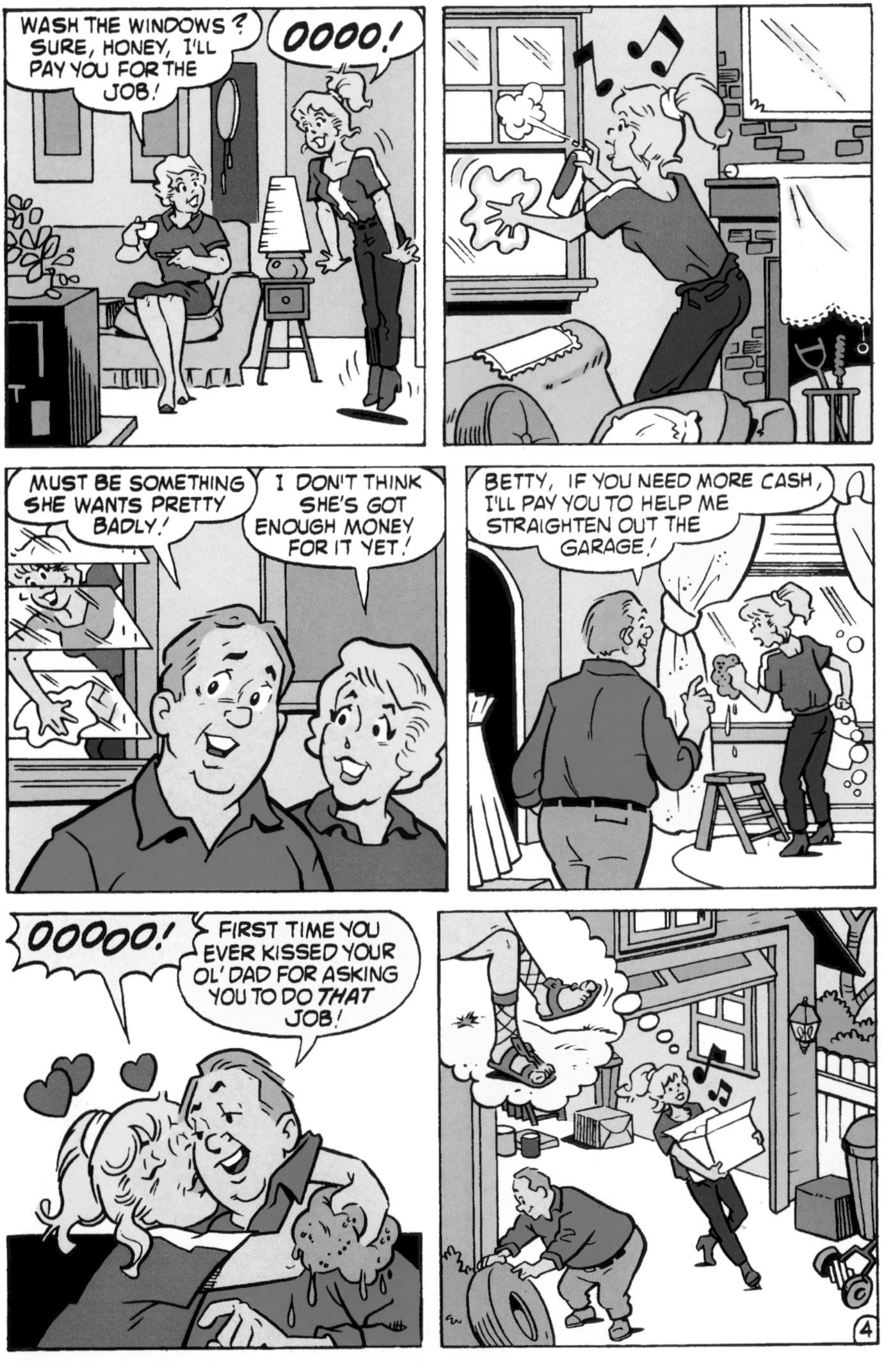
WASH THE WINDOWS? SURE, HONEY, I'LL PAY YOU FOR THE JOB!
OOOO!
MUST BE SOMETHING SHE WANTS PRETTY BADLY!
I DON'T THINK SHE'S GOT ENOUGH MONEY FOR IT YET!
BETTY, IF YOU NEED MORE CASH, I'LL PAY YOU TO HELP ME STRAIGHTEN OUT THE GARAGE!
OOOOO!
FIRST TIME YOU EVER KISSED YOUR OL' DAD FOR ASKING YOU TO DO THAT JOB!
4

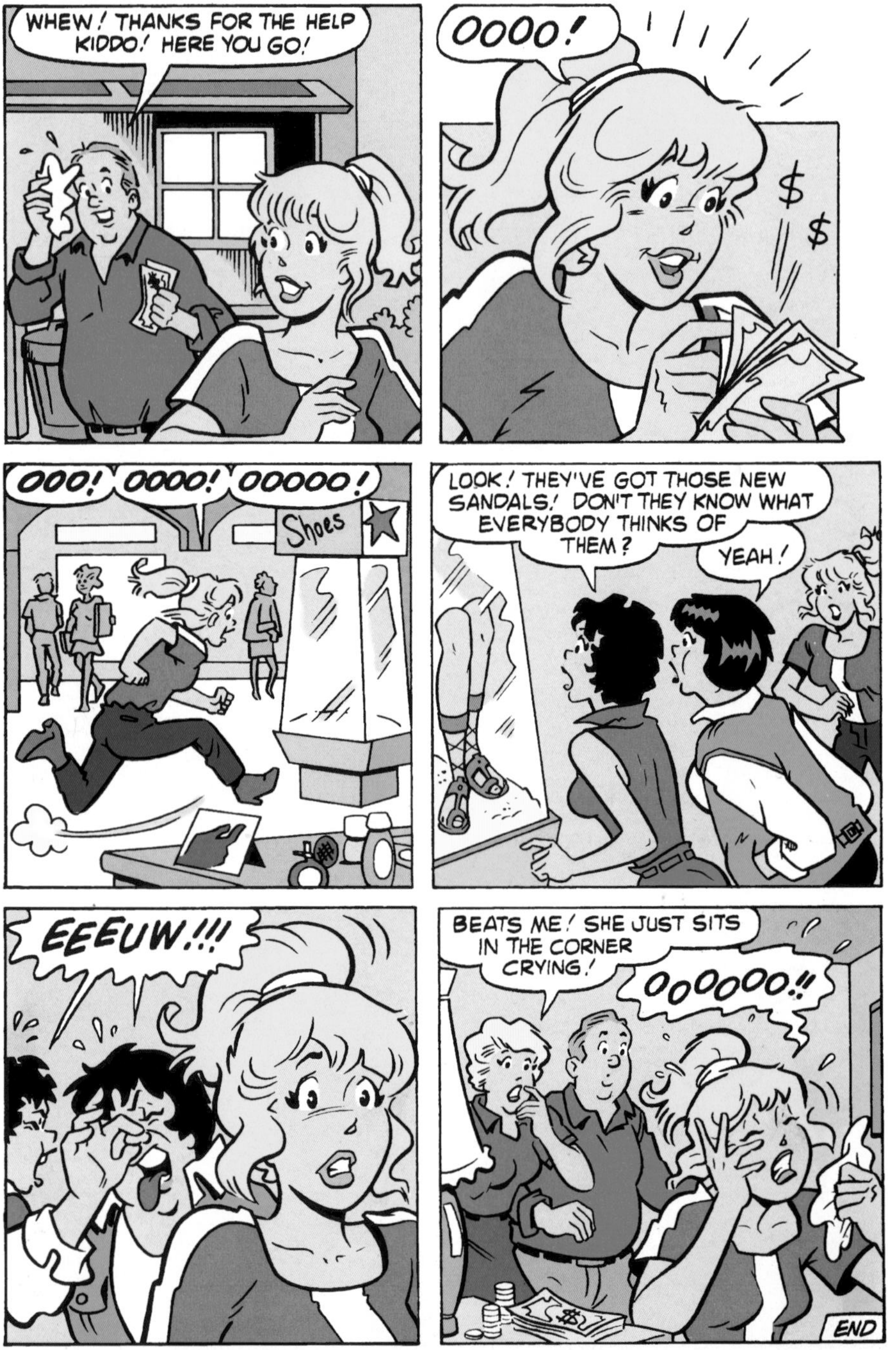
WHEW! THANKS FOR THE HELP KIDDO! HERE YOU GO!
OOOO!
$ $
OOO! OOOO! OOOOO!
Shoes
LOOK! THEY'VE GOT THOSE NEW SANDALS! DON'T THEY KNOW WHAT EVERYBODY THINKS OF THEM?
YEAH!
EEEUW!!!
BEATS ME! SHE JUST SITS IN THE CORNER CRYING!
OOOOOO!!
END

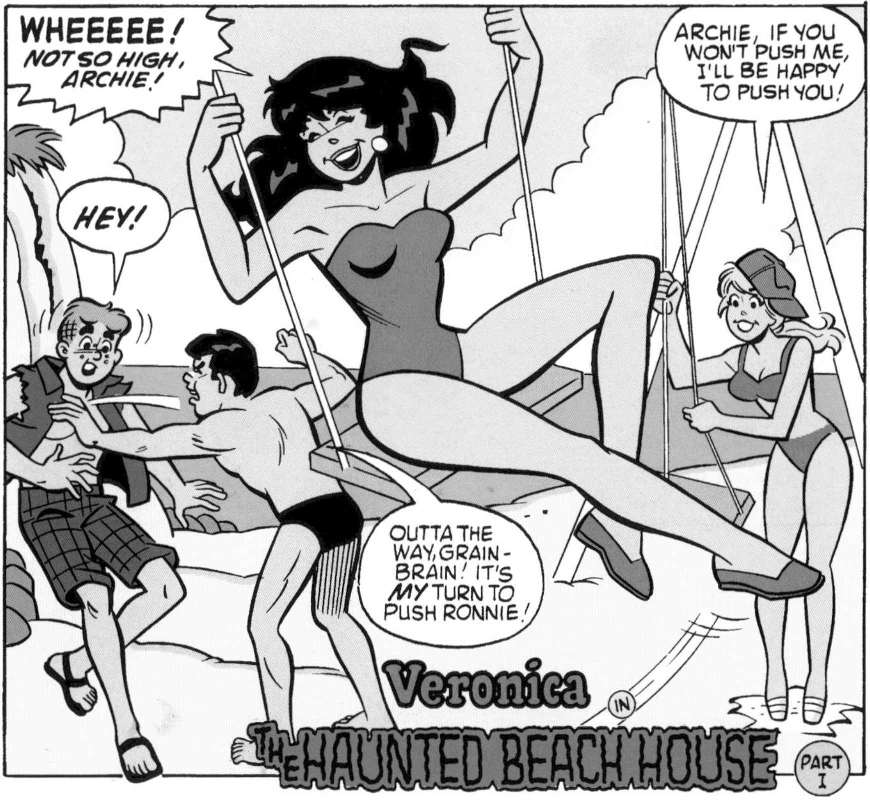
WHEEEEEE! NOT SO HIGH, ARCHIE!
HEY!
ARCHIE, IF YOU WON'T PUSH ME, I'LL BE HAPPY TO PUSH YOU!
OUTTA THE WAY, GRAIN-BRAIN! IT'S MY TURN TO PUSH RONNIE!
Veronica IN THE HAUNTED BEACH HOUSE PART I

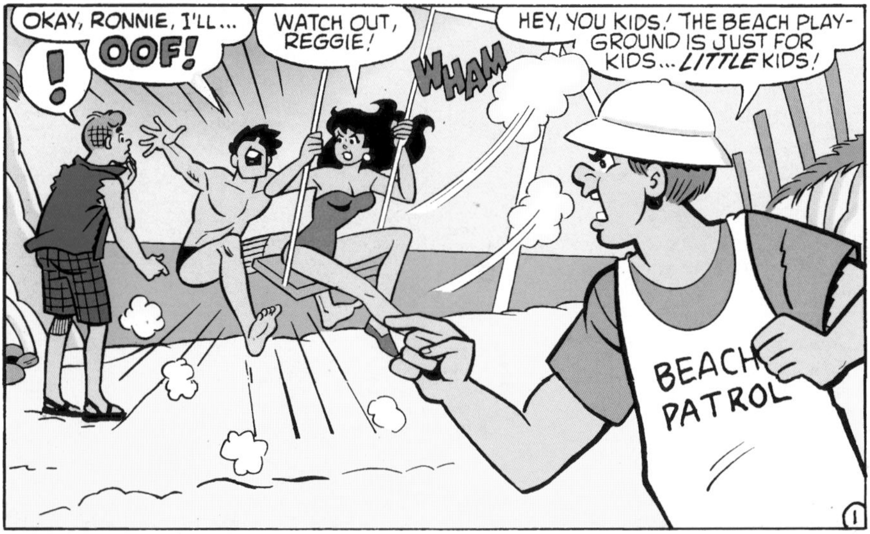
!
OKAY, RONNIE, I'LL... OOF!
WATCH OUT, REGGIE!
WHAM
HEY, YOU KIDS! THE BEACH PLAY-GROUND IS JUST FOR KIDS... LITTLE KIDS!
BEACH PATROL
1

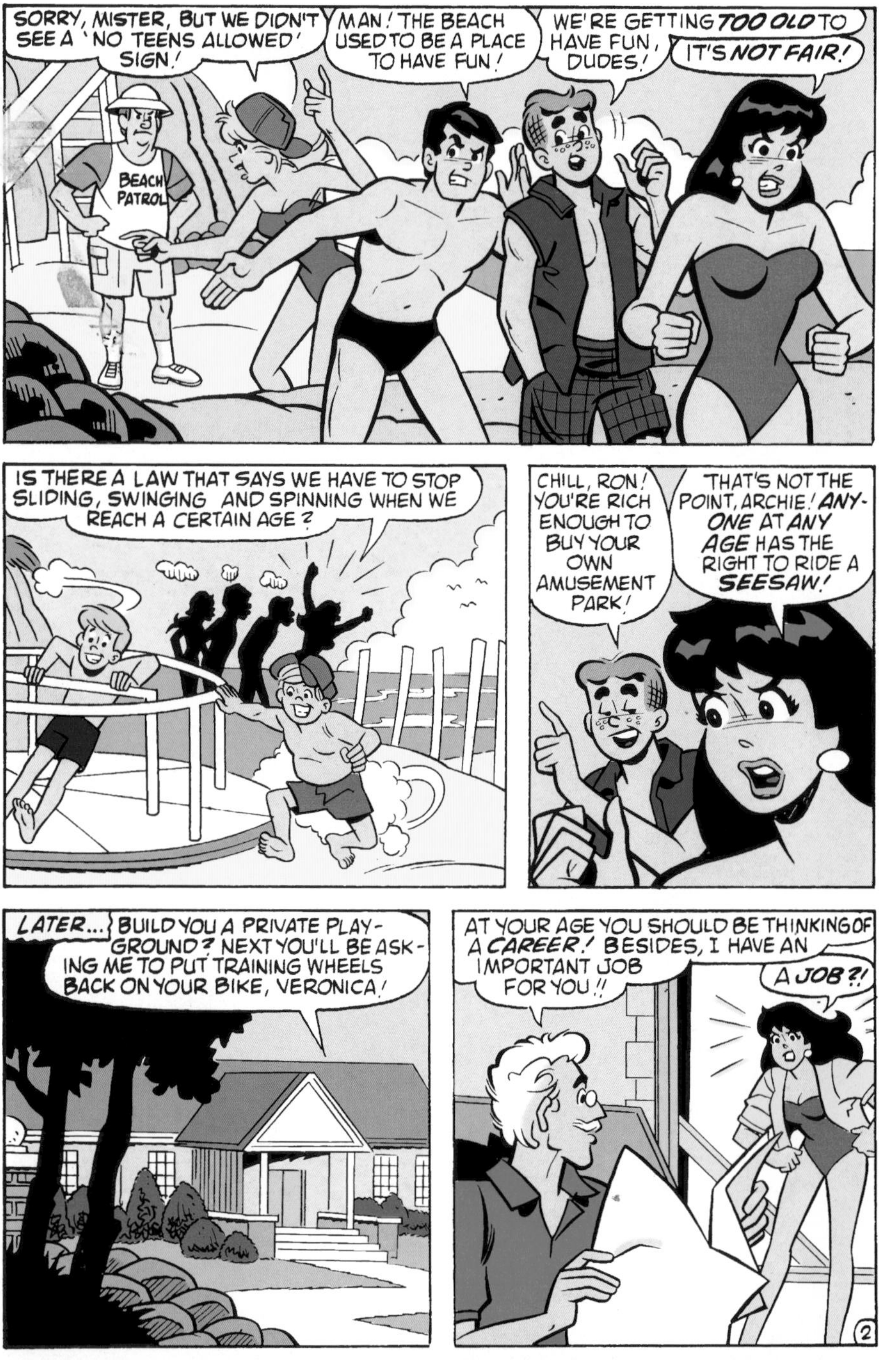
SORRY, MISTER, BUT WE DIDN'T SEE A 'NO TEENS ALLOWED' SIGN!
MAN! THE BEACH USED TO BE A PLACE TO HAVE FUN!
WE'RE GETTING TOO OLD TO HAVE FUN, DUDES!
IT'S NOT FAIR!
BEACH PATROL
IS THERE A LAW THAT SAYS WE HAVE TO STOP SLIDING, SWINGING AND SPINNING WHEN WE REACH A CERTAIN AGE?
CHILL, RON! YOU'RE RICH ENOUGH TO BUY YOUR OWN AMUSEMENT PARK!
THAT'S NOT THE POINT, ARCHIE! ANY-ONE AT ANY AGE HAS THE RIGHT TO RIDE A SEESAW!
LATER...
BUILD YOU A PRIVATE PLAY-GROUND? NEXT YOU'LL BE ASK-ING ME TO PUT TRAINING WHEELS BACK ON YOUR BIKE, VERONICA!
AT YOUR AGE YOU SHOULD BE THINKING OF A CAREER! BESIDES, I HAVE AN IMPORTANT JOB FOR YOU!!
A JOB?!
2

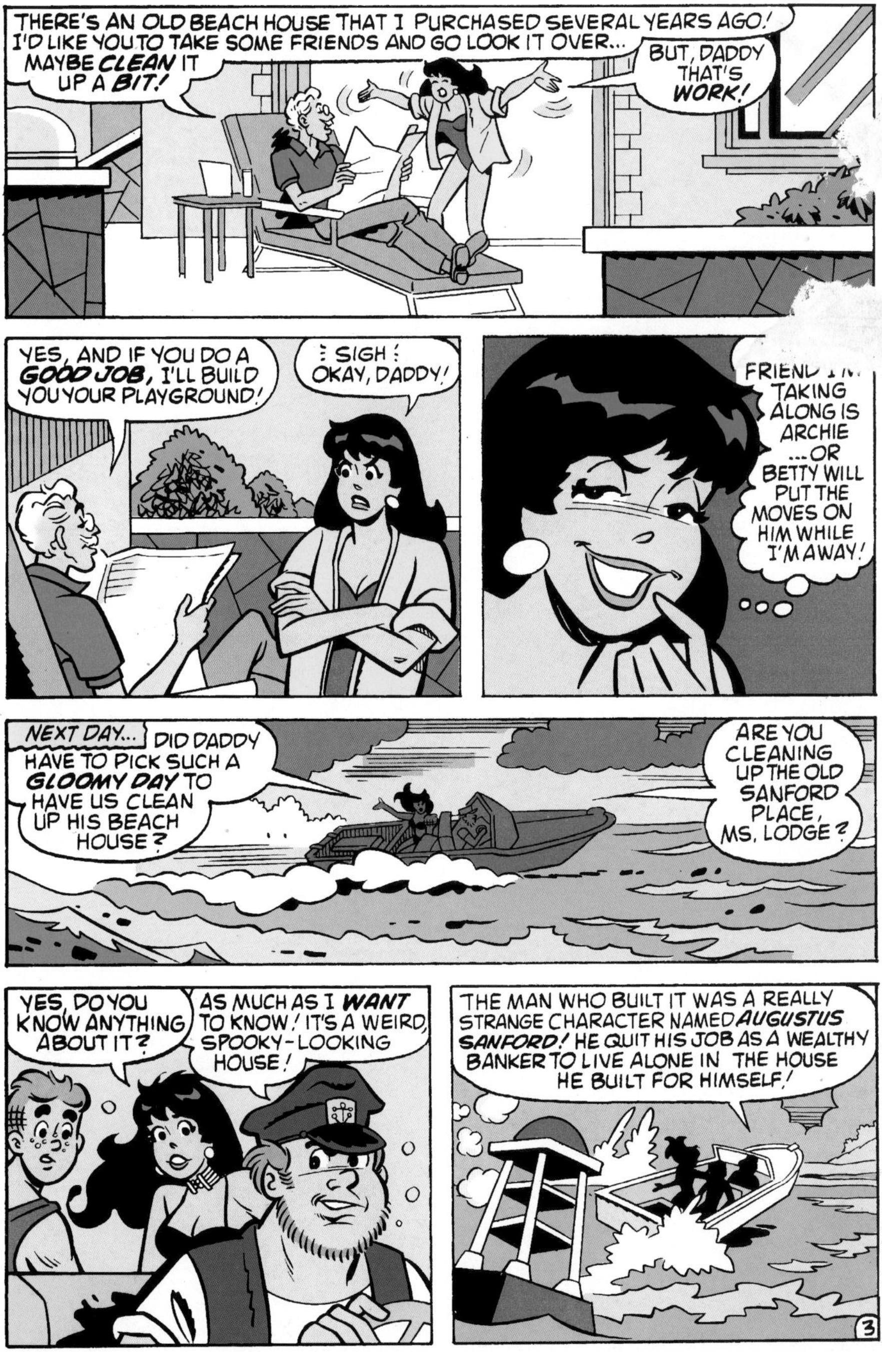
THERE'S AN OLD BEACH HOUSE THAT I PURCHASED SEVERAL YEARS AGO! I'D LIKE YOU TO TAKE SOME FRIENDS AND GO LOOK IT OVER... MAYBE CLEAN IT UP A BIT!
BUT, DADDY THAT'S WORK!
YES, AND IF YOU DO A GOOD JOB, I'LL BUILD YOU YOUR PLAYGROUND!
SIGH OKAY, DADDY!
FRIEND
TAKING ALONG IS ARCHIE ...OR BETTY WILL PUT THE MOVES ON HIM WHILE I'M AWAY!
NEXT DAY...
DID DADDY HAVE TO PICK SUCH A GLOOMY DAY TO HAVE US CLEAN UP HIS BEACH HOUSE?
ARE YOU CLEANING UP THE OLD SANFORD PLACE, MS. LODGE?
YES, DO YOU KNOW ANYTHING ABOUT IT?
AS MUCH AS I WANT TO KNOW! IT'S A WEIRD, SPOOKY-LOOKING HOUSE!
THE MAN WHO BUILT IT WAS A REALLY STRANGE CHARACTER NAMED AUGUSTUS SANFORD! HE QUIT HIS JOB AS A WEALTHY BANKER TO LIVE ALONE IN THE HOUSE HE BUILT FOR HIMSELF!

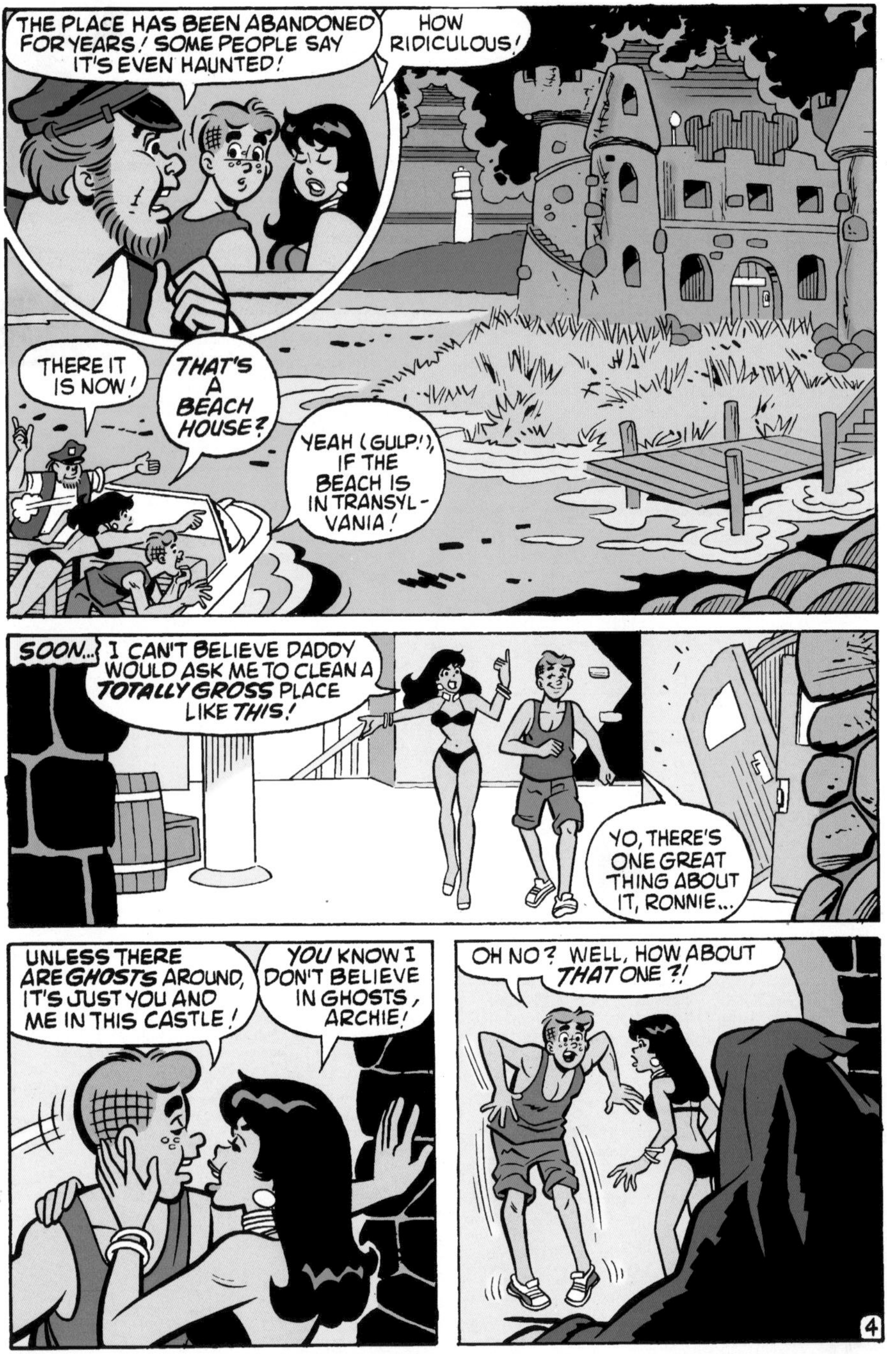
THE PLACE HAS BEEN ABANDONED FOR YEARS! SOME PEOPLE SAY IT'S EVEN HAUNTED!
HOW RIDICULOUS!
THERE IT IS NOW!
THAT'S A BEACH HOUSE?
YEAH (GULP!), IF THE BEACH IS IN TRANSYLVANIA!
SOON...
I CAN'T BELIEVE DADDY WOULD ASK ME TO CLEAN A TOTALLY GROSS PLACE LIKE THIS!
YO, THERE'S ONE GREAT THING ABOUT IT, RONNIE...
UNLESS THERE ARE GHOSTS AROUND, IT'S JUST YOU AND ME IN THIS CASTLE!
YOU KNOW I DON'T BELIEVE IN GHOSTS, ARCHIE!
OH NO? WELL, HOW ABOUT THAT ONE?!
4

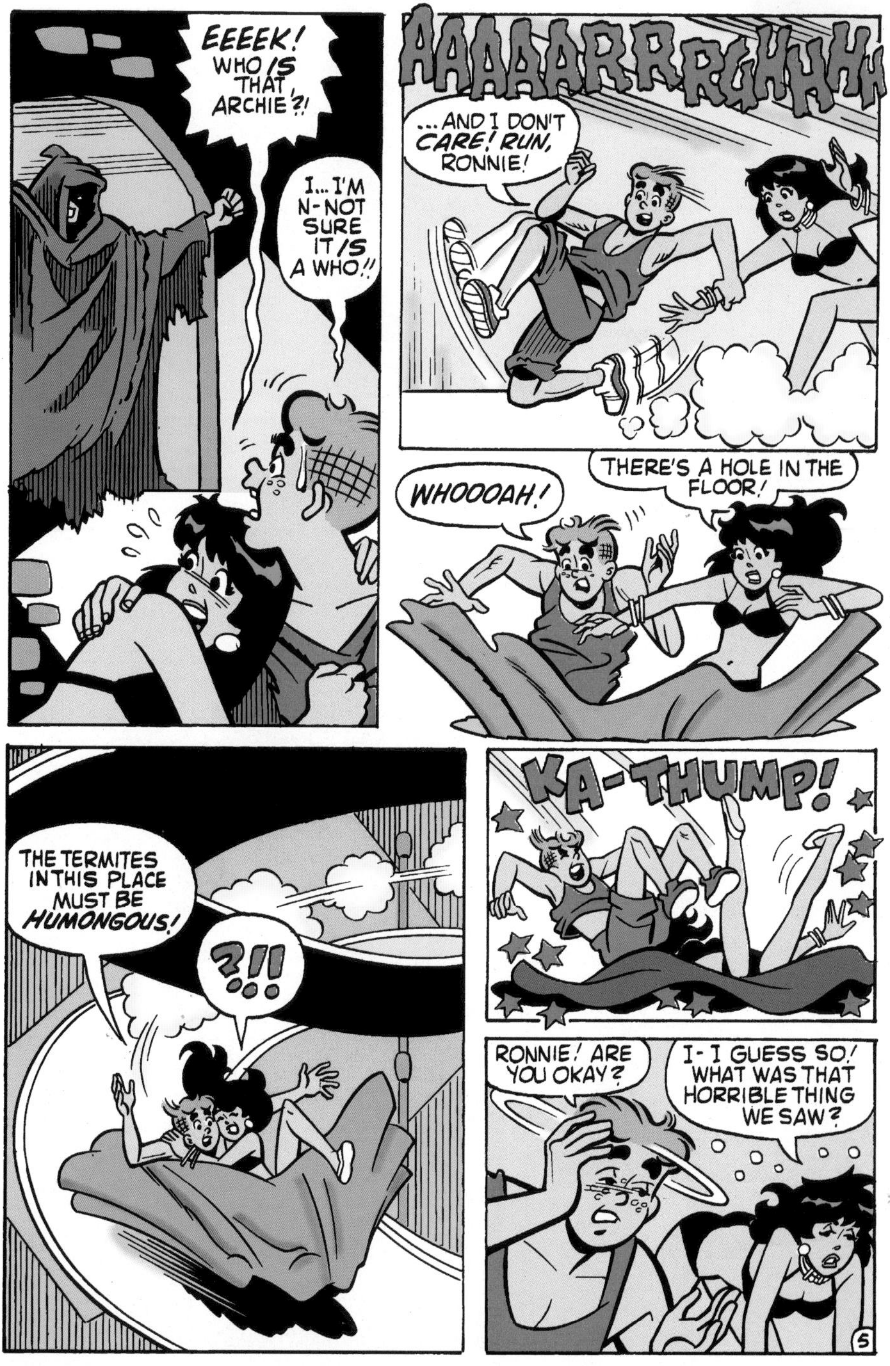
EEEEK! WHO IS THAT, ARCHIE?!
I... I'M N-NOT SURE IT IS A WHO!!
AAAAARRRGHHHH
...AND I DON'T CARE! RUN, RONNIE!
WHOOOAH!
THERE'S A HOLE IN THE FLOOR!
THE TERMITES IN THIS PLACE MUST BE HUMONGOUS!
?!!
KA-THUMP!
RONNIE! ARE YOU OKAY?
I- I GUESS SO! WHAT WAS THAT HORRIBLE THING WE SAW?
5

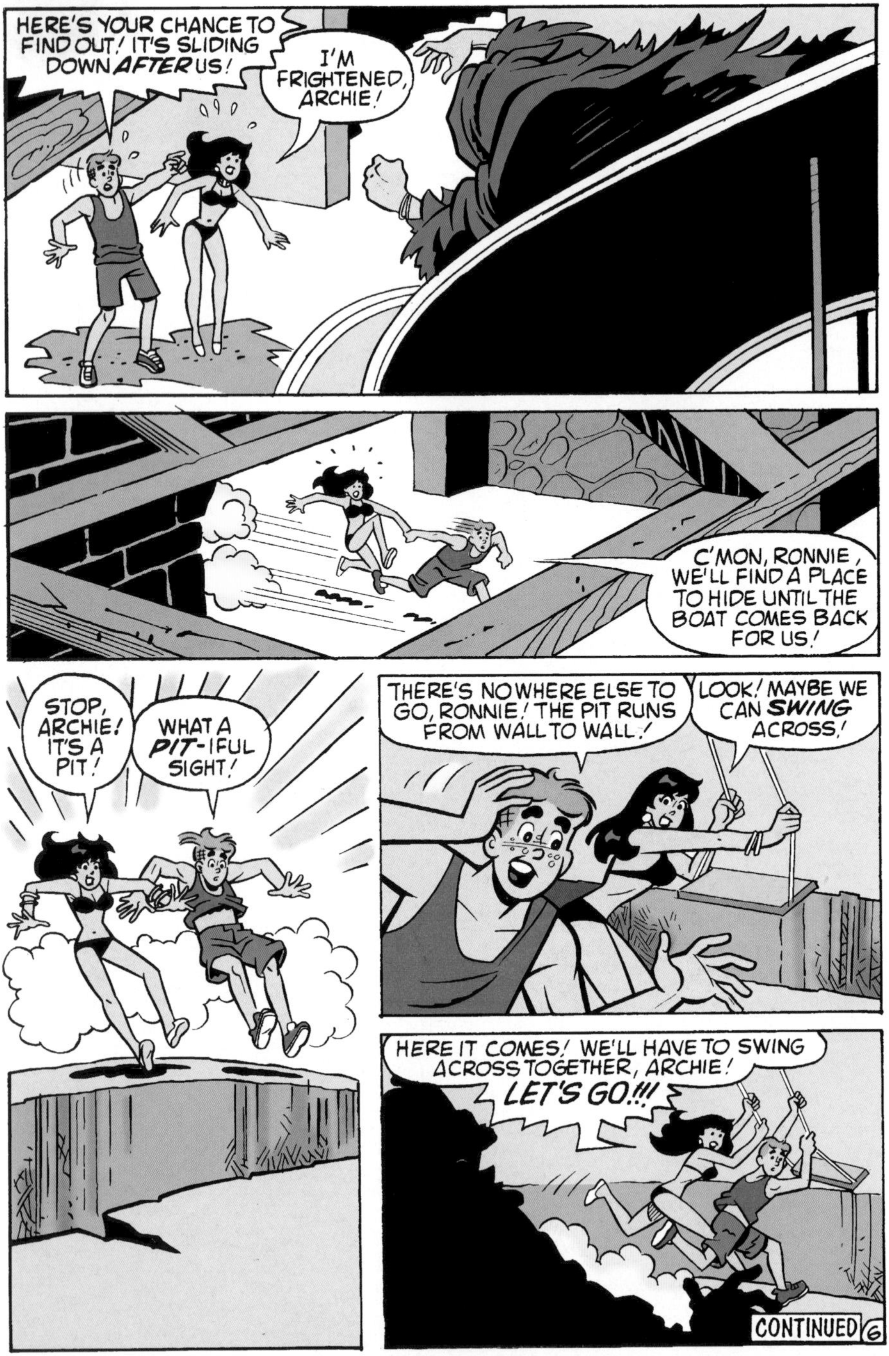
HERE'S YOUR CHANCE TO FIND OUT! IT'S SLIDING DOWN AFTER US!
I'M FRIGHTENED, ARCHIE!
C'MON, RONNIE, WE'LL FIND A PLACE TO HIDE UNTIL THE BOAT COMES BACK FOR US!
STOP, ARCHIE! IT'S A PIT!
WHAT A PIT-IFUL SIGHT!
THERE'S NOWHERE ELSE TO GO, RONNIE! THE PIT RUNS FROM WALL TO WALL!
LOOK! MAYBE WE CAN SWING ACROSS!
HERE IT COMES! WE'LL HAVE TO SWING ACROSS TOGETHER, ARCHIE!
LET'S GO!!!
CONTINUED
6

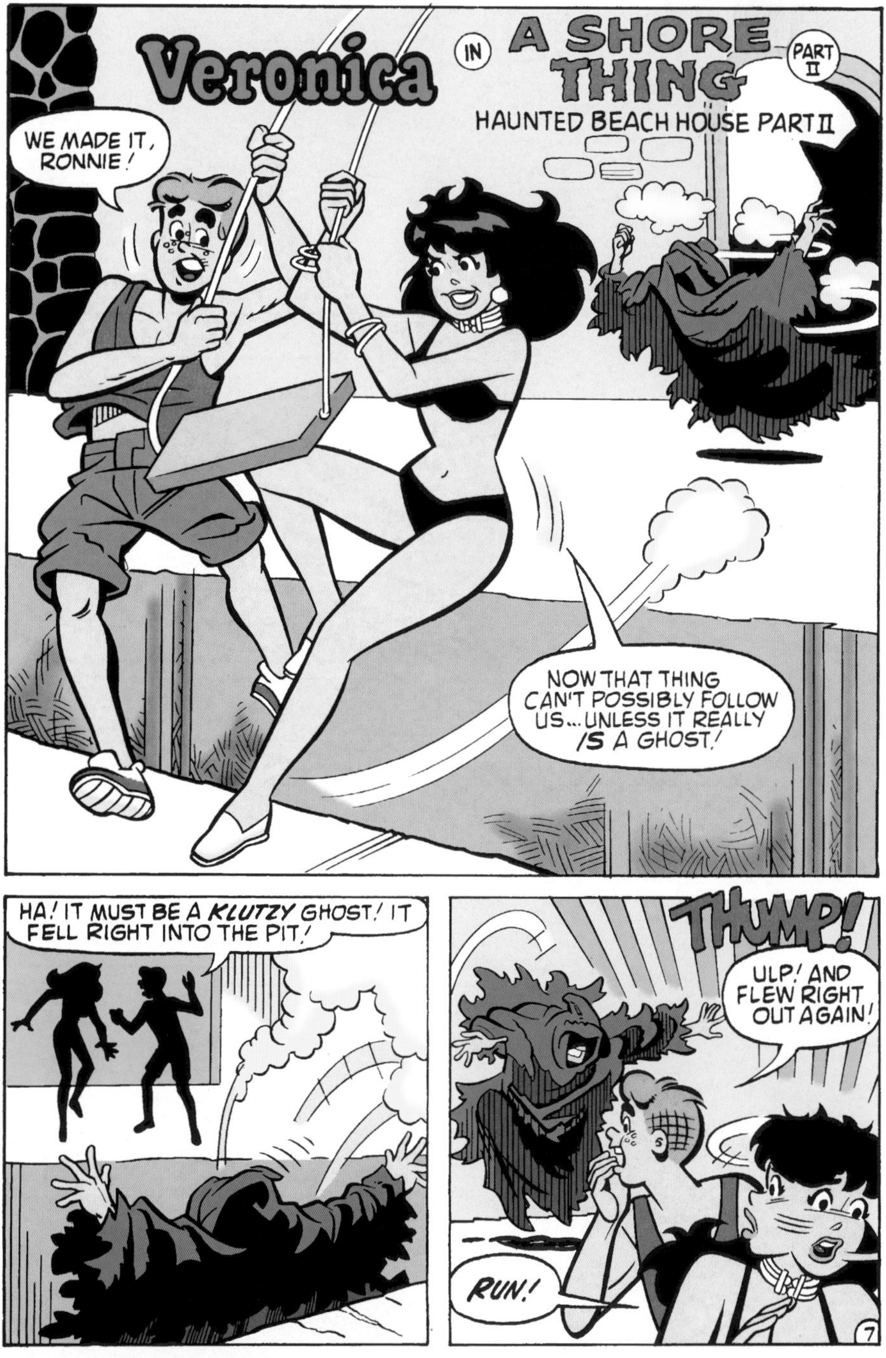
Veronica
IN
A SHORE THING
PART II
HAUNTED BEACH HOUSE PART II
WE MADE IT, RONNIE!
NOW THAT THING CAN'T POSSIBLY FOLLOW US... UNLESS IT REALLY IS A GHOST!
HA! IT MUST BE A KLUTZY GHOST! IT FELL RIGHT INTO THE PIT!
THUMP!
ULP! AND FLEW RIGHT OUT AGAIN!
RUN!
7

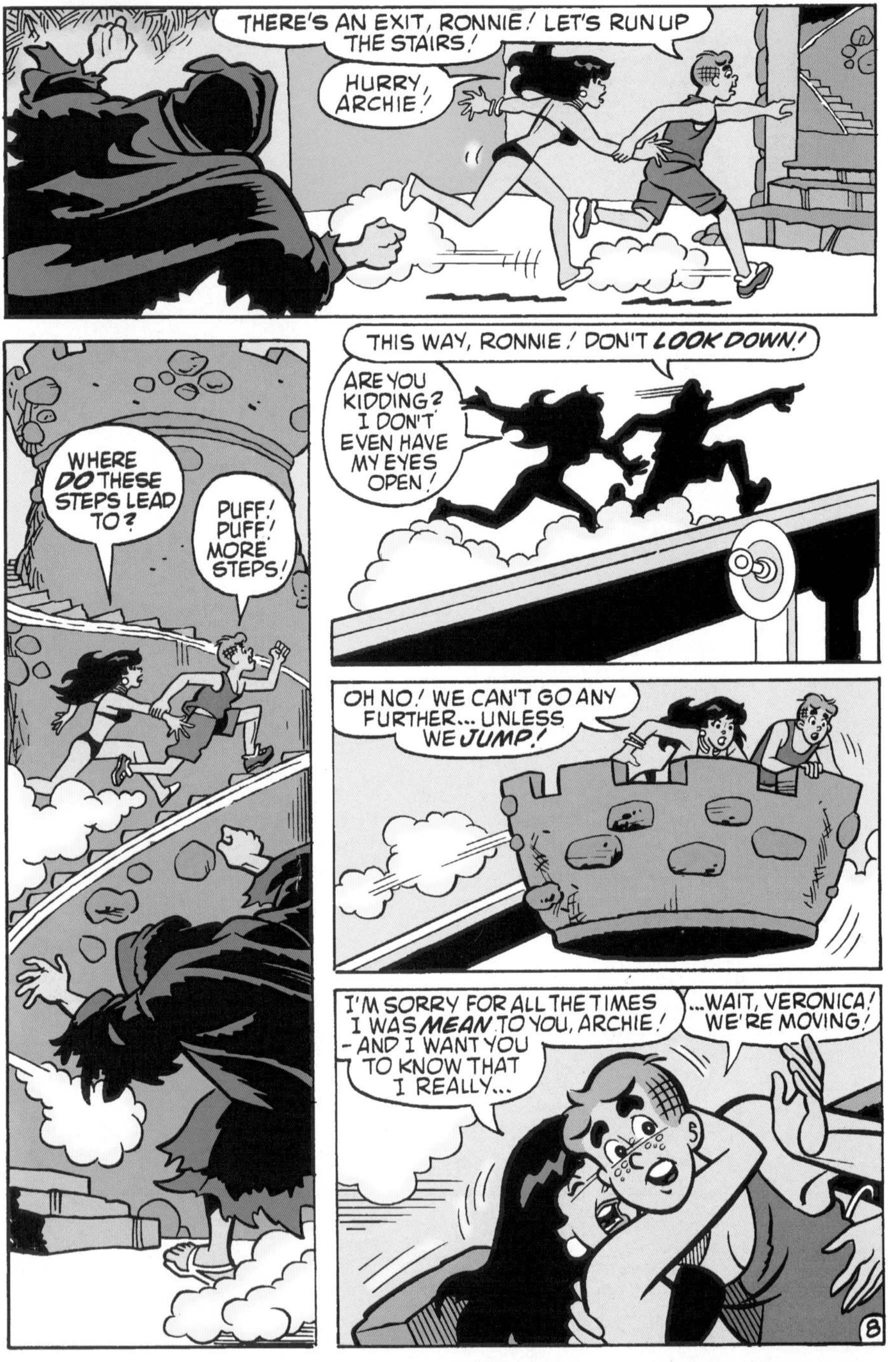

THERE'S AN EXIT, RONNIE! LET'S RUN UP THE STAIRS!
HURRY, ARCHIE!
WHERE DO THESE STEPS LEAD TO?
PUFF! PUFF! MORE STEPS!
THIS WAY, RONNIE! DON'T LOOK DOWN!
ARE YOU KIDDING? I DON'T EVEN HAVE MY EYES OPEN!
OH NO! WE CAN'T GO ANY FURTHER... UNLESS WE JUMP!
I'M SORRY FOR ALL THE TIMES I WAS MEAN TO YOU, ARCHIE! - AND I WANT YOU TO KNOW THAT I REALLY...
...WAIT, VERONICA! WE'RE MOVING!
8

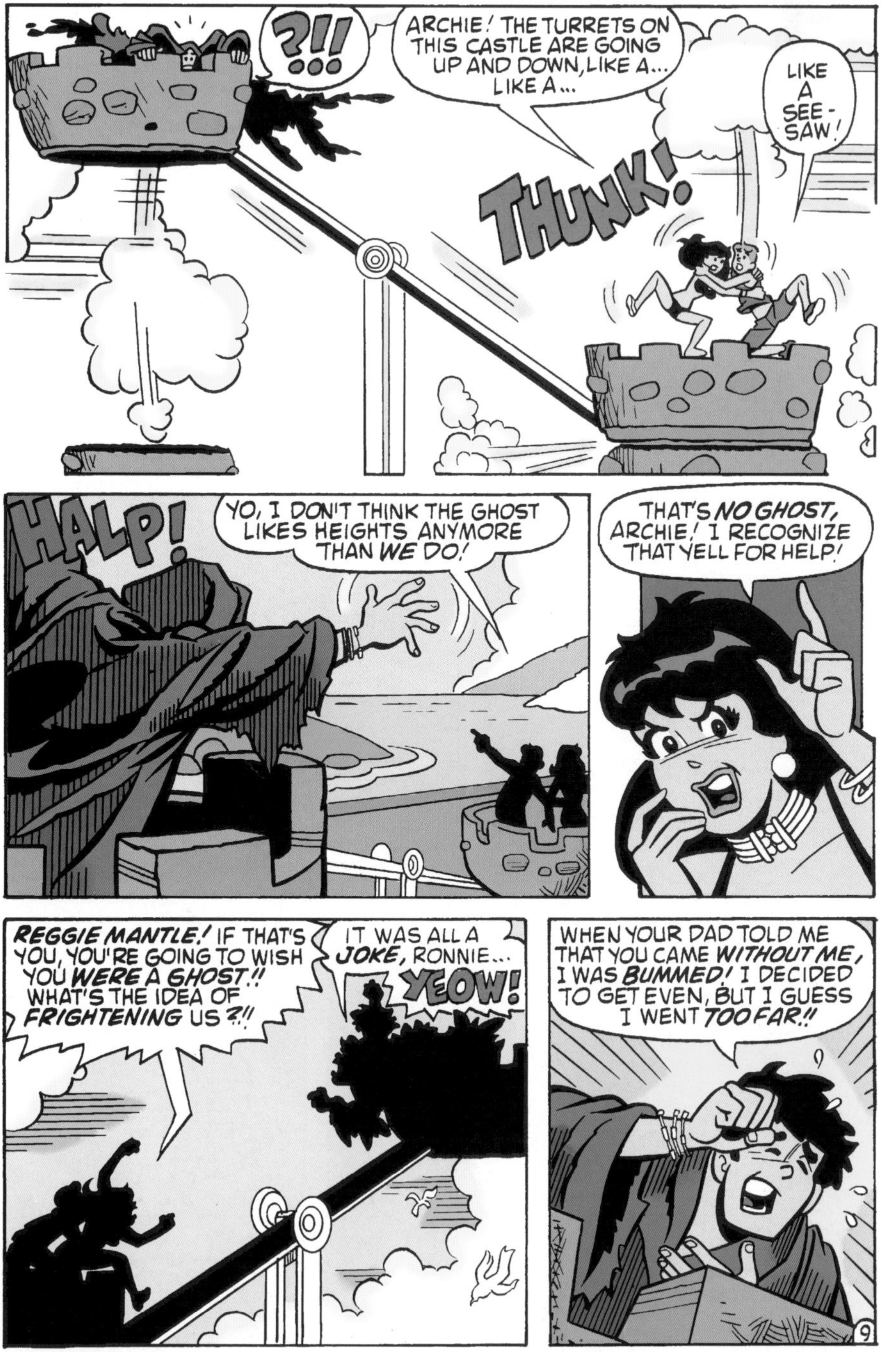
?!!
ARCHIE! THE TURRETS ON THIS CASTLE ARE GOING UP AND DOWN, LIKE A... LIKE A...
LIKE A SEE-SAW!
THUNK!
HALP!
YO, I DON'T THINK THE GHOST LIKES HEIGHTS ANYMORE THAN WE DO!
THAT'S NO GHOST, ARCHIE! I RECOGNIZE THAT YELL FOR HELP!
REGGIE MANTLE! IF THAT'S YOU, YOU'RE GOING TO WISH YOU WERE A GHOST!! WHAT'S THE IDEA OF FRIGHTENING US?!!
IT WAS ALL A JOKE, RONNIE...
YEOW!
WHEN YOUR DAD TOLD ME THAT YOU CAME WITHOUT ME, I WAS BUMMED! I DECIDED TO GET EVEN, BUT I GUESS I WENT TOO FAR!!
9

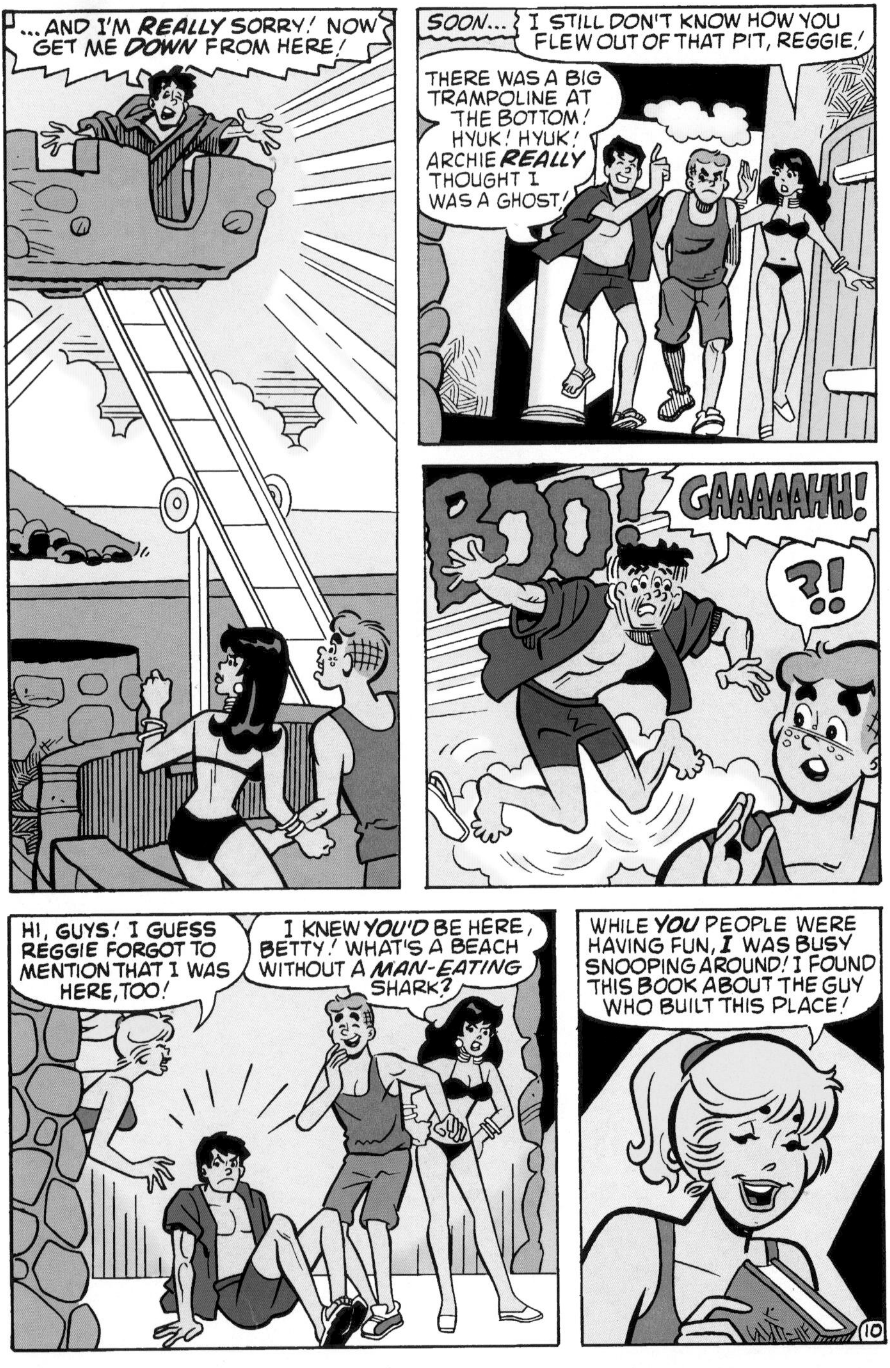
...AND I'M REALLY SORRY! NOW GET ME DOWN FROM HERE!
SOON...
I STILL DON'T KNOW HOW YOU FLEW OUT OF THAT PIT, REGGIE!
THERE WAS A BIG TRAMPOLINE AT THE BOTTOM! HYUK! HYUK! ARCHIE REALLY THOUGHT I WAS A GHOST!
BOO!
GAAAAAHH!
?!
HI, GUYS! I GUESS REGGIE FORGOT TO MENTION THAT I WAS HERE, TOO!
I KNEW YOU'D BE HERE, BETTY! WHAT'S A BEACH WITHOUT A MAN-EATING SHARK?
WHILE YOU PEOPLE WERE HAVING FUN, I WAS BUSY SNOOPING AROUND! I FOUND THIS BOOK ABOUT THE GUY WHO BUILT THIS PLACE!
10

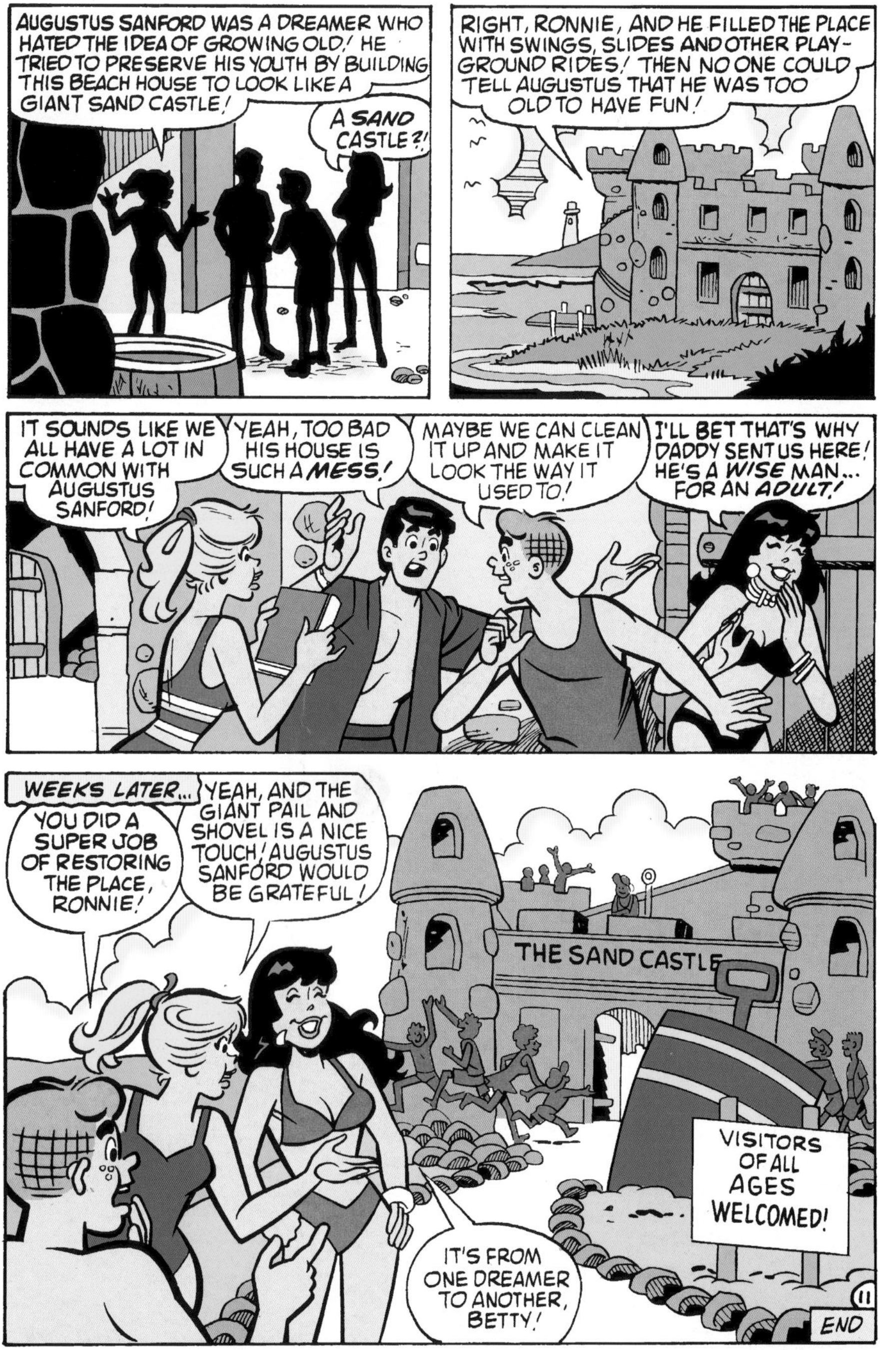
AUGUSTUS SANFORD WAS A DREAMER WHO HATED THE IDEA OF GROWING OLD! HE TRIED TO PRESERVE HIS YOUTH BY BUILDING THIS BEACH HOUSE TO LOOK LIKE A GIANT SAND CASTLE!
A SAND CASTLE?!
RIGHT, RONNIE, AND HE FILLED THE PLACE WITH SWINGS, SLIDES AND OTHER PLAY-GROUND RIDES! THEN NO ONE COULD TELL AUGUSTUS THAT HE WAS TOO OLD TO HAVE FUN!
IT SOUNDS LIKE WE ALL HAVE A LOT IN COMMON WITH AUGUSTUS SANFORD!
YEAH, TOO BAD HIS HOUSE IS SUCH A MESS!
MAYBE WE CAN CLEAN IT UP AND MAKE IT LOOK THE WAY IT USED TO!
I'LL BET THAT'S WHY DADDY SENT US HERE! HE'S A WISE MAN... FOR AN ADULT!
WEEKS LATER...
YOU DID A SUPER JOB OF RESTORING THE PLACE, RONNIE!
YEAH, AND THE GIANT PAIL AND SHOVEL IS A NICE TOUCH! AUGUSTUS SANFORD WOULD BE GRATEFUL!
THE SAND CASTLE
VISITORS OF ALL AGES WELCOMED!
IT'S FROM ONE DREAMER TO ANOTHER, BETTY!
11
END

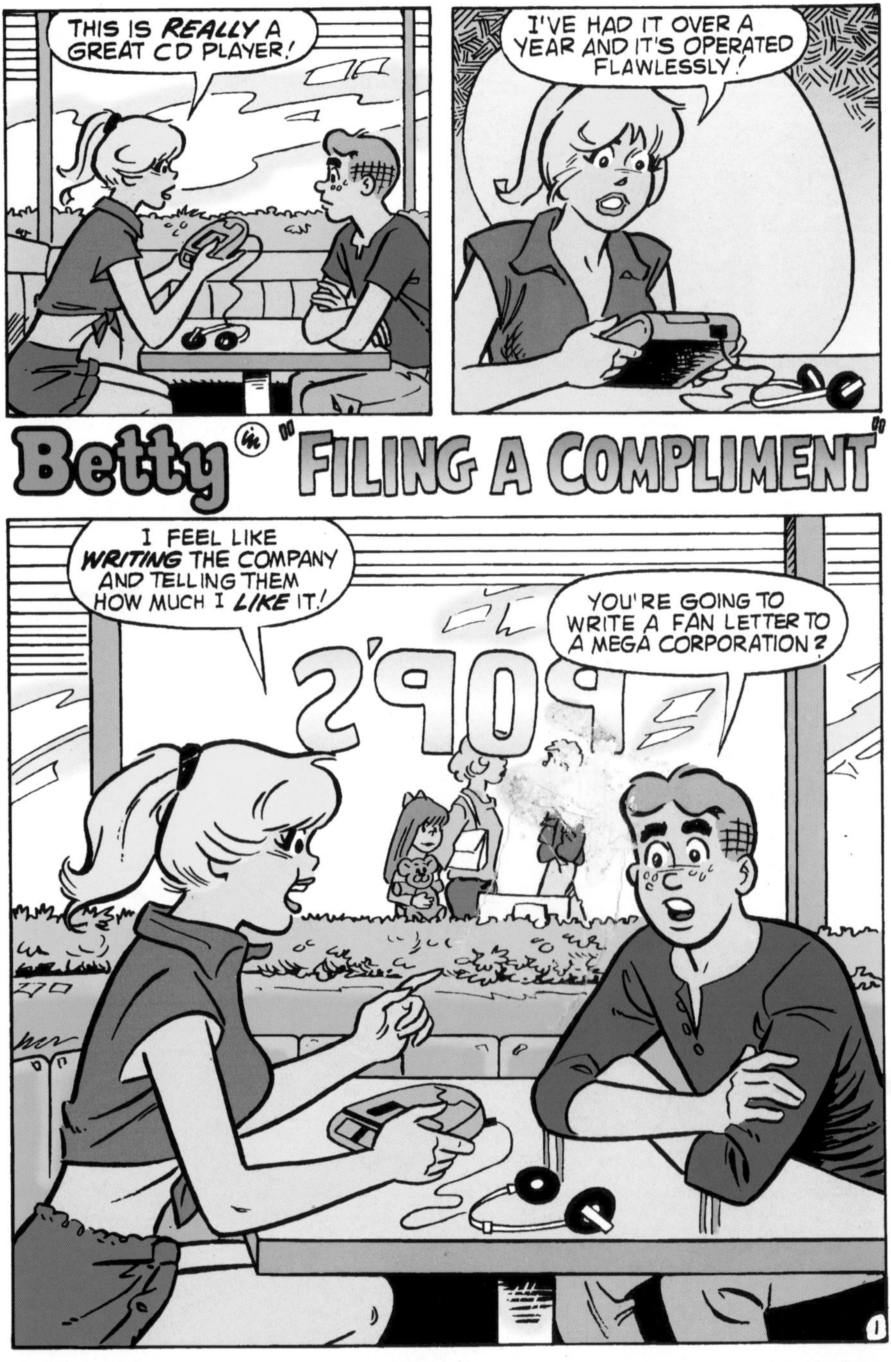
THIS IS REALLY A GREAT CD PLAYER!
I'VE HAD IT OVER A YEAR AND IT'S OPERATED FLAWLESSLY!
Betty in "FILING A COMPLIMENT"
I FEEL LIKE WRITING THE COMPANY AND TELLING THEM HOW MUCH I LIKE IT!
YOU'RE GOING TO WRITE A FAN LETTER TO A MEGA CORPORATION?
POP'S
1

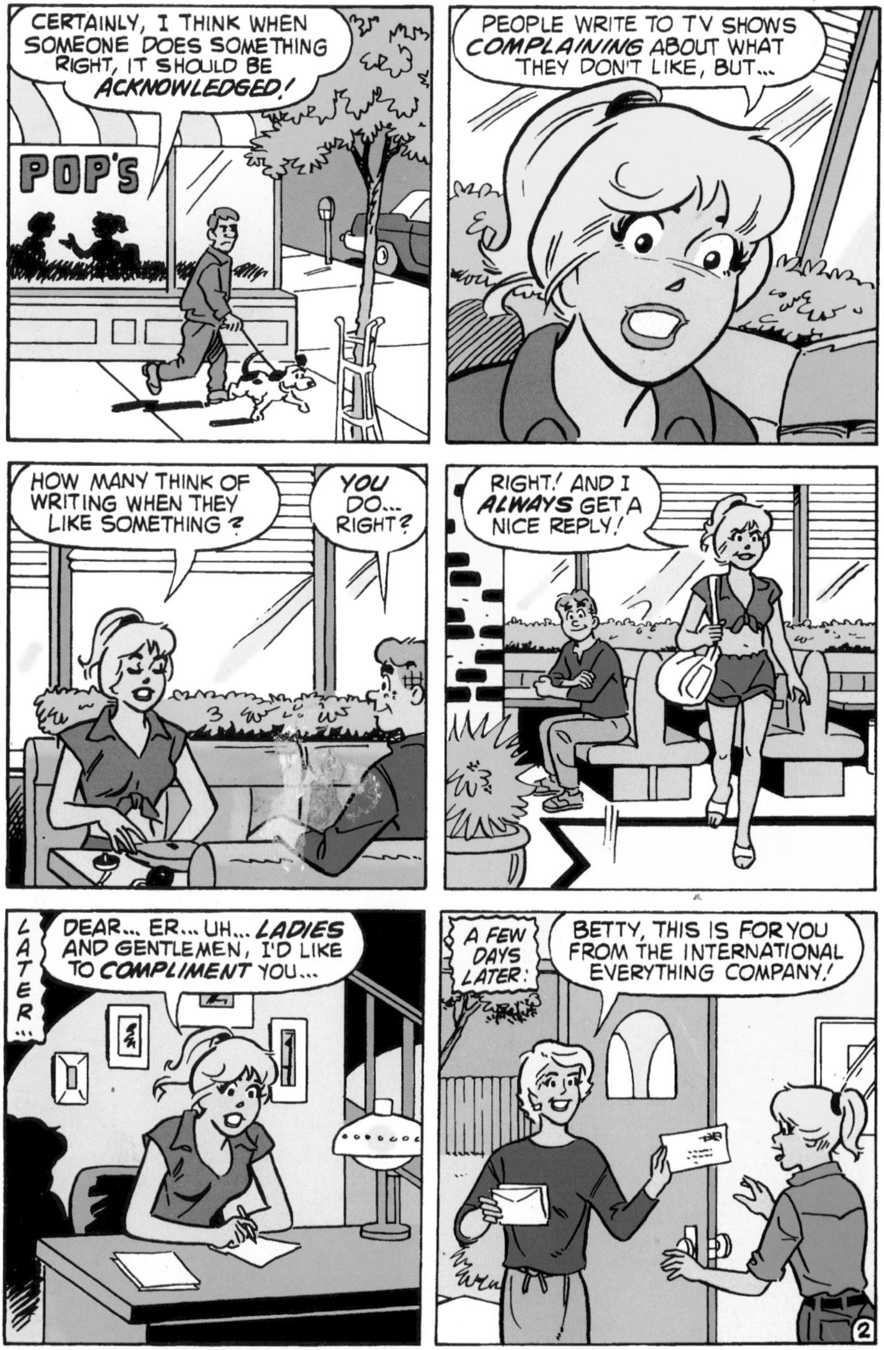
CERTAINLY, I THINK WHEN SOMEONE DOES SOMETHING RIGHT, IT SHOULD BE ACKNOWLEDGED!
POP'S
PEOPLE WRITE TO TV SHOWS COMPLAINING ABOUT WHAT THEY DON'T LIKE, BUT...
HOW MANY THINK OF WRITING WHEN THEY LIKE SOMETHING?
YOU DO... RIGHT?
RIGHT! AND I ALWAYS GET A NICE REPLY!
LATER...
DEAR... ER... UH... LADIES AND GENTLEMEN, I'D LIKE TO COMPLIMENT YOU...
A FEW DAYS LATER:
BETTY, THIS IS FOR YOU FROM THE INTERNATIONAL EVERYTHING COMPANY!
2

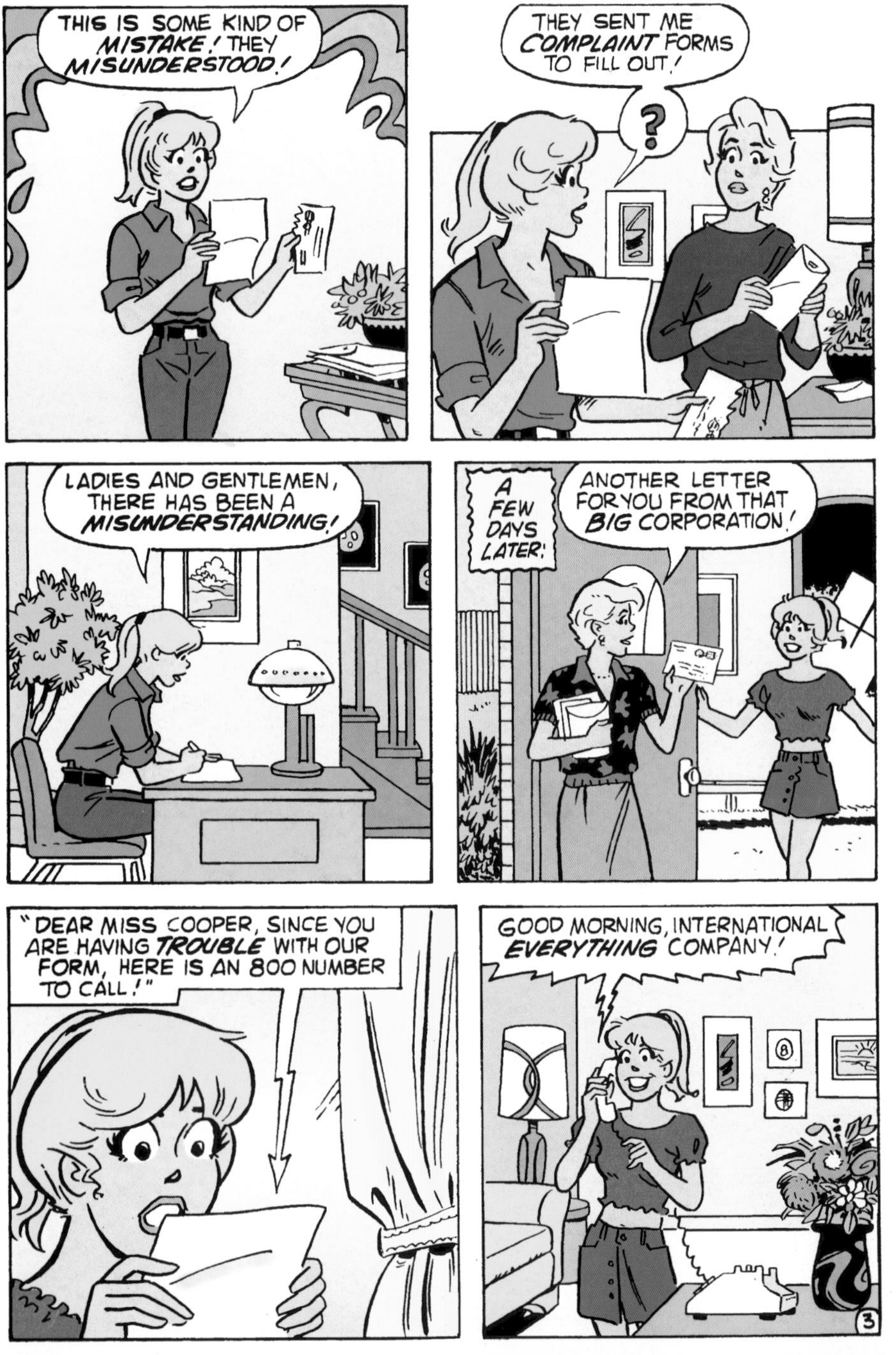
THIS IS SOME KIND OF MISTAKE! THEY MISUNDERSTOOD!
THEY SENT ME COMPLAINT FORMS TO FILL OUT!
?
LADIES AND GENTLEMEN, THERE HAS BEEN A MISUNDERSTANDING!
A FEW DAYS LATER!
ANOTHER LETTER FOR YOU FROM THAT BIG CORPORATION!
"DEAR MISS COOPER, SINCE YOU ARE HAVING TROUBLE WITH OUR FORM, HERE IS AN 800 NUMBER TO CALL!"
GOOD MORNING, INTERNATIONAL EVERYTHING COMPANY!
3

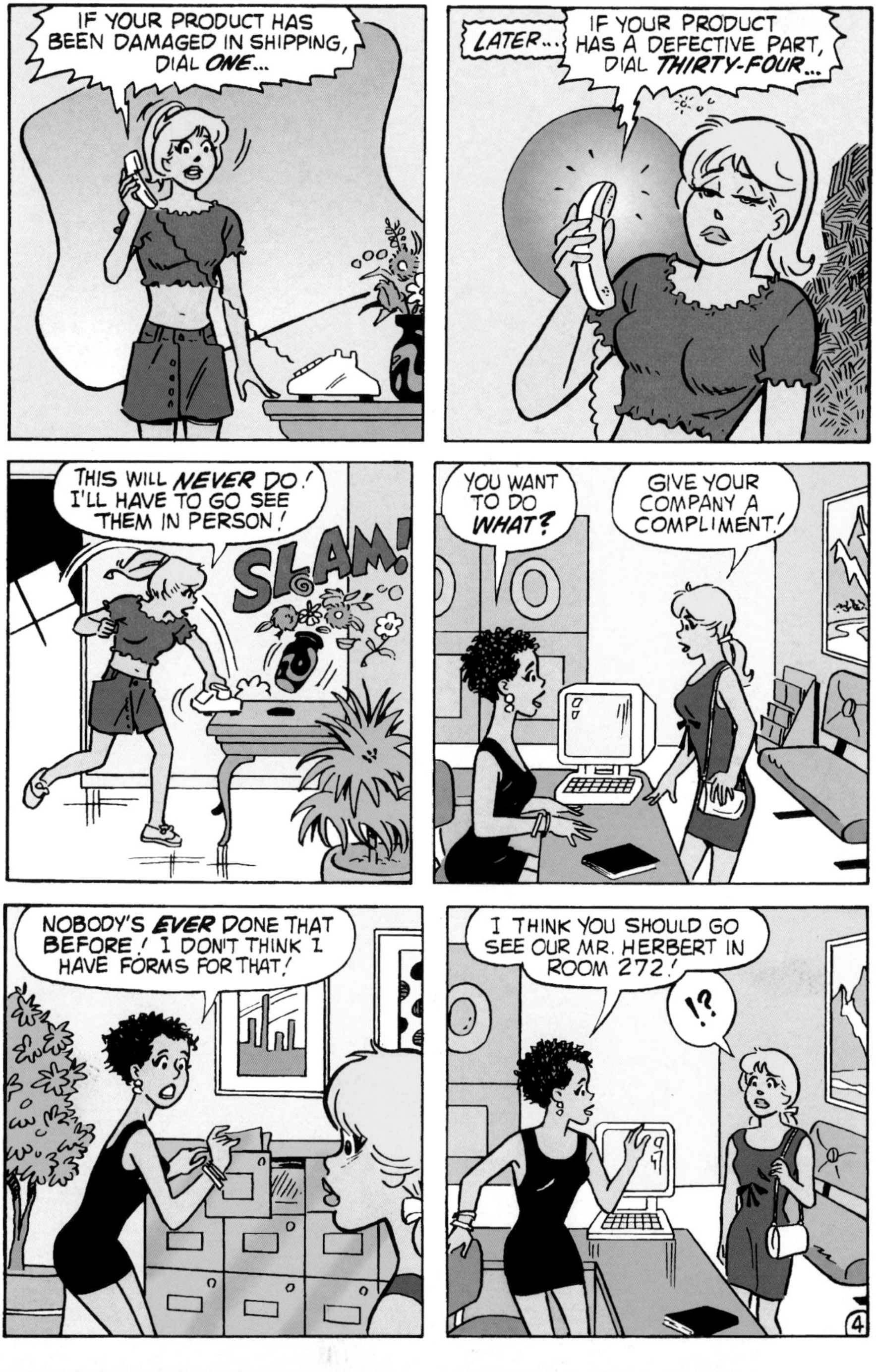
IF YOUR PRODUCT HAS BEEN DAMAGED IN SHIPPING, DIAL ONE...
LATER...
IF YOUR PRODUCT HAS A DEFECTIVE PART, DIAL THIRTY-FOUR...
THIS WILL NEVER DO! I'LL HAVE TO GO SEE THEM IN PERSON!
SLAM!
YOU WANT TO DO WHAT?
GIVE YOUR COMPANY A COMPLIMENT!
NOBODY'S EVER DONE THAT BEFORE! I DON'T THINK I HAVE FORMS FOR THAT!
I THINK YOU SHOULD GO SEE OUR MR. HERBERT IN ROOM 272!
!?
4

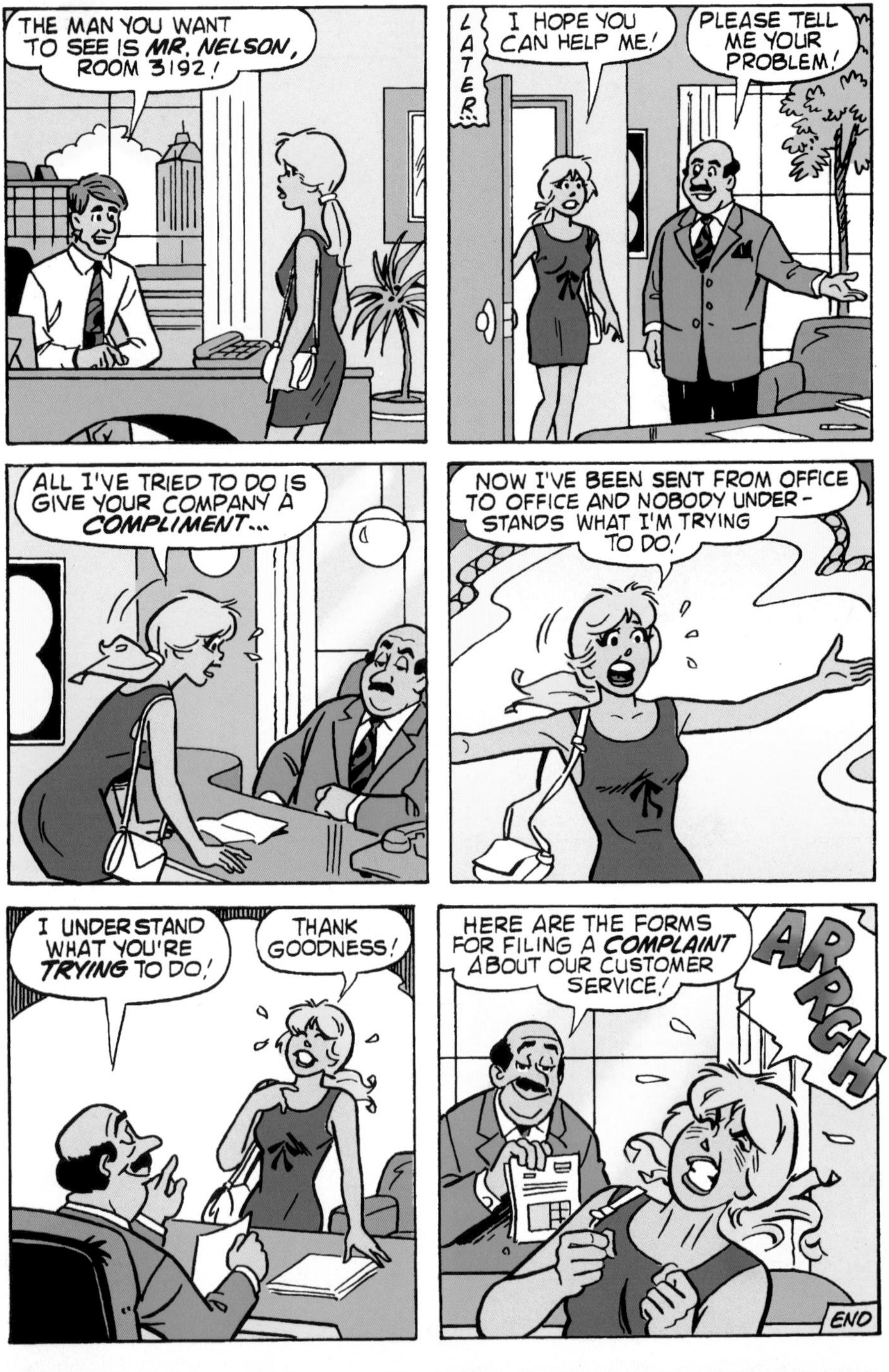
THE MAN YOU WANT TO SEE IS MR. NELSON, ROOM 3192!
LATER...
I HOPE YOU CAN HELP ME!
PLEASE TELL ME YOUR PROBLEM!
ALL I'VE TRIED TO DO IS GIVE YOUR COMPANY A COMPLIMENT...
NOW I'VE BEEN SENT FROM OFFICE TO OFFICE AND NOBODY UNDERSTANDS WHAT I'M TRYING TO DO!
I UNDERSTAND WHAT YOU'RE TRYING TO DO!
THANK GOODNESS!
HERE ARE THE FORMS FOR FILING A COMPLAINT ABOUT OUR CUSTOMER SERVICE!
ARRGH
END

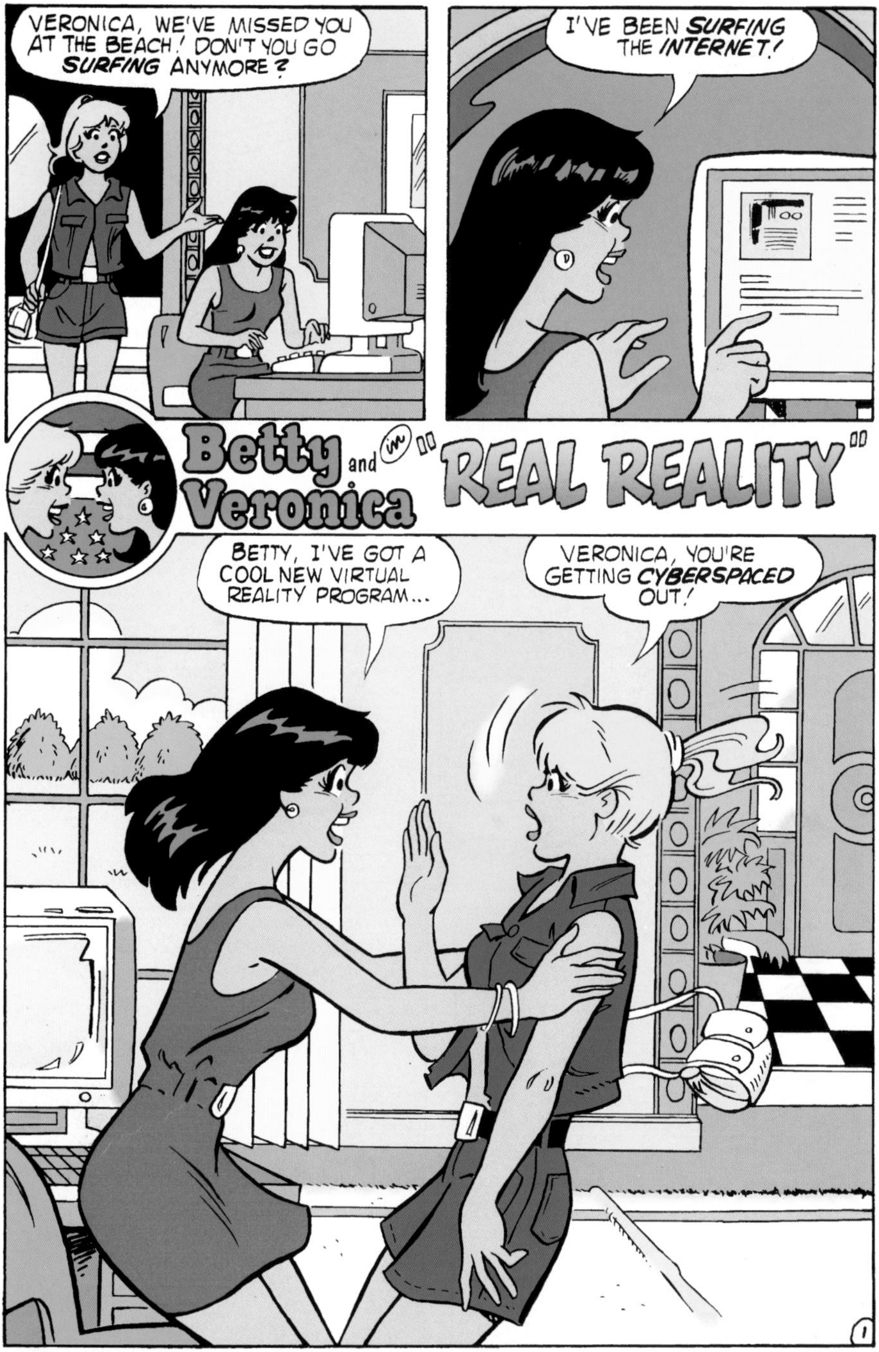
VERONICA, WE'VE MISSED YOU AT THE BEACH! DON'T YOU GO SURFING ANYMORE?
I'VE BEEN SURFING THE INTERNET!
Betty and Veronica in "REAL REALITY"
BETTY, I'VE GOT A COOL NEW VIRTUAL REALITY PROGRAM...
VERONICA, YOU'RE GETTING CYBERSPACED OUT!
1

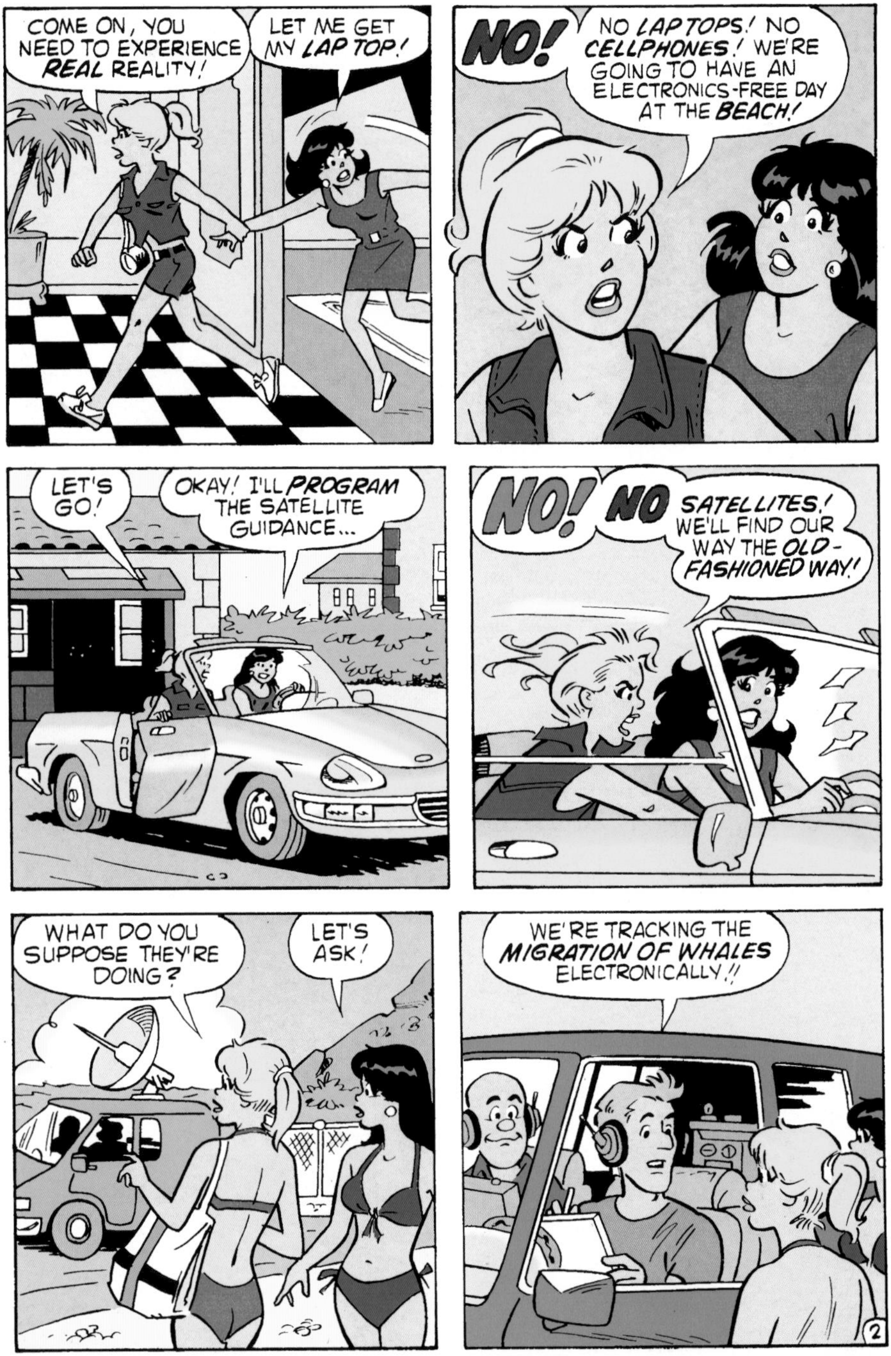
COME ON, YOU NEED TO EXPERIENCE REAL REALITY!
LET ME GET MY LAP TOP!
NO!
NO LAPTOPS! NO CELLPHONES! WE'RE GOING TO HAVE AN ELECTRONICS-FREE DAY AT THE BEACH!
LET'S GO!
OKAY! I'LL PROGRAM THE SATELLITE GUIDANCE...
NO!
NO SATELLITES! WE'LL FIND OUR WAY THE OLD-FASHIONED WAY!
WHAT DO YOU SUPPOSE THEY'RE DOING?
LET'S ASK!
WE'RE TRACKING THE MIGRATION OF WHALES ELECTRONICALLY!!
2

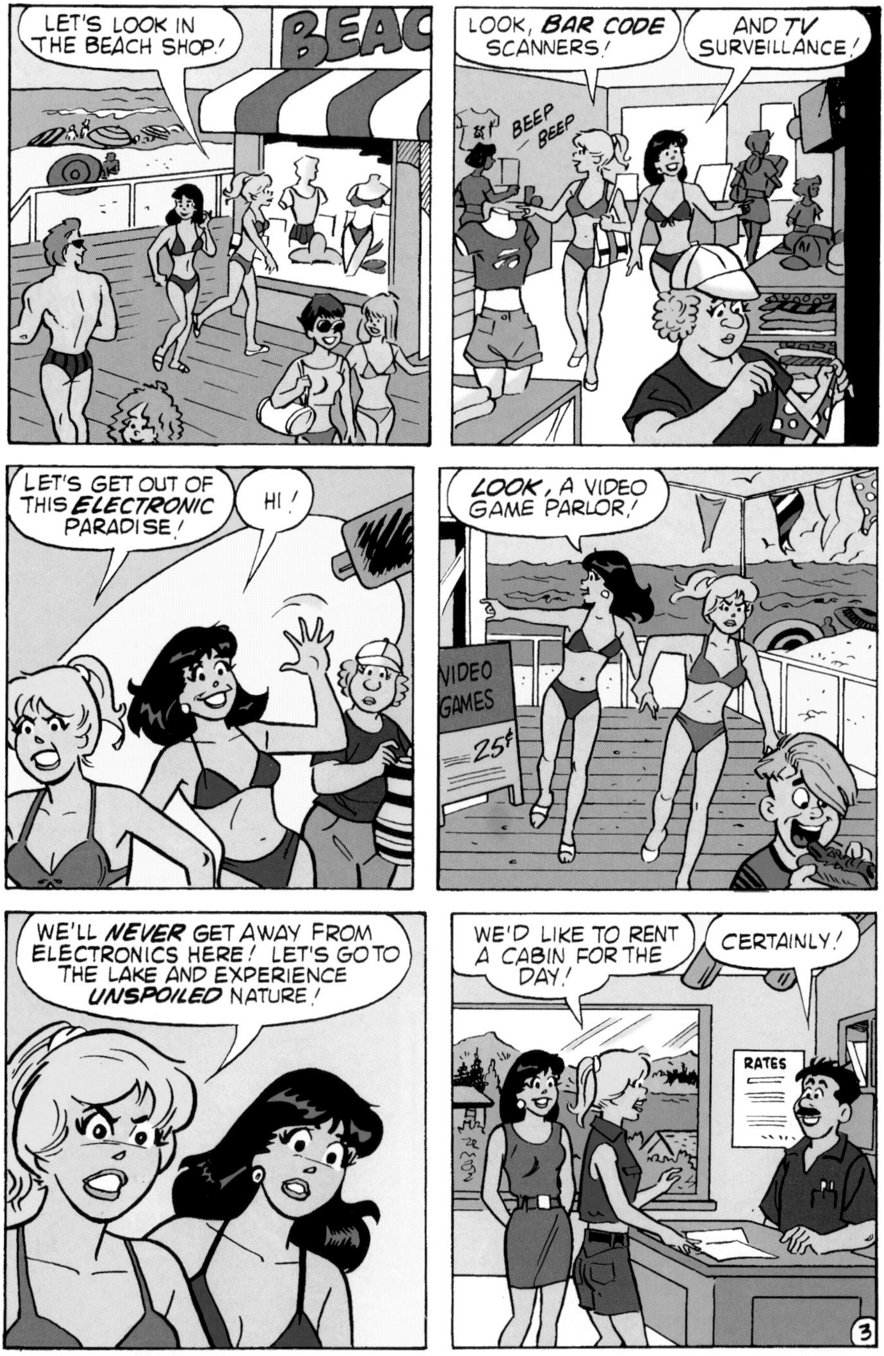
LET'S LOOK IN THE BEACH SHOP!
BEAC
LOOK, BAR CODE SCANNERS!
AND TV SURVEILLANCE!
BEEP BEEP
LET'S GET OUT OF THIS ELECTRONIC PARADISE!
HI!
LOOK, A VIDEO GAME PARLOR!
VIDEO GAMES
25¢
WE'LL NEVER GET AWAY FROM ELECTRONICS HERE! LET'S GO TO THE LAKE AND EXPERIENCE UNSPOILED NATURE!
WE'D LIKE TO RENT A CABIN FOR THE DAY!
CERTAINLY!
RATES
3

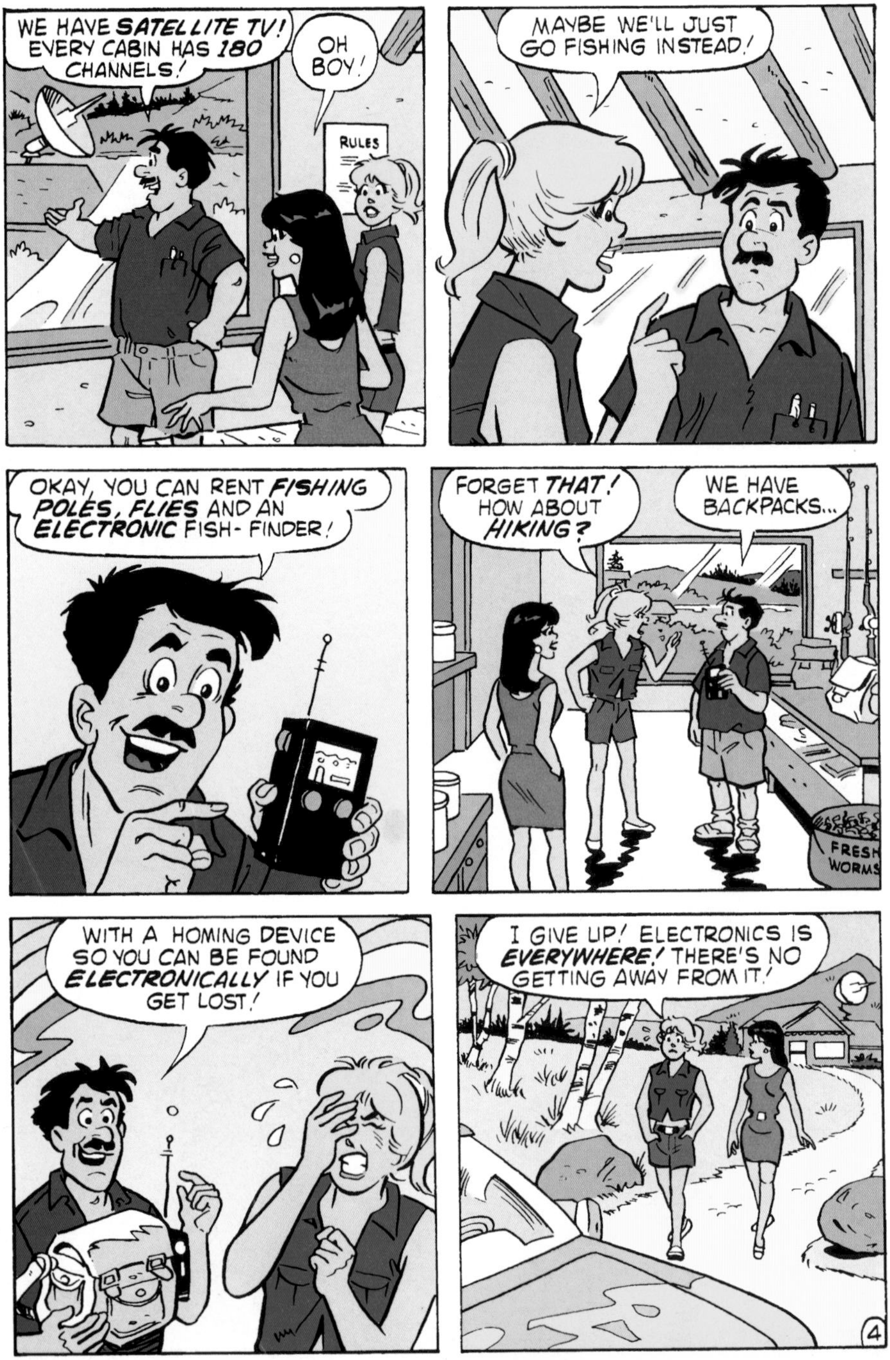
WE HAVE SATELLITE TV! EVERY CABIN HAS 180 CHANNELS!
OH BOY!
RULES
MAYBE WE'LL JUST GO FISHING INSTEAD!
OKAY, YOU CAN RENT FISHING POLES, FLIES AND AN ELECTRONIC FISH-FINDER!
FORGET THAT! HOW ABOUT HIKING?
WE HAVE BACKPACKS...
FRESH WORMS
WITH A HOMING DEVICE SO YOU CAN BE FOUND ELECTRONICALLY IF YOU GET LOST!
I GIVE UP! ELECTRONICS IS EVERYWHERE! THERE'S NO GETTING AWAY FROM IT!
4

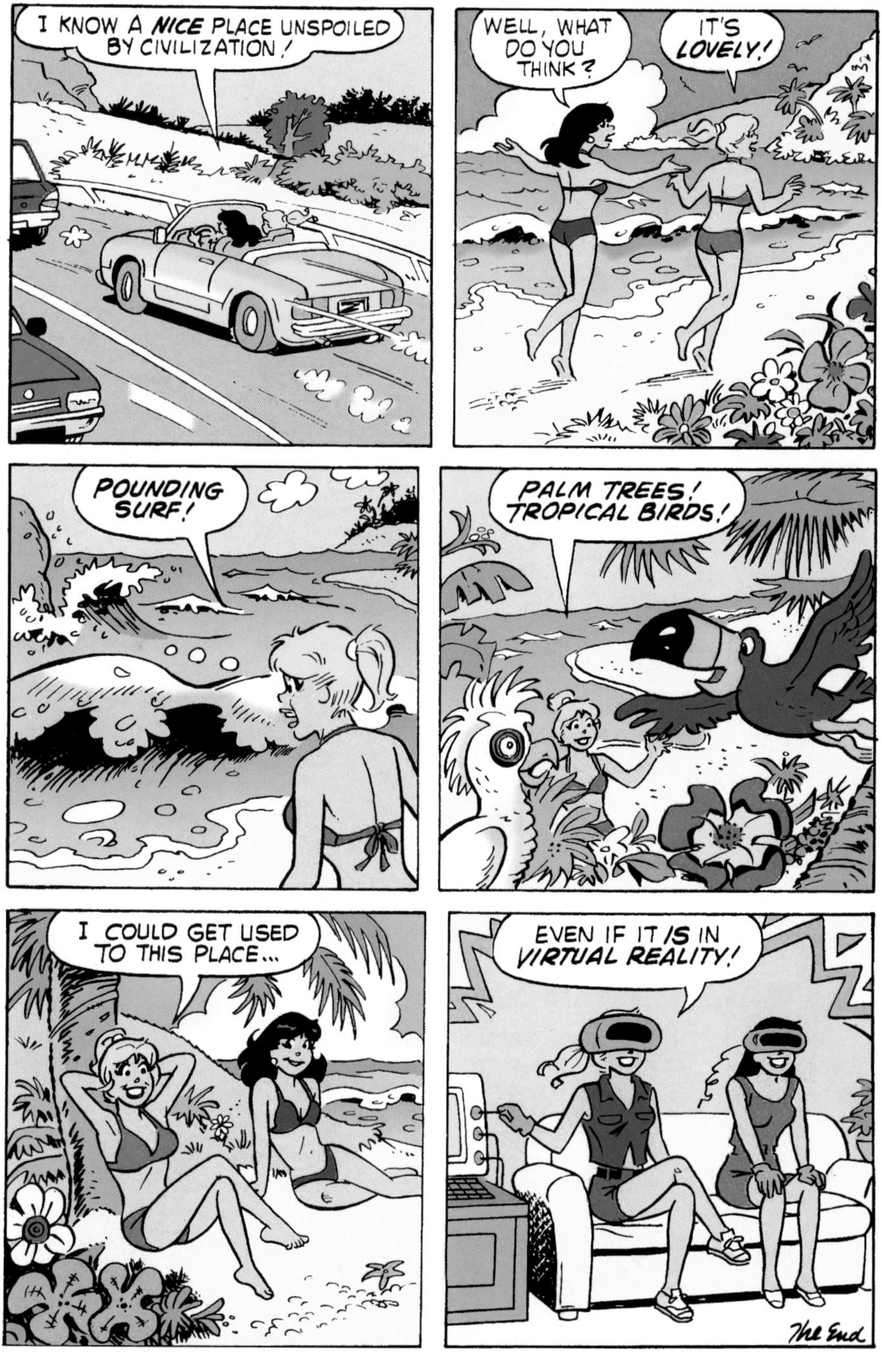
I KNOW A NICE PLACE UNSPOILED BY CIVILIZATION!
WELL, WHAT DO YOU THINK?
IT'S LOVELY!
POUNDING SURF!
PALM TREES! TROPICAL BIRDS!
I COULD GET USED TO THIS PLACE...
EVEN IF IT IS IN VIRTUAL REALITY!
The End

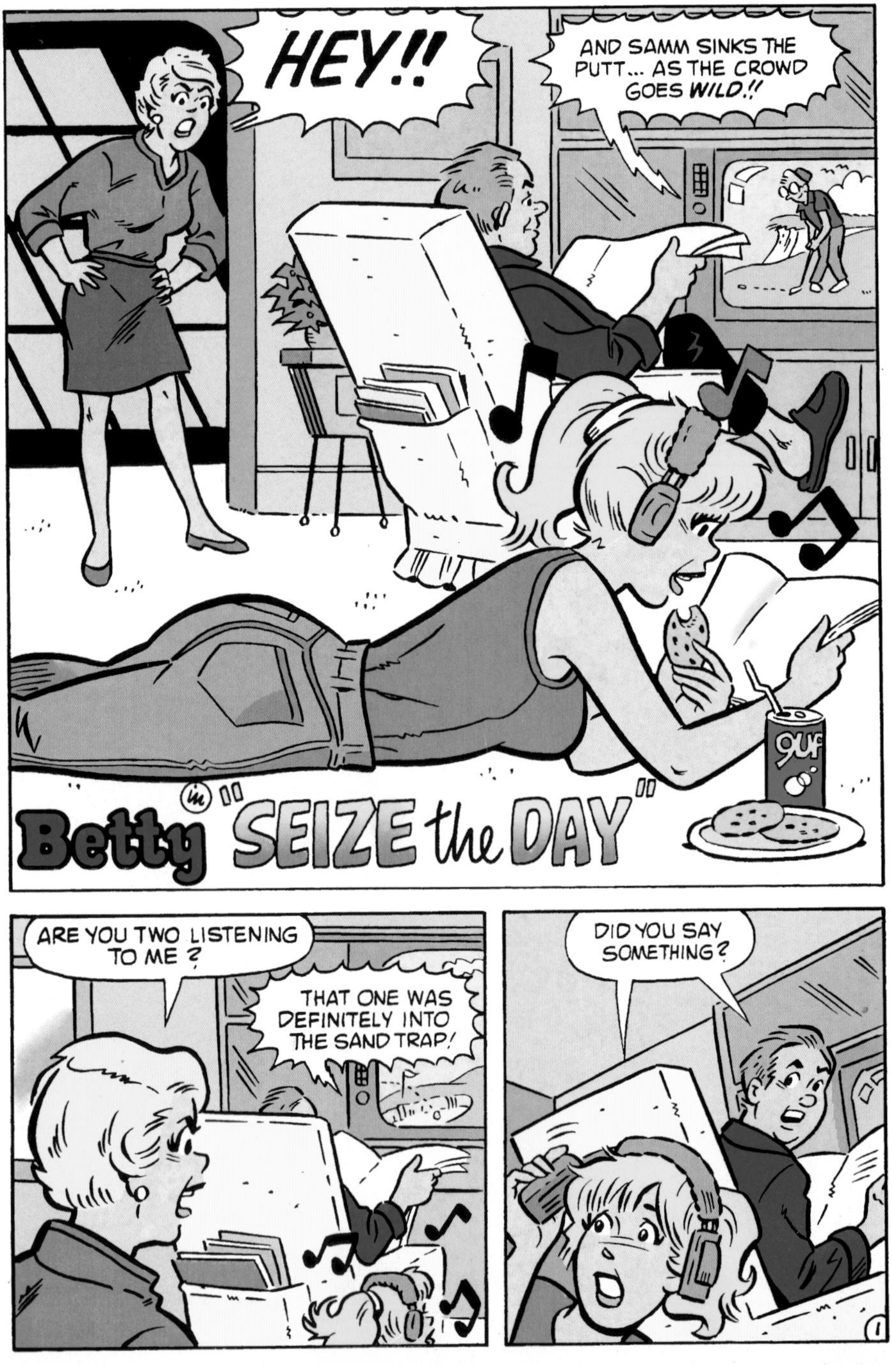
HEY!!
AND SAMM SINKS THE PUTT... AS THE CROWD GOES WILD!!
Betty in "SEIZE the DAY"
ARE YOU TWO LISTENING TO ME?
THAT ONE WAS DEFINITELY INTO THE SAND TRAP!
DID YOU SAY SOMETHING?
1

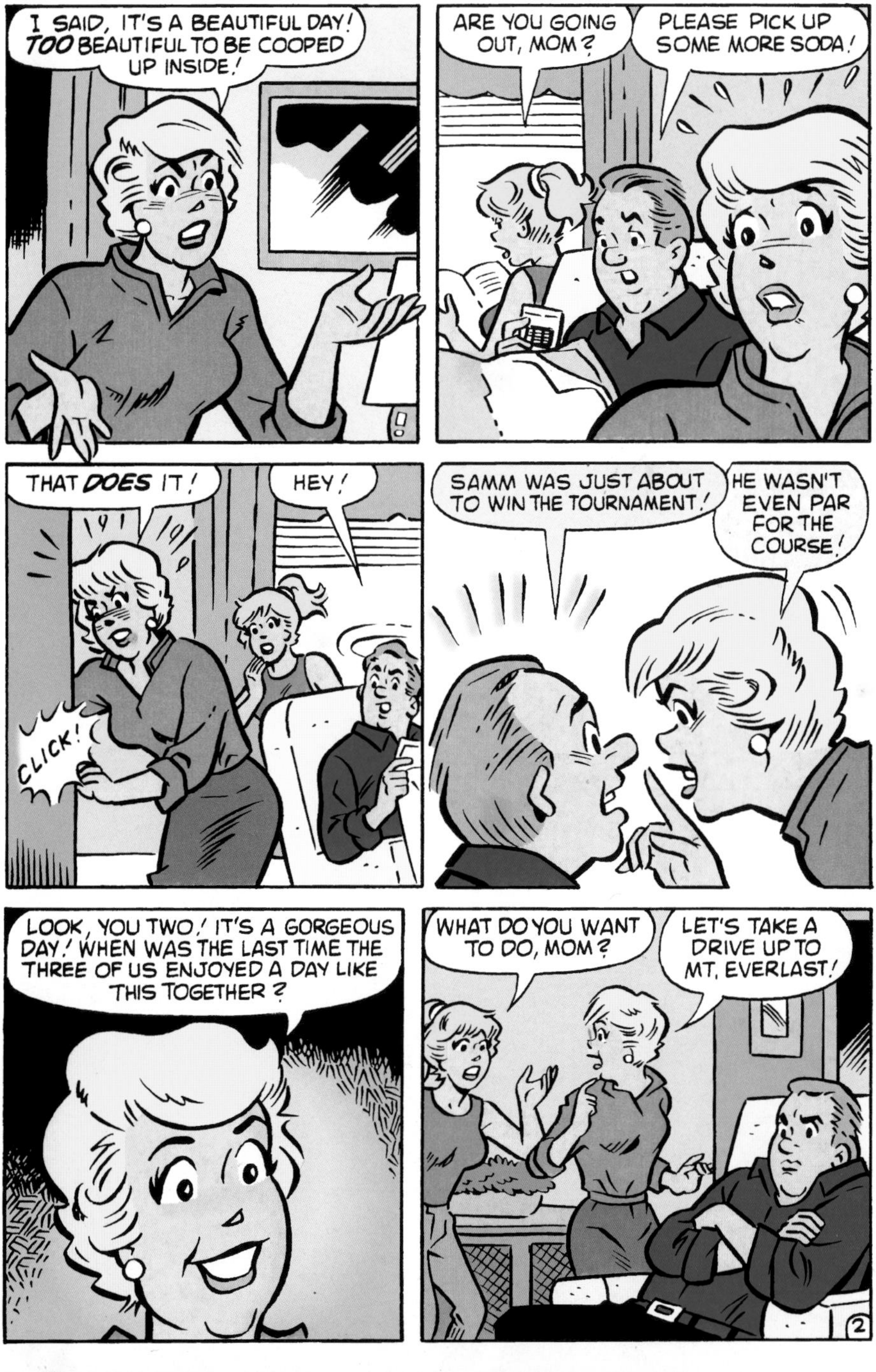
I SAID, IT'S A BEAUTIFUL DAY! TOO BEAUTIFUL TO BE COOPED UP INSIDE!
ARE YOU GOING OUT, MOM?
PLEASE PICK UP SOME MORE SODA!
THAT DOES IT!
HEY!
CLICK!
SAMM WAS JUST ABOUT TO WIN THE TOURNAMENT!
HE WASN'T EVEN PAR FOR THE COURSE!
LOOK, YOU TWO! IT'S A GORGEOUS DAY! WHEN WAS THE LAST TIME THE THREE OF US ENJOYED A DAY LIKE THIS TOGETHER?
WHAT DO YOU WANT TO DO, MOM?
LET'S TAKE A DRIVE UP TO MT. EVERLAST!
2

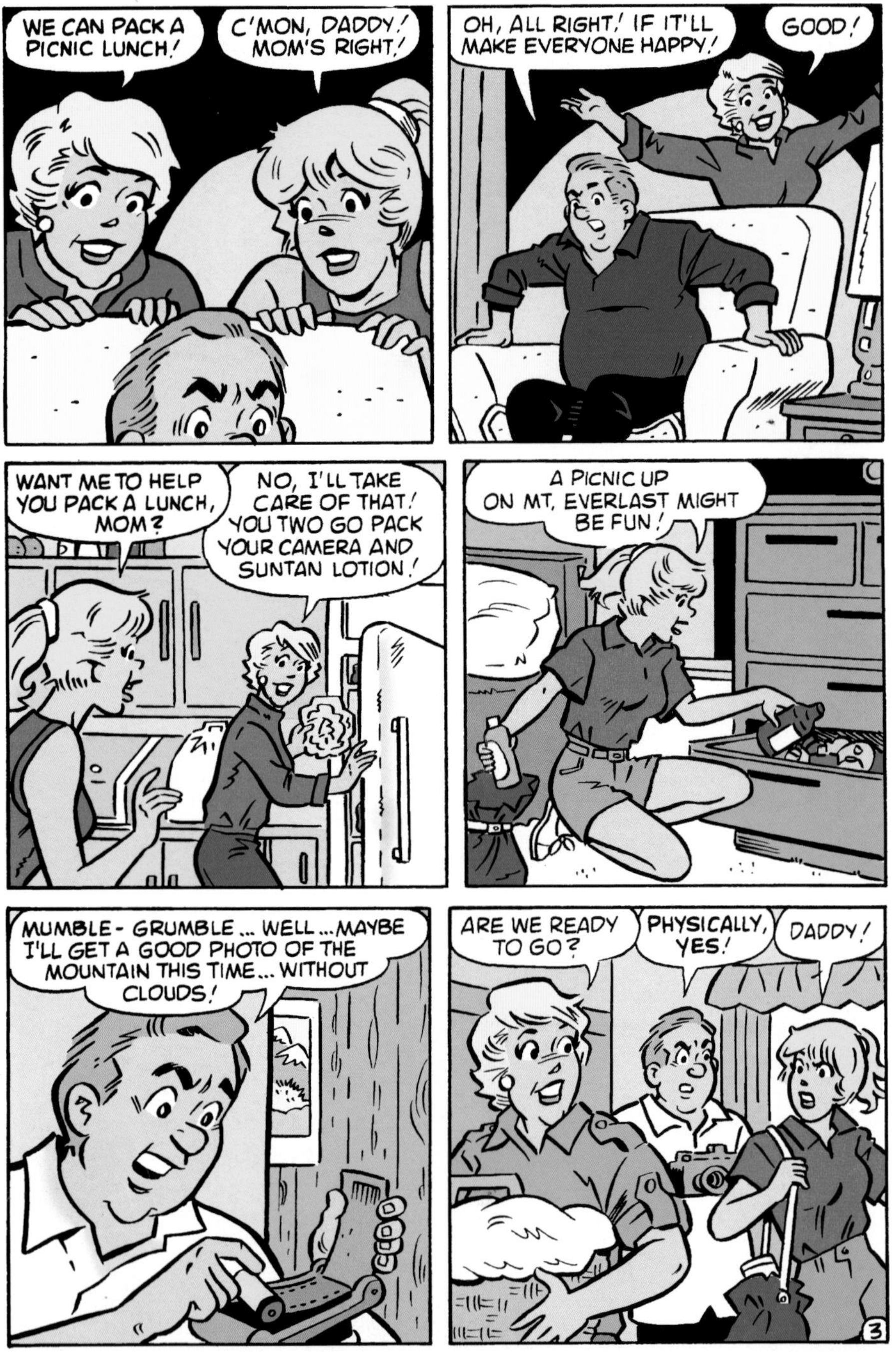
WE CAN PACK A PICNIC LUNCH!
C'MON, DADDY! MOM'S RIGHT!
OH, ALL RIGHT! IF IT'LL MAKE EVERYONE HAPPY!
GOOD!
WANT ME TO HELP YOU PACK A LUNCH, MOM?
NO, I'LL TAKE CARE OF THAT! YOU TWO GO PACK YOUR CAMERA AND SUNTAN LOTION!
A PICNIC UP ON MT. EVERLAST MIGHT BE FUN!
MUMBLE - GRUMBLE ... WELL ... MAYBE I'LL GET A GOOD PHOTO OF THE MOUNTAIN THIS TIME... WITHOUT CLOUDS!
ARE WE READY TO GO?
PHYSICALLY, YES!
DADDY!
3

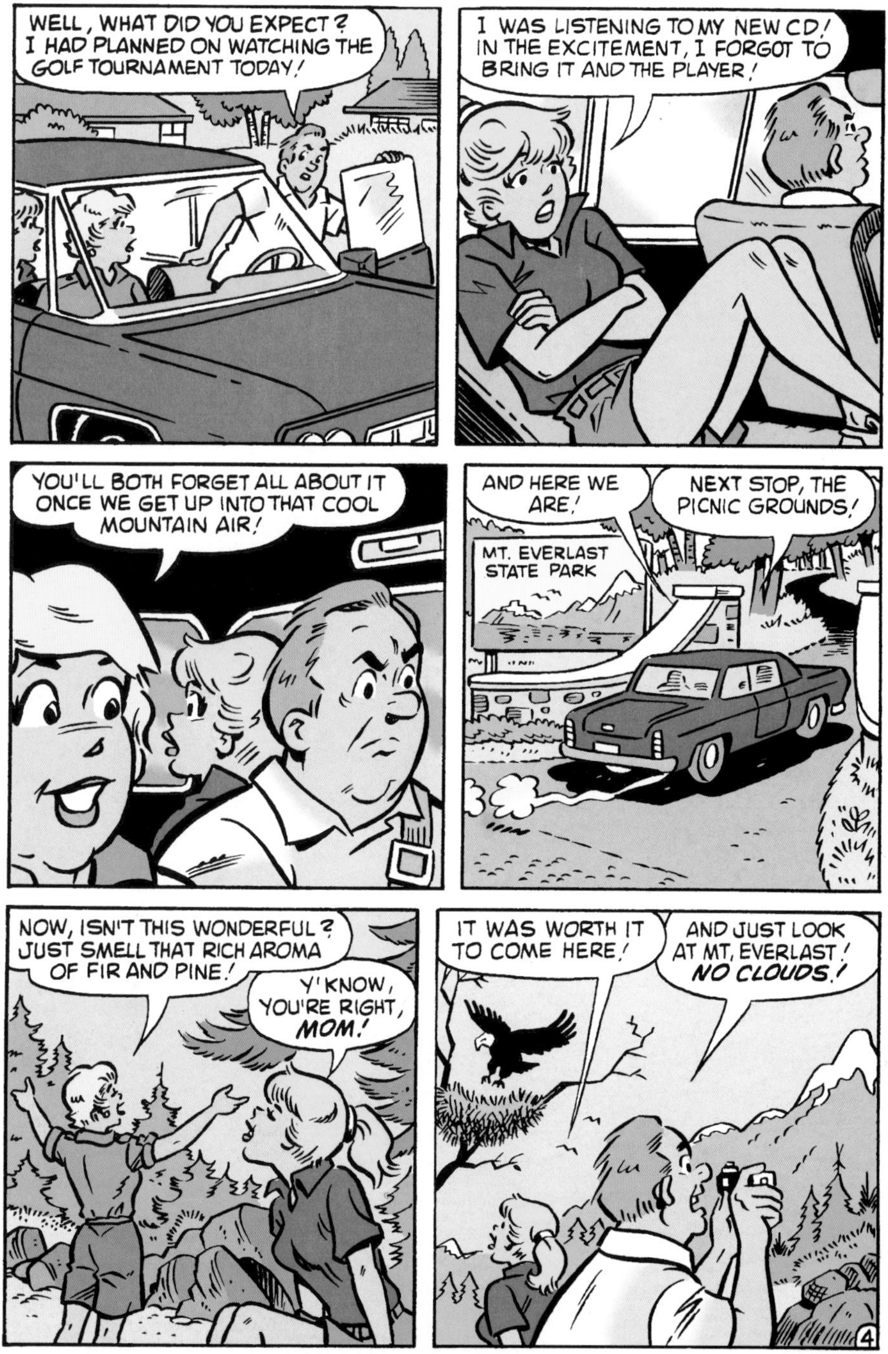
WELL, WHAT DID YOU EXPECT? I HAD PLANNED ON WATCHING THE GOLF TOURNAMENT TODAY!
I WAS LISTENING TO MY NEW CD! IN THE EXCITEMENT, I FORGOT TO BRING IT AND THE PLAYER!
YOU'LL BOTH FORGET ALL ABOUT IT ONCE WE GET UP INTO THAT COOL MOUNTAIN AIR!
AND HERE WE ARE!
NEXT STOP, THE PICNIC GROUNDS!
MT. EVERLAST STATE PARK
NOW, ISN'T THIS WONDERFUL? JUST SMELL THAT RICH AROMA OF FIR AND PINE!
Y'KNOW, YOU'RE RIGHT, MOM!
IT WAS WORTH IT TO COME HERE!
AND JUST LOOK AT MT. EVERLAST! NO CLOUDS!
4

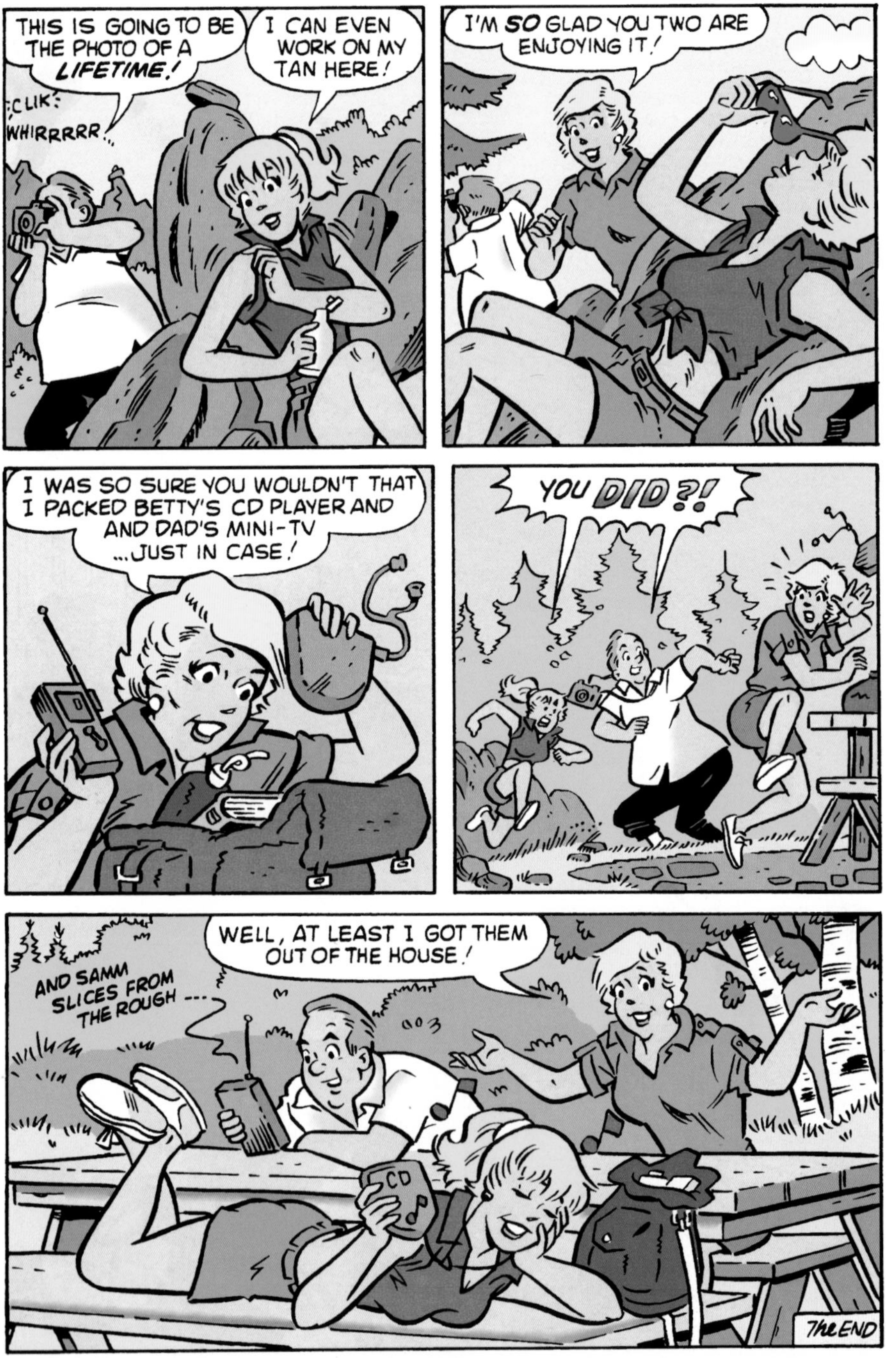
THIS IS GOING TO BE THE PHOTO OF A LIFETIME!
I CAN EVEN WORK ON MY TAN HERE!
CLIK
WHIRRRRR
I'M SO GLAD YOU TWO ARE ENJOYING IT!
I WAS SO SURE YOU WOULDN'T THAT I PACKED BETTY'S CD PLAYER AND AND DAD'S MINI-TV ...JUST IN CASE!
YOU DID?!
WELL, AT LEAST I GOT THEM OUT OF THE HOUSE!
AND SAMM SLICES FROM THE ROUGH ---
CD
The END

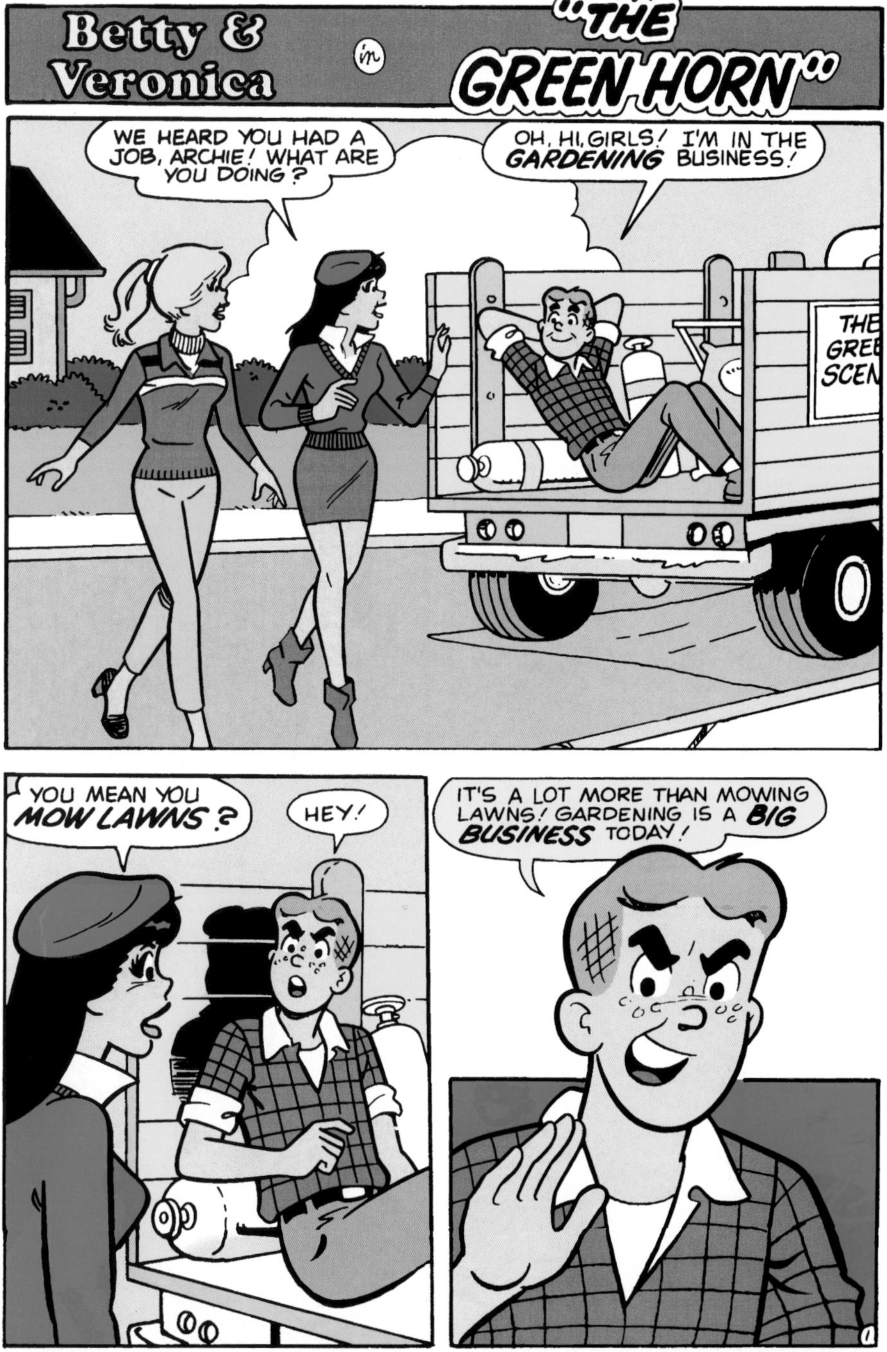
Betty & Veronica
in
"THE GREEN HORN"
WE HEARD YOU HAD A JOB, ARCHIE! WHAT ARE YOU DOING?
OH, HI, GIRLS! I'M IN THE GARDENING BUSINESS!
THE GREE SCEN
YOU MEAN YOU MOW LAWNS?
HEY!
IT'S A LOT MORE THAN MOWING LAWNS! GARDENING IS A BIG BUSINESS TODAY!
1

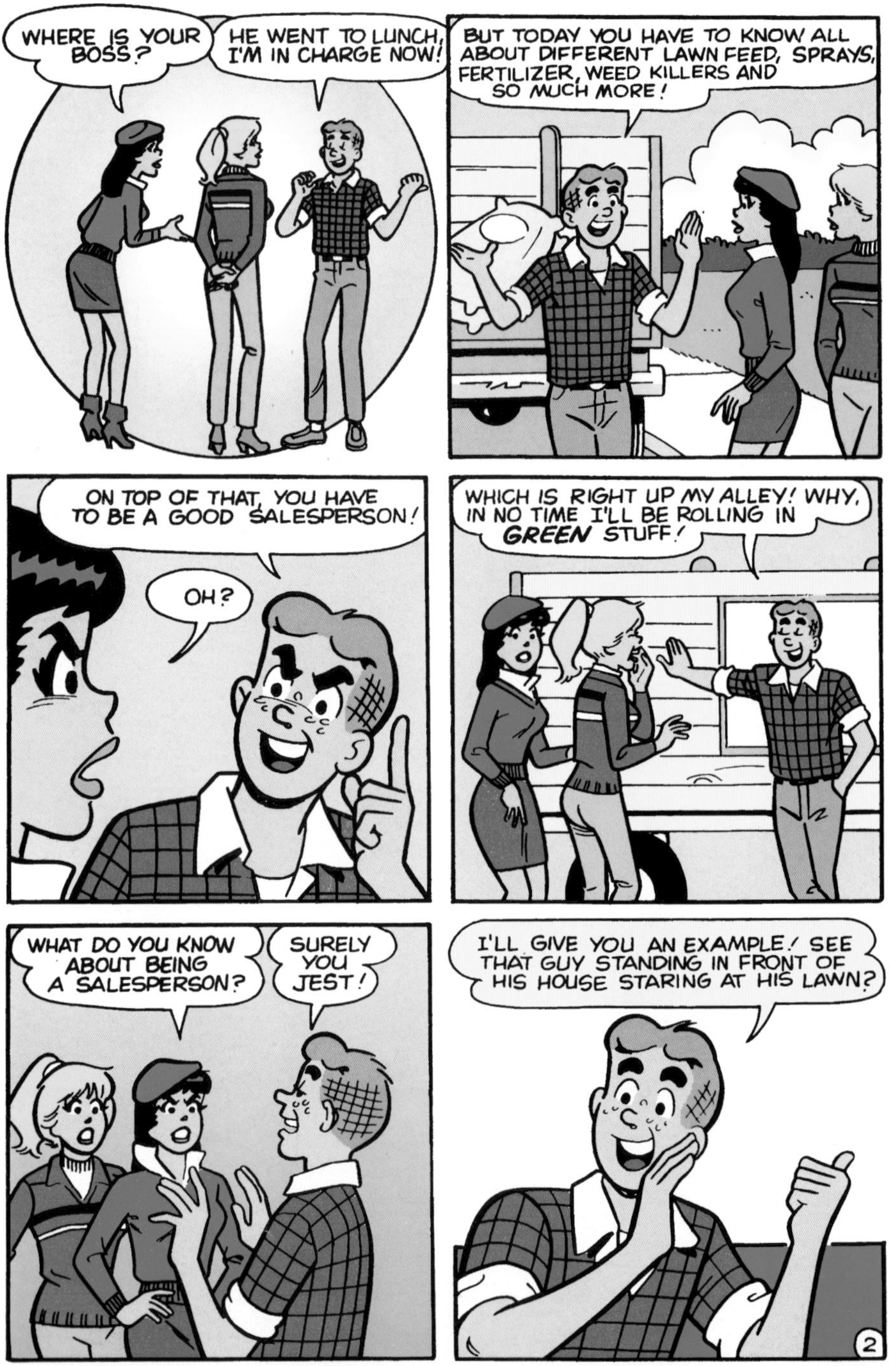
WHERE IS YOUR BOSS?
HE WENT TO LUNCH, I'M IN CHARGE NOW!
BUT TODAY YOU HAVE TO KNOW ALL ABOUT DIFFERENT LAWN FEED, SPRAYS, FERTILIZER, WEED KILLERS AND SO MUCH MORE!
ON TOP OF THAT, YOU HAVE TO BE A GOOD SALESPERSON!
OH?
WHICH IS RIGHT UP MY ALLEY! WHY, IN NO TIME I'LL BE ROLLING IN GREEN STUFF!
WHAT DO YOU KNOW ABOUT BEING A SALESPERSON?
SURELY YOU JEST!
I'LL GIVE YOU AN EXAMPLE! SEE THAT GUY STANDING IN FRONT OF HIS HOUSE STARING AT HIS LAWN?
2

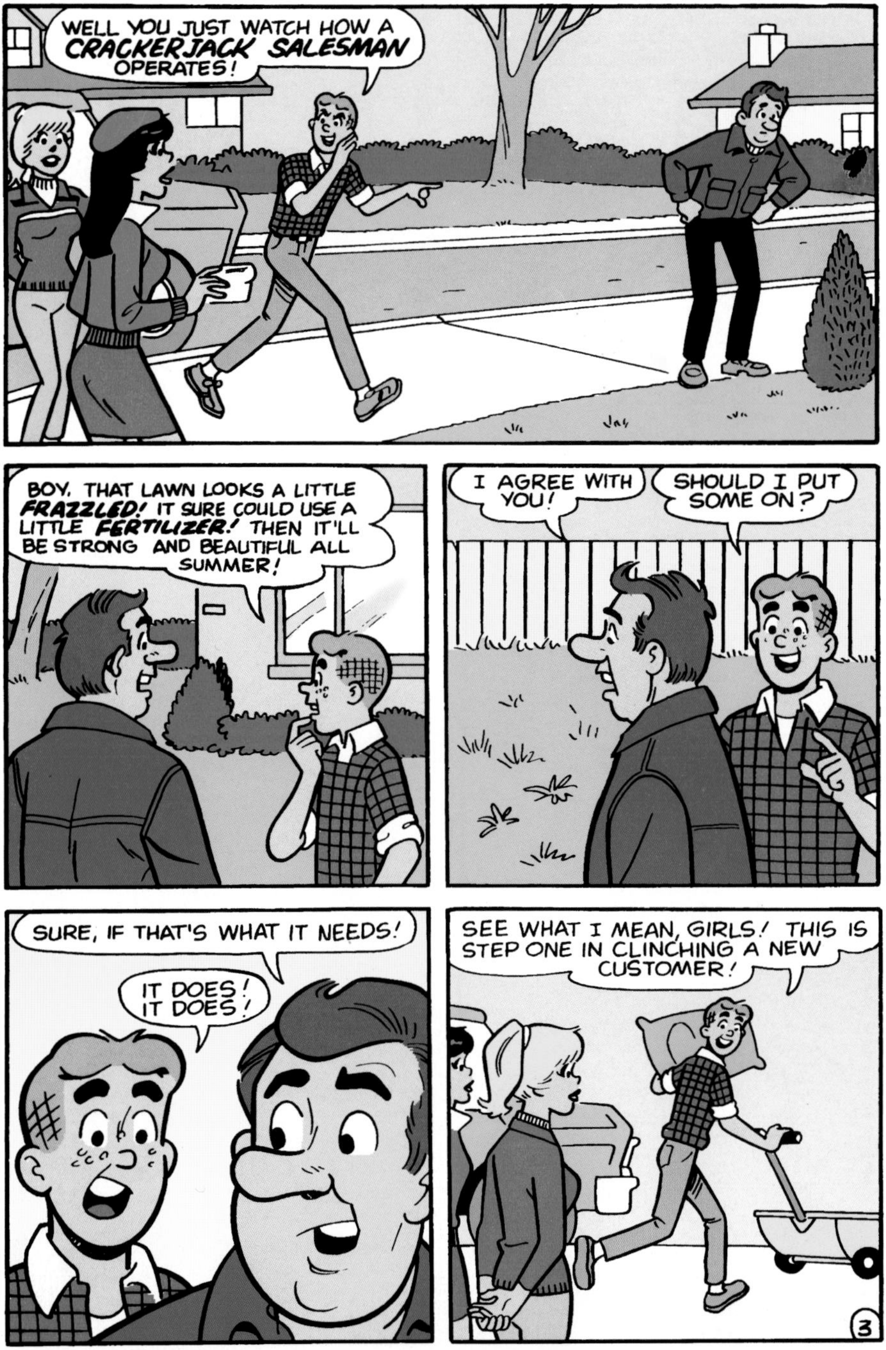
WELL YOU JUST WATCH HOW A CRACKERJACK SALESMAN OPERATES!
BOY, THAT LAWN LOOKS A LITTLE FRAZZLED! IT SURE COULD USE A LITTLE FERTILIZER! THEN IT'LL BE STRONG AND BEAUTIFUL ALL SUMMER!
I AGREE WITH YOU!
SHOULD I PUT SOME ON?
SURE, IF THAT'S WHAT IT NEEDS!
IT DOES! IT DOES!
SEE WHAT I MEAN, GIRLS! THIS IS STEP ONE IN CLINCHING A NEW CUSTOMER!
3

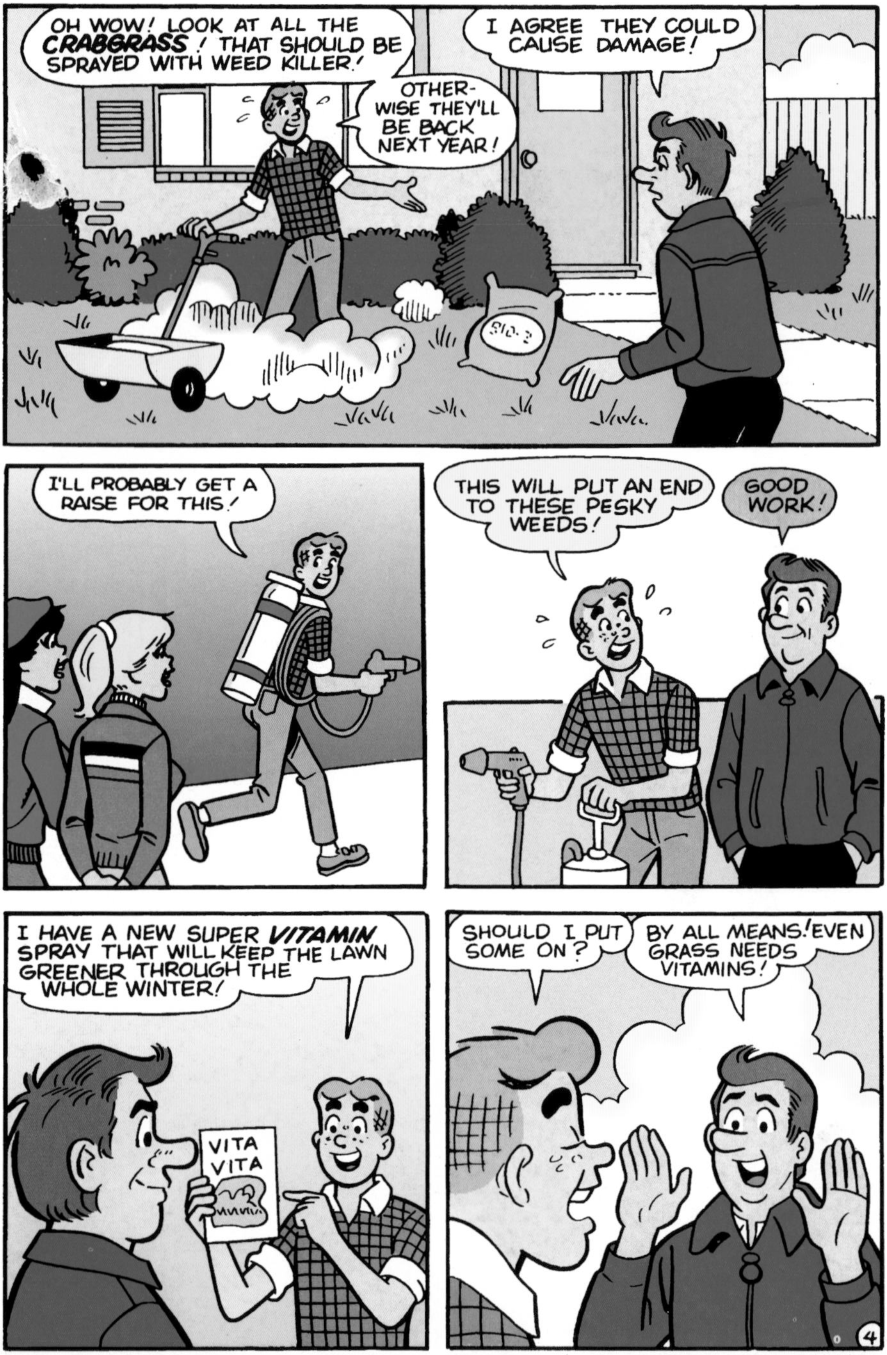
OH WOW! LOOK AT ALL THE CRABGRASS! THAT SHOULD BE SPRAYED WITH WEED KILLER!
OTHER-WISE THEY'LL BE BACK NEXT YEAR!
I AGREE THEY COULD CAUSE DAMAGE!
I'LL PROBABLY GET A RAISE FOR THIS!
THIS WILL PUT AN END TO THESE PESKY WEEDS!
GOOD WORK!
I HAVE A NEW SUPER VITAMIN SPRAY THAT WILL KEEP THE LAWN GREENER THROUGH THE WHOLE WINTER!
VITA VITA
SHOULD I PUT SOME ON?
BY ALL MEANS! EVEN GRASS NEEDS VITAMINS!
4

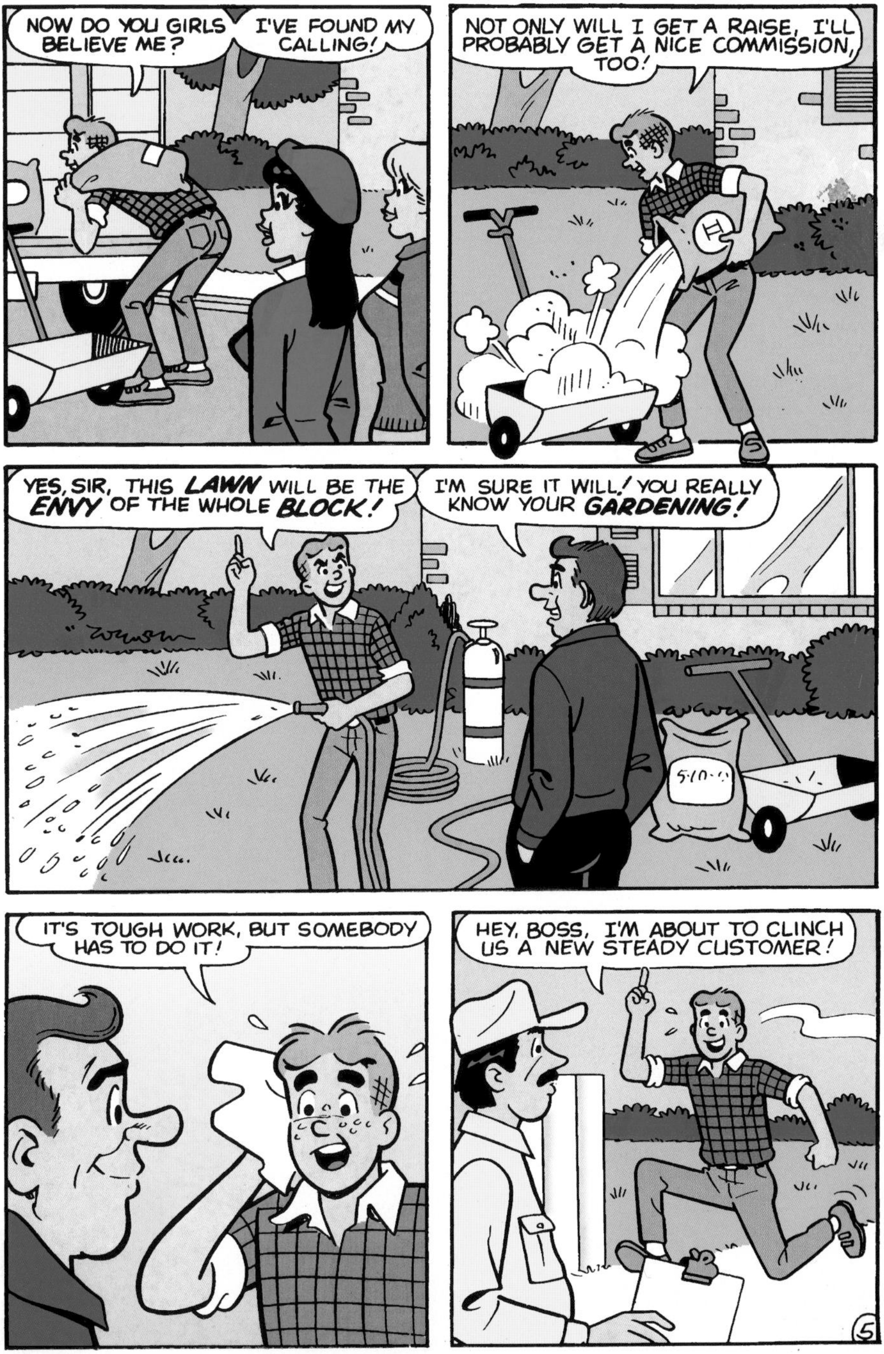
NOW DO YOU GIRLS BELIEVE ME?
I'VE FOUND MY CALLING!
NOT ONLY WILL I GET A RAISE, I'LL PROBABLY GET A NICE COMMISSION, TOO!
YES, SIR, THIS LAWN WILL BE THE ENVY OF THE WHOLE BLOCK!
I'M SURE IT WILL! YOU REALLY KNOW YOUR GARDENING!
IT'S TOUGH WORK, BUT SOMEBODY HAS TO DO IT!
HEY, BOSS, I'M ABOUT TO CLINCH US A NEW STEADY CUSTOMER!
5

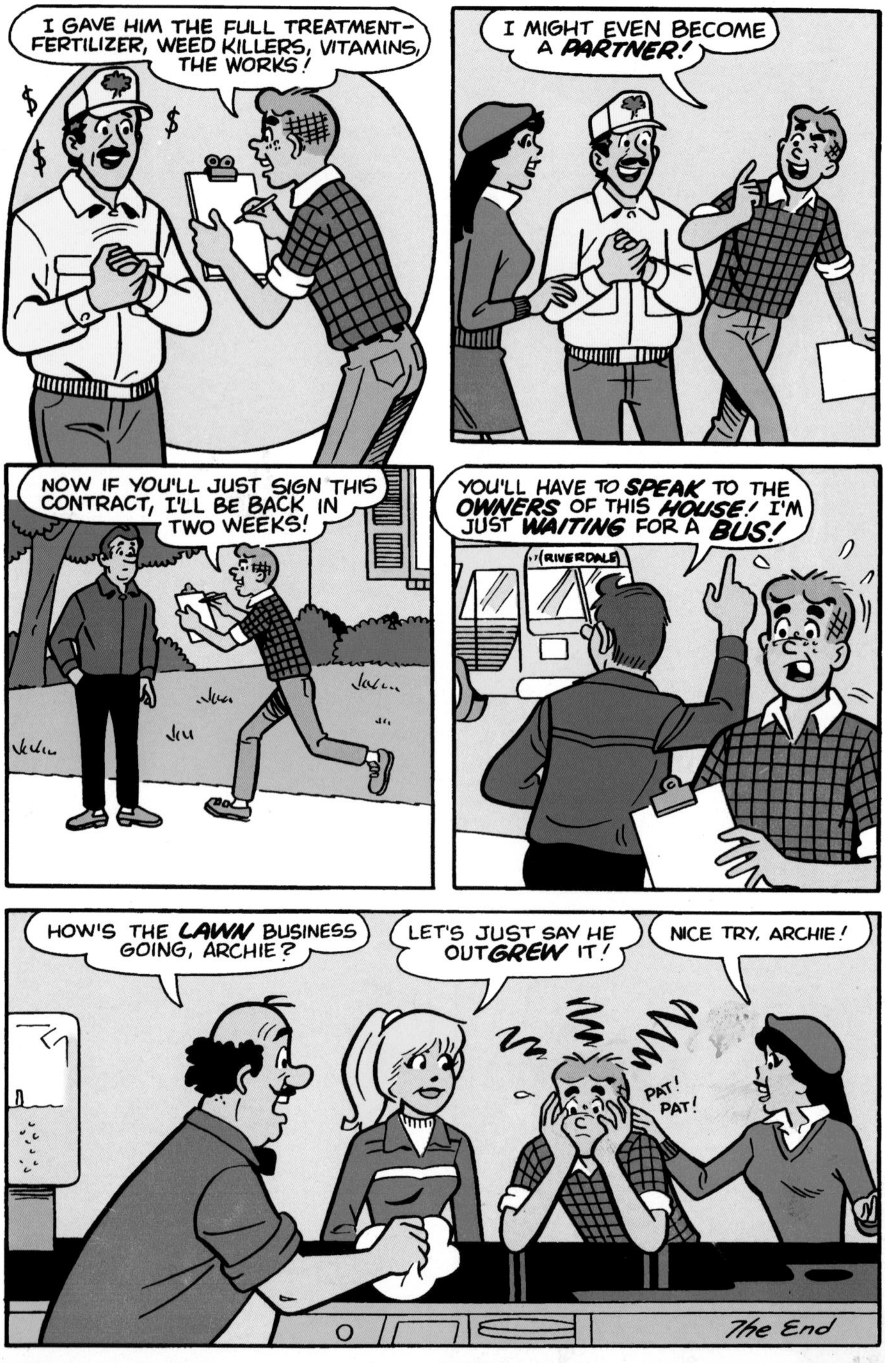
I GAVE HIM THE FULL TREATMENT- FERTILIZER, WEED KILLERS, VITAMINS, THE WORKS!
I MIGHT EVEN BECOME A PARTNER!
NOW IF YOU'LL JUST SIGN THIS CONTRACT, I'LL BE BACK IN TWO WEEKS!
YOU'LL HAVE TO SPEAK TO THE OWNERS OF THIS HOUSE! I'M JUST WAITING FOR A BUS!
RIVERDALE
HOW'S THE LAWN BUSINESS GOING, ARCHIE?
LET'S JUST SAY HE OUTGREW IT!
NICE TRY, ARCHIE!
PAT! PAT!
The End

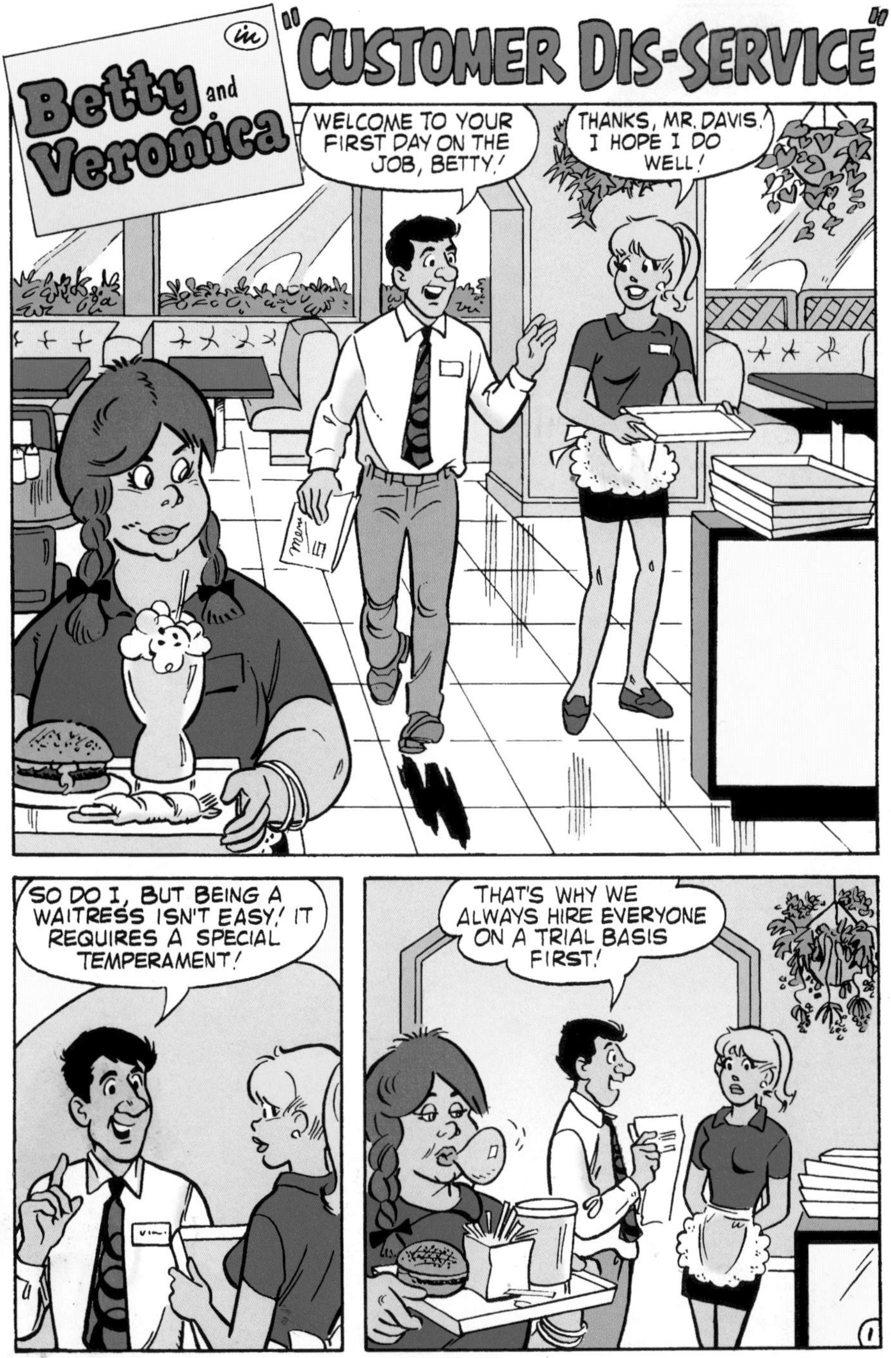
Betty and Veronica in
"CUSTOMER DIS-SERVICE"
WELCOME TO YOUR FIRST DAY ON THE JOB, BETTY!
THANKS, MR. DAVIS! I HOPE I DO WELL!
SO DO I, BUT BEING A WAITRESS ISN'T EASY! IT REQUIRES A SPECIAL TEMPERAMENT!
THAT'S WHY WE ALWAYS HIRE EVERYONE ON A TRIAL BASIS FIRST!
1

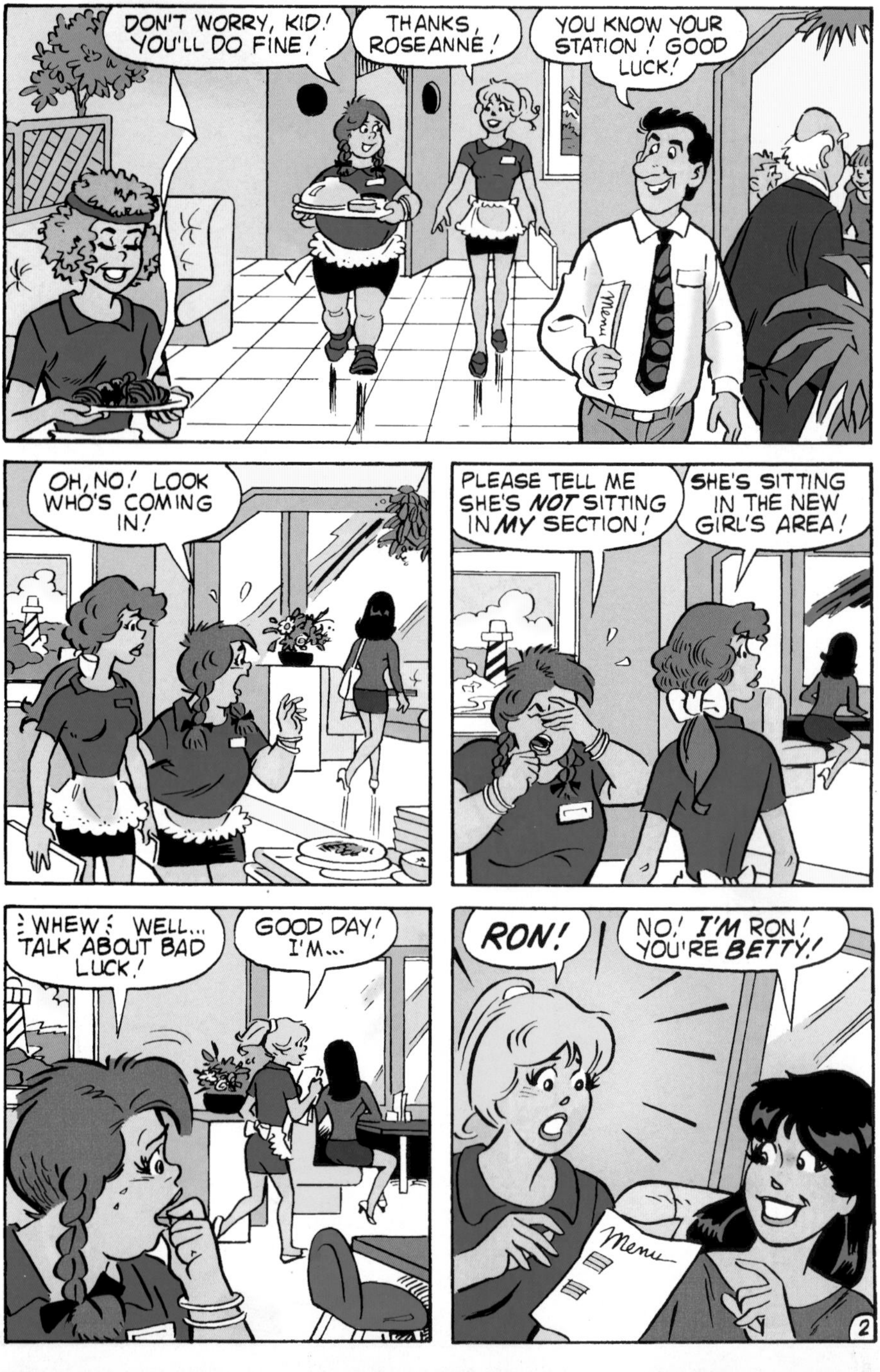
DON'T WORRY, KID! YOU'LL DO FINE!
THANKS, ROSEANNE!
YOU KNOW YOUR STATION! GOOD LUCK!
Menu
OH, NO! LOOK WHO'S COMING IN!
PLEASE TELL ME SHE'S *NOT* SITTING IN *MY* SECTION!
SHE'S SITTING IN THE NEW GIRL'S AREA!
WHEW! WELL... TALK ABOUT BAD LUCK!
GOOD DAY! I'M...
RON!
NO! *I'M* RON! YOU'RE *BETTY*!
Menu
2

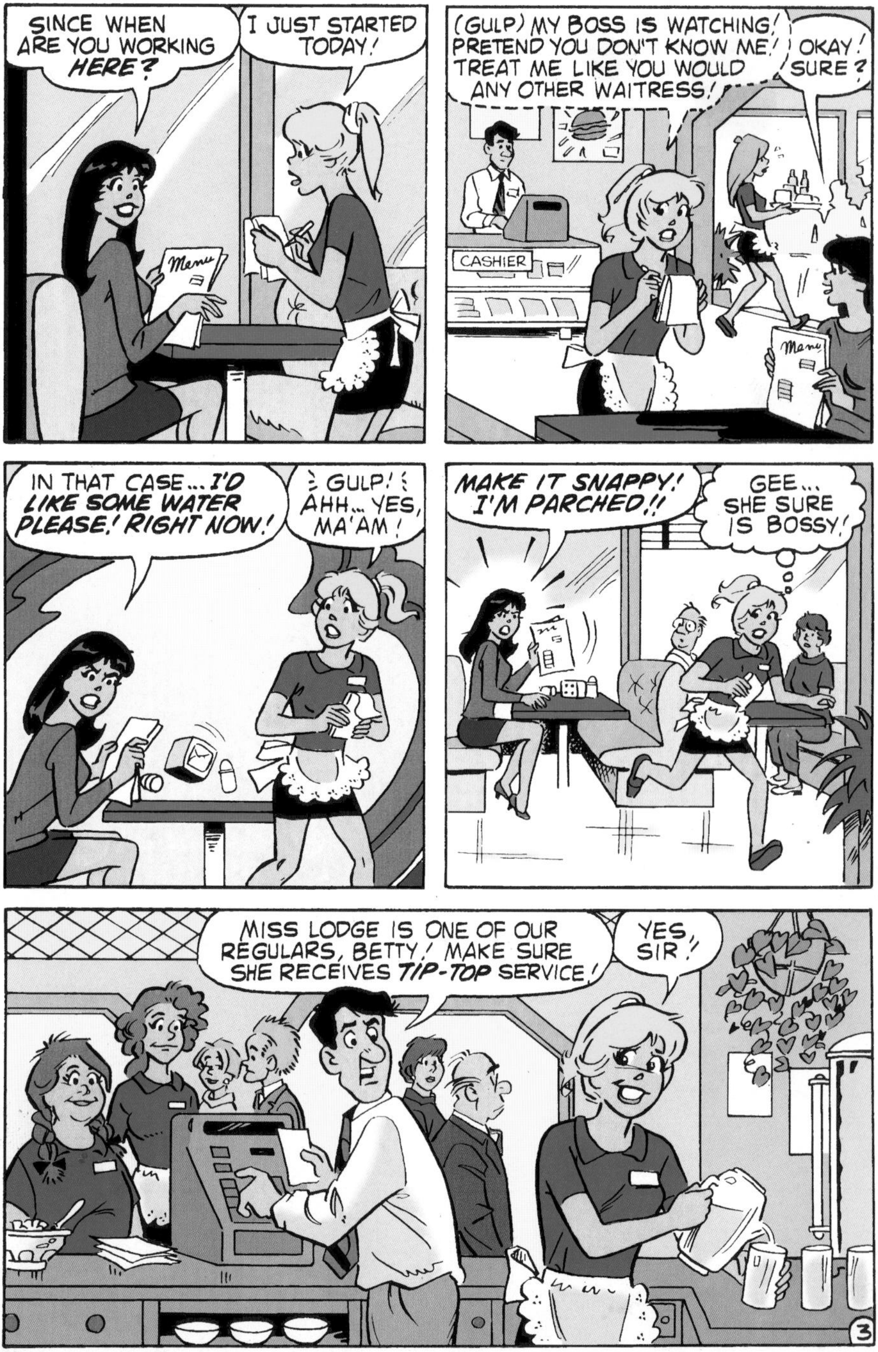
SINCE WHEN ARE YOU WORKING *HERE?*
I JUST STARTED TODAY!
Menu
(GULP) MY BOSS IS WATCHING! PRETEND YOU DON'T KNOW ME! TREAT ME LIKE YOU WOULD ANY OTHER WAITRESS!
OKAY! SURE?
CASHIER
Menu
IN THAT CASE... *I'D LIKE SOME WATER PLEASE! RIGHT NOW!*
GULP! AHH... YES, MA'AM!
MAKE IT SNAPPY! I'M PARCHED!!
GEE... SHE SURE IS BOSSY!
MISS LODGE IS ONE OF OUR REGULARS, BETTY! MAKE SURE SHE RECEIVES *TIP-TOP* SERVICE!
YES, SIR!
3

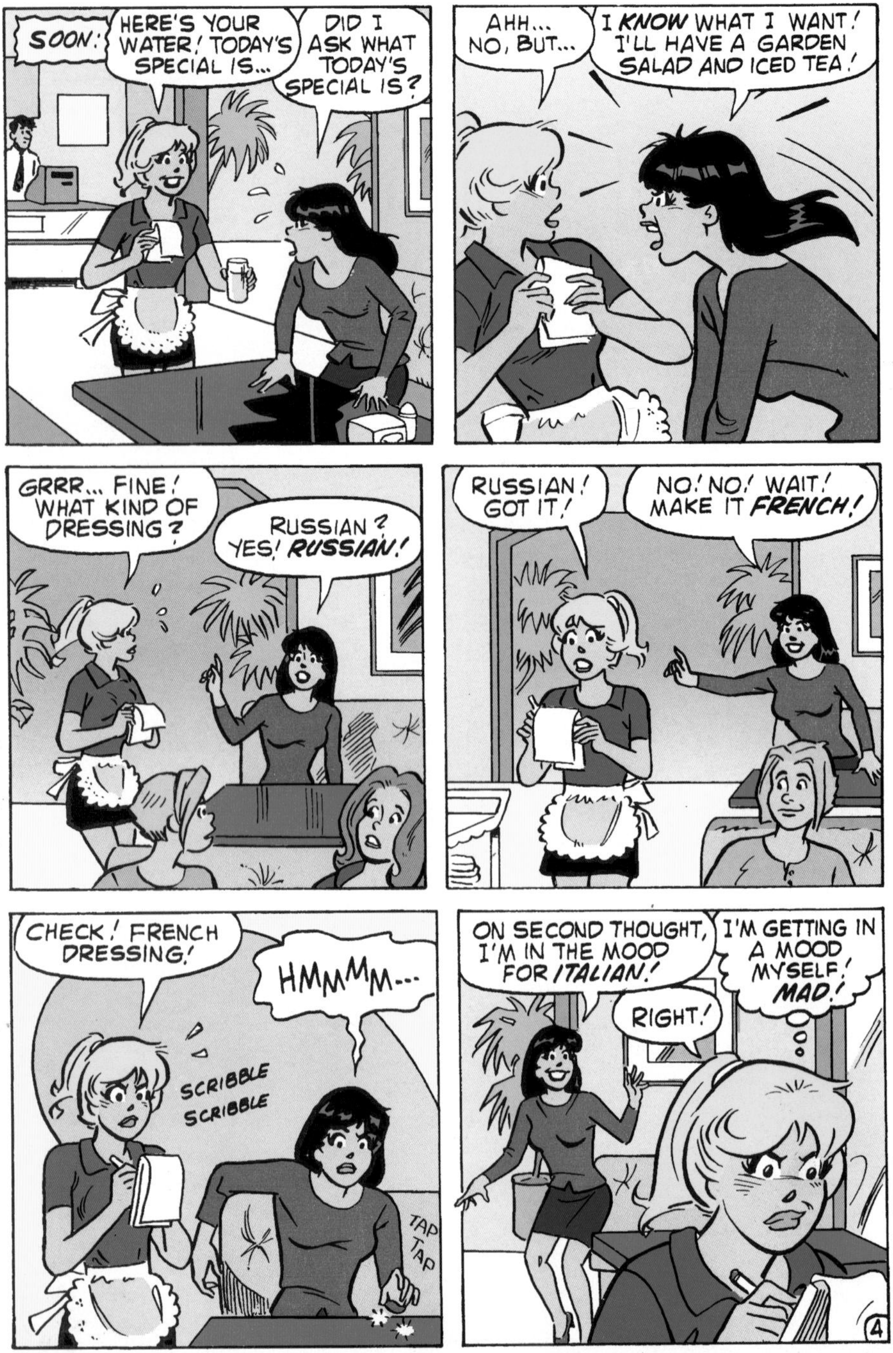
SOON:
HERE'S YOUR WATER! TODAY'S SPECIAL IS...
DID I ASK WHAT TODAY'S SPECIAL IS?
AHH... NO, BUT...
I KNOW WHAT I WANT! I'LL HAVE A GARDEN SALAD AND ICED TEA!
GRRR... FINE! WHAT KIND OF DRESSING?
RUSSIAN? YES! RUSSIAN!
RUSSIAN! GOT IT!
NO! NO! WAIT! MAKE IT FRENCH!
CHECK! FRENCH DRESSING!
HMMMM...
SCRIBBLE SCRIBBLE
TAP TAP
ON SECOND THOUGHT, I'M IN THE MOOD FOR ITALIAN!
RIGHT!
I'M GETTING IN A MOOD MYSELF! MAD!
4

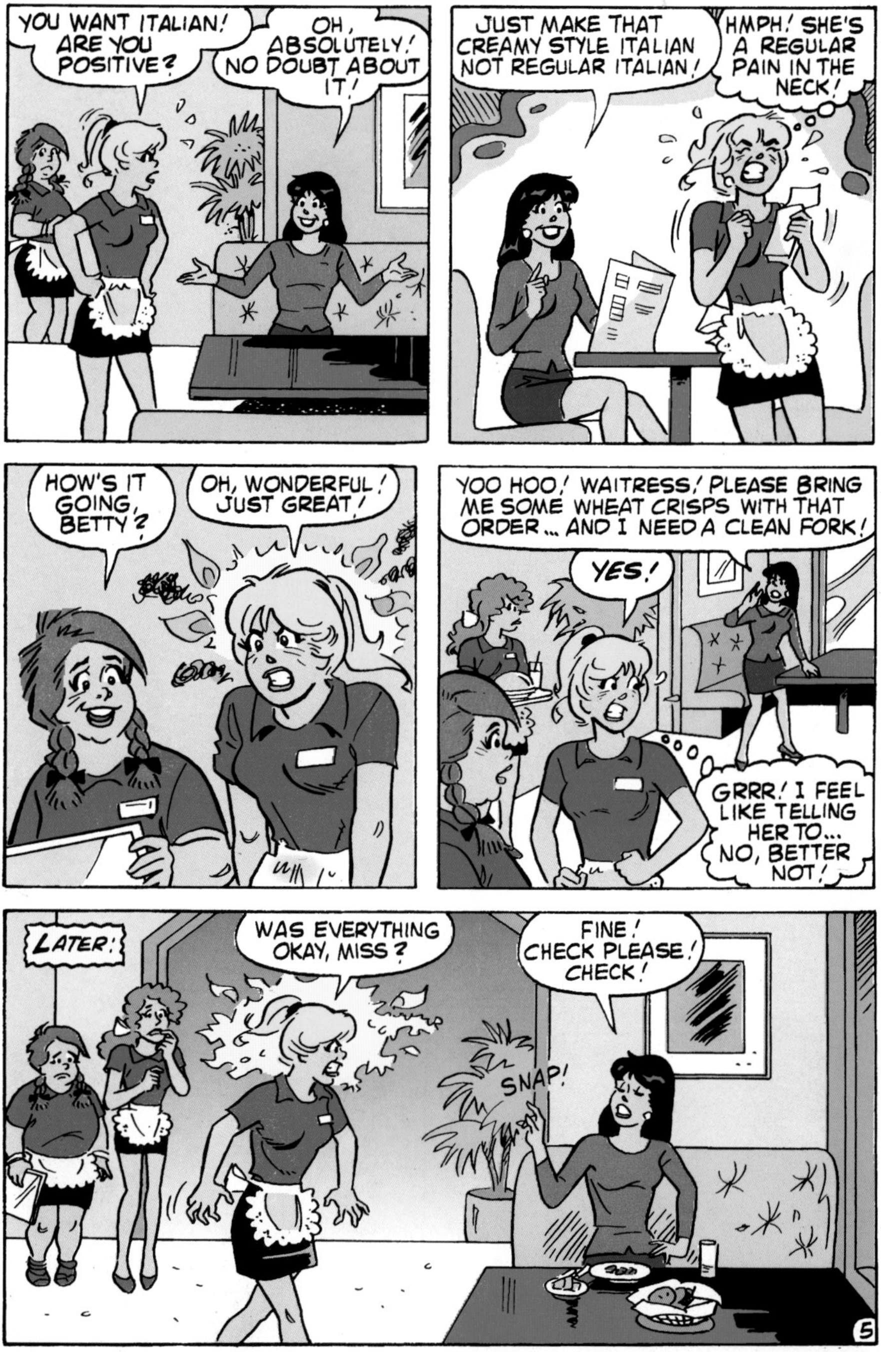
YOU WANT ITALIAN! ARE YOU POSITIVE?
OH, ABSOLUTELY! NO DOUBT ABOUT IT!
JUST MAKE THAT CREAMY STYLE ITALIAN NOT REGULAR ITALIAN!
HMPH! SHE'S A REGULAR PAIN IN THE NECK!
HOW'S IT GOING, BETTY?
OH, WONDERFUL! JUST GREAT!
YOO HOO! WAITRESS! PLEASE BRING ME SOME WHEAT CRISPS WITH THAT ORDER... AND I NEED A CLEAN FORK!
YES!
GRRR! I FEEL LIKE TELLING HER TO... NO, BETTER NOT!
LATER!
WAS EVERYTHING OKAY, MISS?
FINE! CHECK PLEASE! CHECK!
SNAP!
5

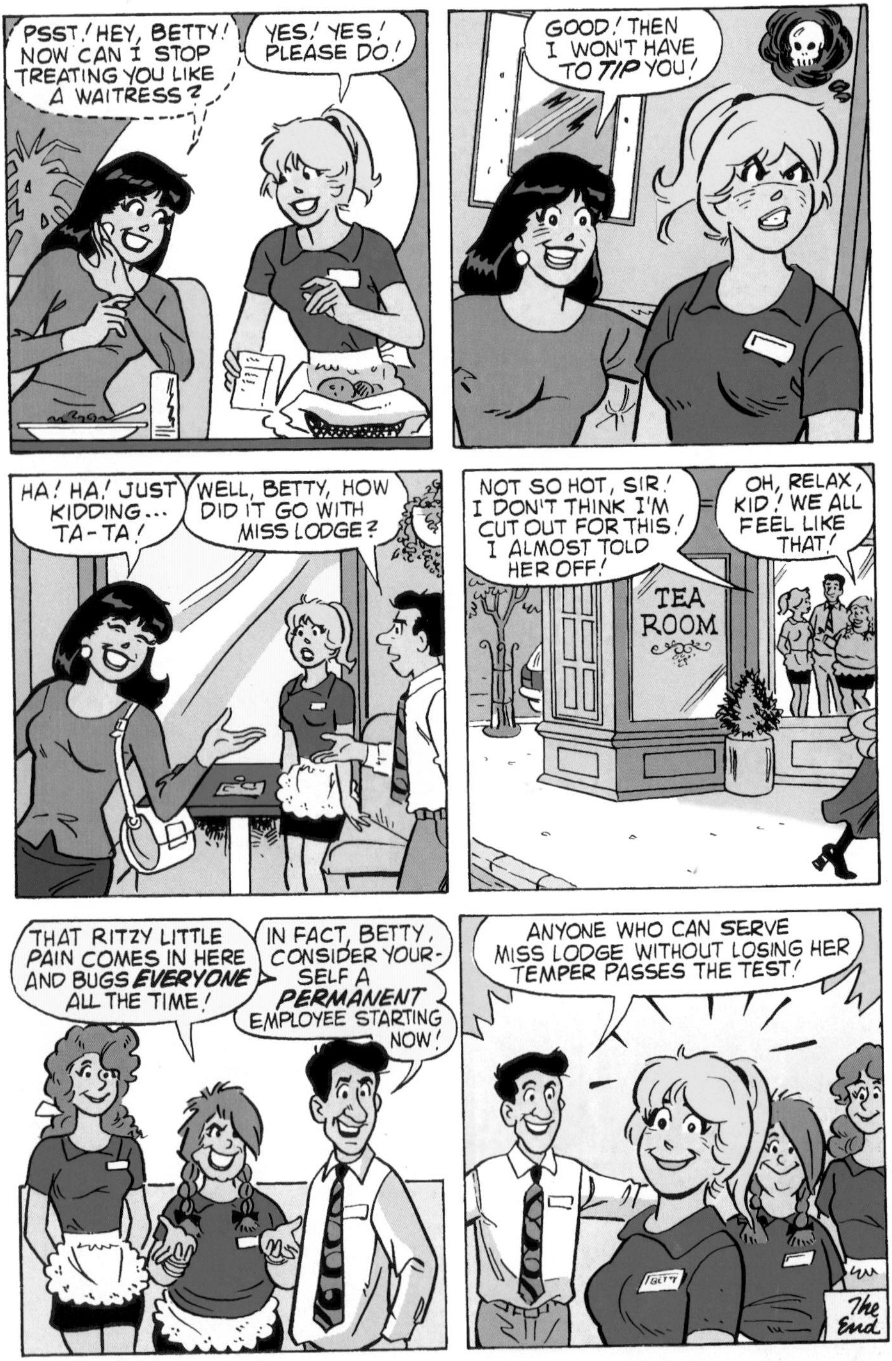
PSST! HEY, BETTY! NOW CAN I STOP TREATING YOU LIKE A WAITRESS?
YES! YES! PLEASE DO!
GOOD! THEN I WON'T HAVE TO TIP YOU!
HA! HA! JUST KIDDING... TA-TA!
WELL, BETTY, HOW DID IT GO WITH MISS LODGE?
NOT SO HOT, SIR! I DON'T THINK I'M CUT OUT FOR THIS! I ALMOST TOLD HER OFF!
OH, RELAX, KID! WE ALL FEEL LIKE THAT!
TEA ROOM
THAT RITZY LITTLE PAIN COMES IN HERE AND BUGS EVERYONE ALL THE TIME!
IN FACT, BETTY, CONSIDER YOURSELF A PERMANENT EMPLOYEE STARTING NOW!
ANYONE WHO CAN SERVE MISS LODGE WITHOUT LOSING HER TEMPER PASSES THE TEST!
BETTY
The End

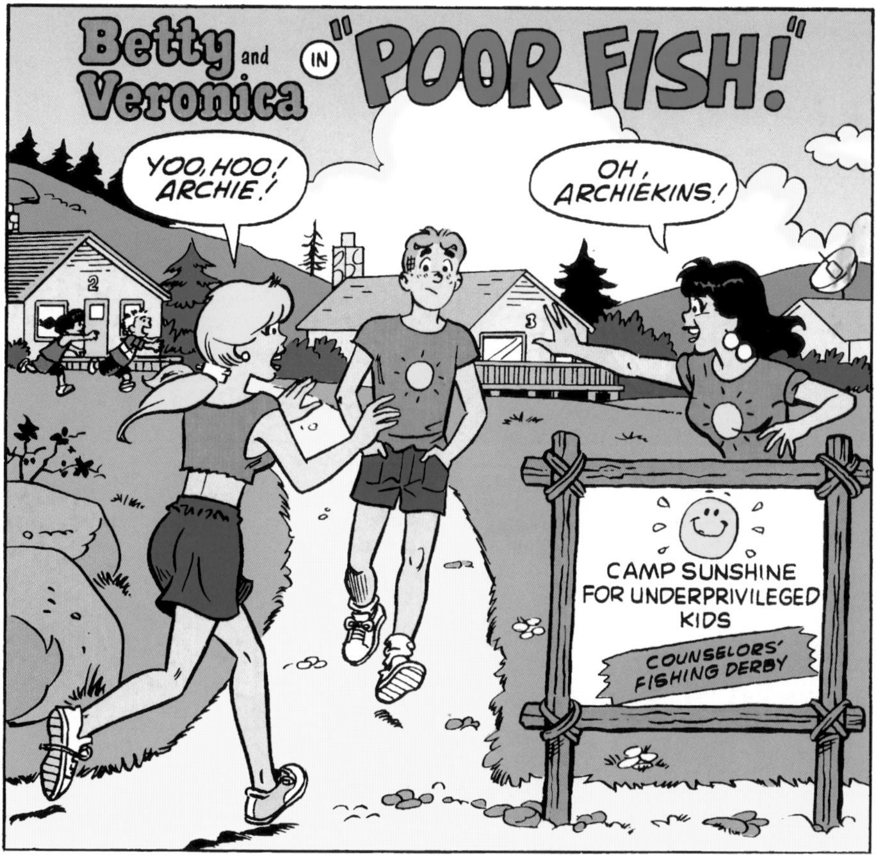
Betty and Veronica IN "POOR FISH!"
YOO, HOO! ARCHIE!
OH, ARCHIEKINS!
CAMP SUNSHINE FOR UNDERPRIVILEGED KIDS
COUNSELORS' FISHING DERBY

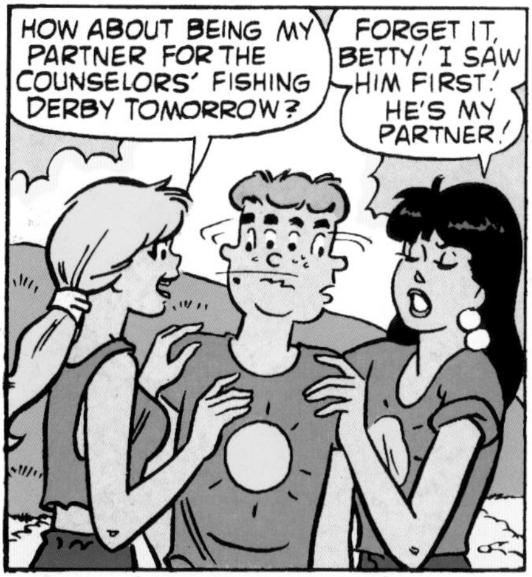
HOW ABOUT BEING MY PARTNER FOR THE COUNSELORS' FISHING DERBY TOMORROW?
FORGET IT, BETTY! I SAW HIM FIRST! HE'S MY PARTNER!

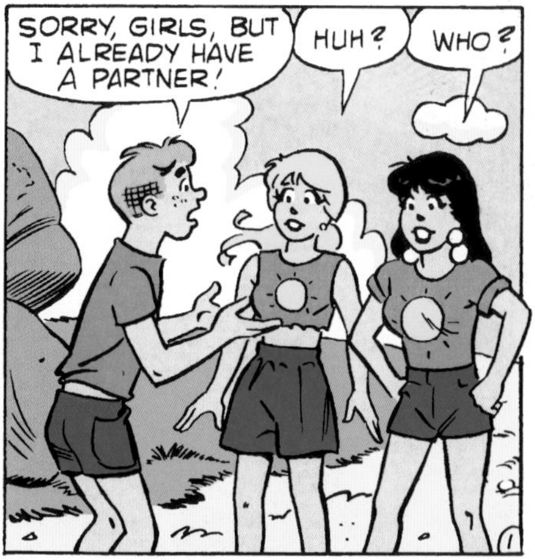
SORRY, GIRLS, BUT I ALREADY HAVE A PARTNER!
HUH?
WHO?

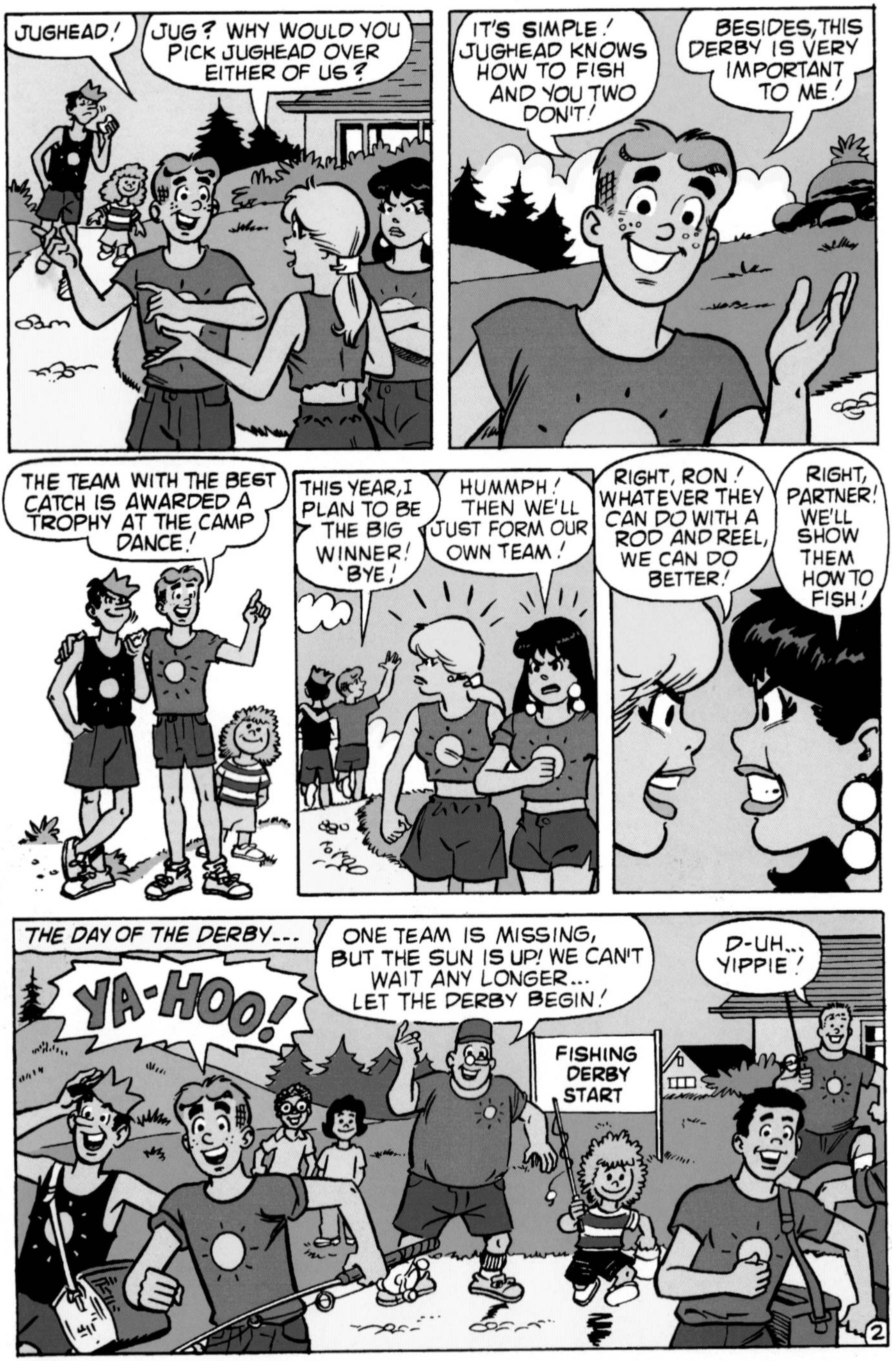
JUGHEAD!
JUG? WHY WOULD YOU PICK JUGHEAD OVER EITHER OF US?
IT'S SIMPLE! JUGHEAD KNOWS HOW TO FISH AND YOU TWO DON'T!
BESIDES, THIS DERBY IS VERY IMPORTANT TO ME!
THE TEAM WITH THE BEST CATCH IS AWARDED A TROPHY AT THE CAMP DANCE!
THIS YEAR, I PLAN TO BE THE BIG WINNER! 'BYE!
HUMMPH! THEN WE'LL JUST FORM OUR OWN TEAM!
RIGHT, RON! WHATEVER THEY CAN DO WITH A ROD AND REEL, WE CAN DO BETTER!
RIGHT, PARTNER! WE'LL SHOW THEM HOW TO FISH!
THE DAY OF THE DERBY...
YA-HOO!
ONE TEAM IS MISSING, BUT THE SUN IS UP! WE CAN'T WAIT ANY LONGER... LET THE DERBY BEGIN!
FISHING DERBY START
D-UH... YIPPIE!
2

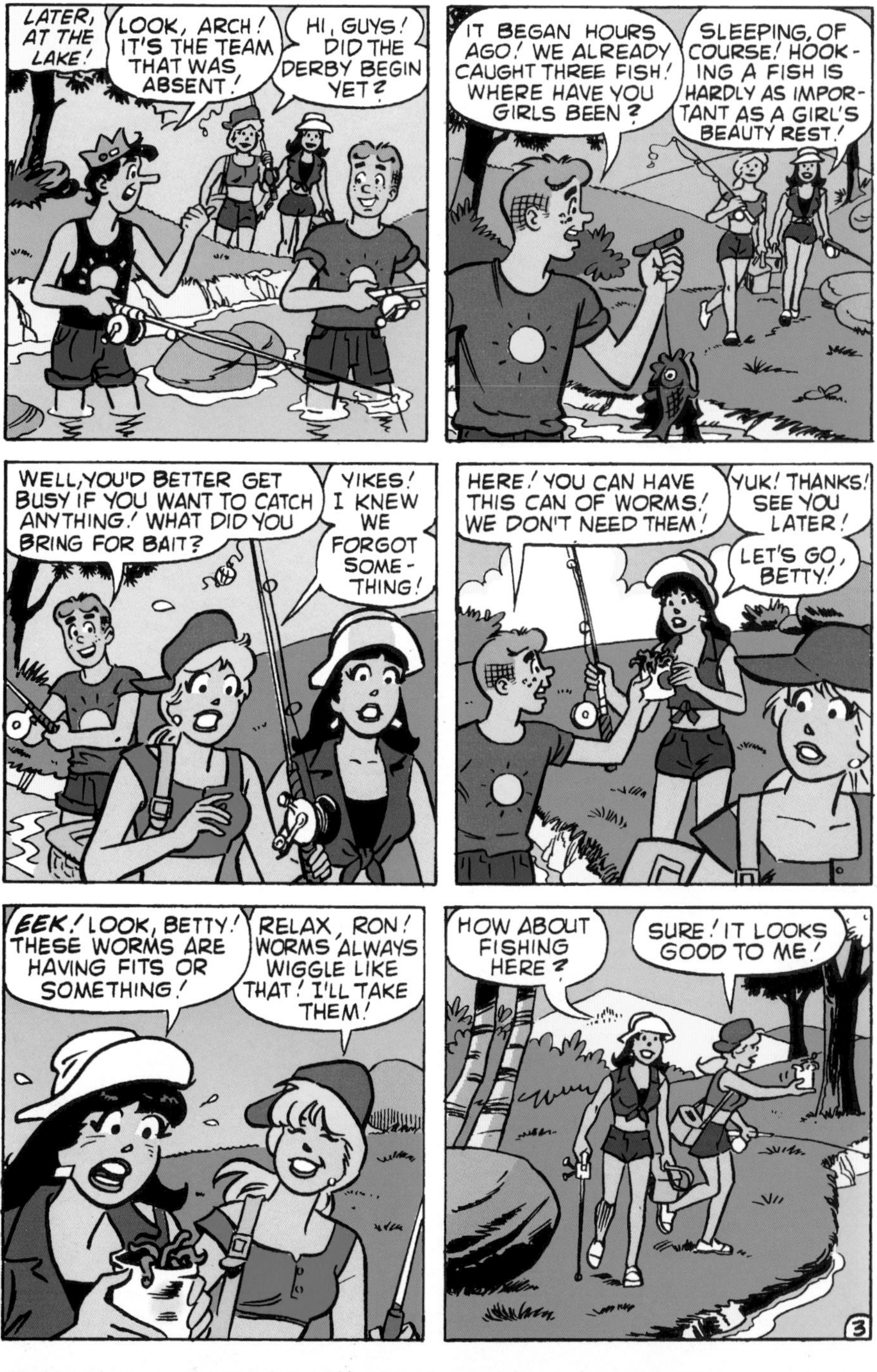
LATER, AT THE LAKE!
LOOK, ARCH! IT'S THE TEAM THAT WAS ABSENT!
HI, GUYS! DID THE DERBY BEGIN YET?
IT BEGAN HOURS AGO! WE ALREADY CAUGHT THREE FISH! WHERE HAVE YOU GIRLS BEEN?
SLEEPING, OF COURSE! HOOKING A FISH IS HARDLY AS IMPORTANT AS A GIRL'S BEAUTY REST!
WELL, YOU'D BETTER GET BUSY IF YOU WANT TO CATCH ANYTHING! WHAT DID YOU BRING FOR BAIT?
YIKES! I KNEW WE FORGOT SOMETHING!
HERE! YOU CAN HAVE THIS CAN OF WORMS! WE DON'T NEED THEM!
YUK! THANKS! SEE YOU LATER!
LET'S GO, BETTY!
EEK! LOOK, BETTY! THESE WORMS ARE HAVING FITS OR SOMETHING!
RELAX, RON! WORMS ALWAYS WIGGLE LIKE THAT! I'LL TAKE THEM!
HOW ABOUT FISHING HERE?
SURE! IT LOOKS GOOD TO ME!
3

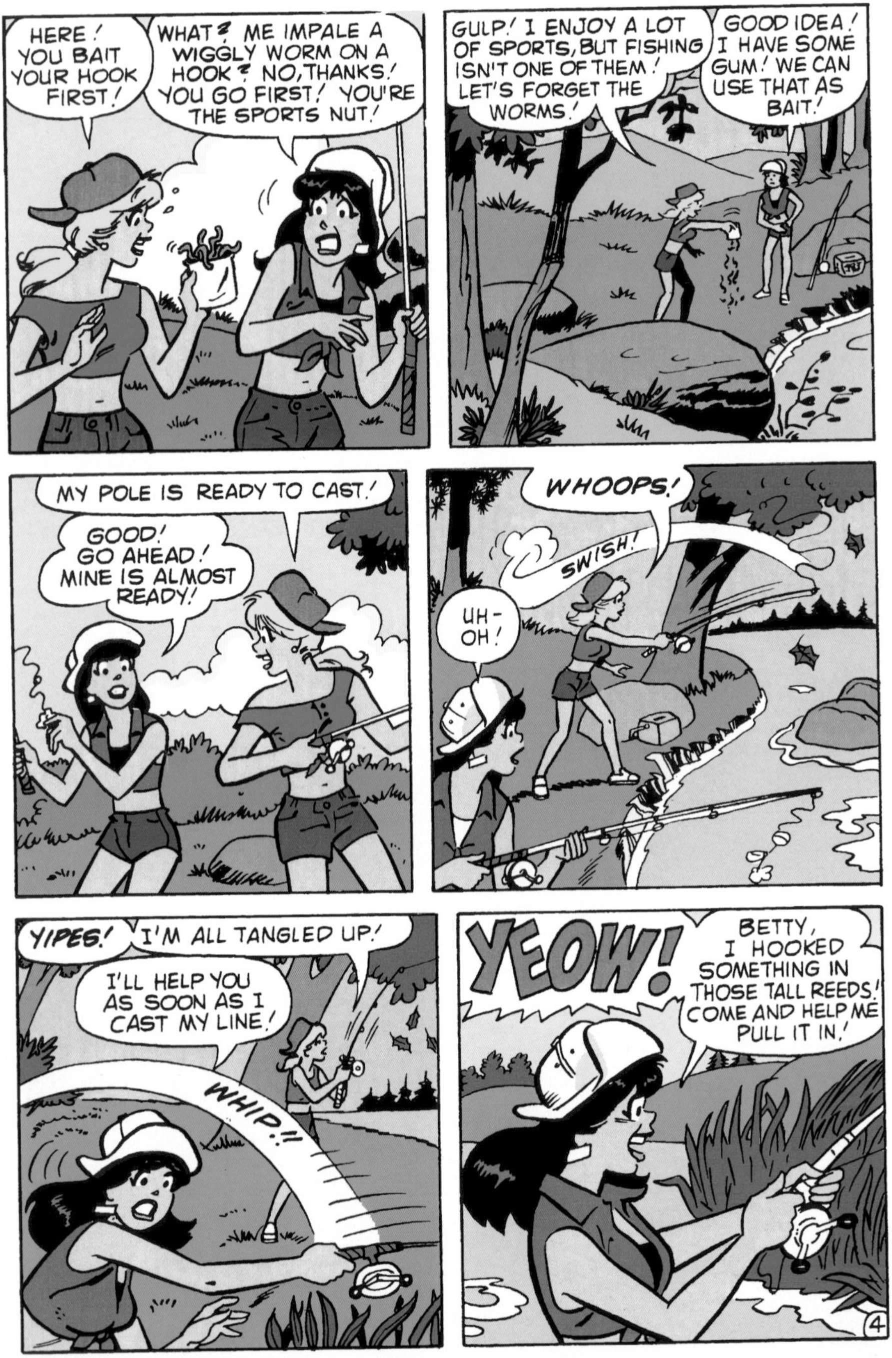
HERE! YOU BAIT YOUR HOOK FIRST!
WHAT? ME IMPALE A WIGGLY WORM ON A HOOK? NO, THANKS! YOU GO FIRST! YOU'RE THE SPORTS NUT!
GULP! I ENJOY A LOT OF SPORTS, BUT FISHING ISN'T ONE OF THEM! LET'S FORGET THE WORMS!
GOOD IDEA! I HAVE SOME GUM! WE CAN USE THAT AS BAIT!
MY POLE IS READY TO CAST!
GOOD! GO AHEAD! MINE IS ALMOST READY!
WHOOPS!
SWISH!
UH-OH!
YIPES!
I'M ALL TANGLED UP!
I'LL HELP YOU AS SOON AS I CAST MY LINE!
WHIP!!
YEOW!
BETTY, I HOOKED SOMETHING IN THOSE TALL REEDS! COME AND HELP ME PULL IT IN!
4

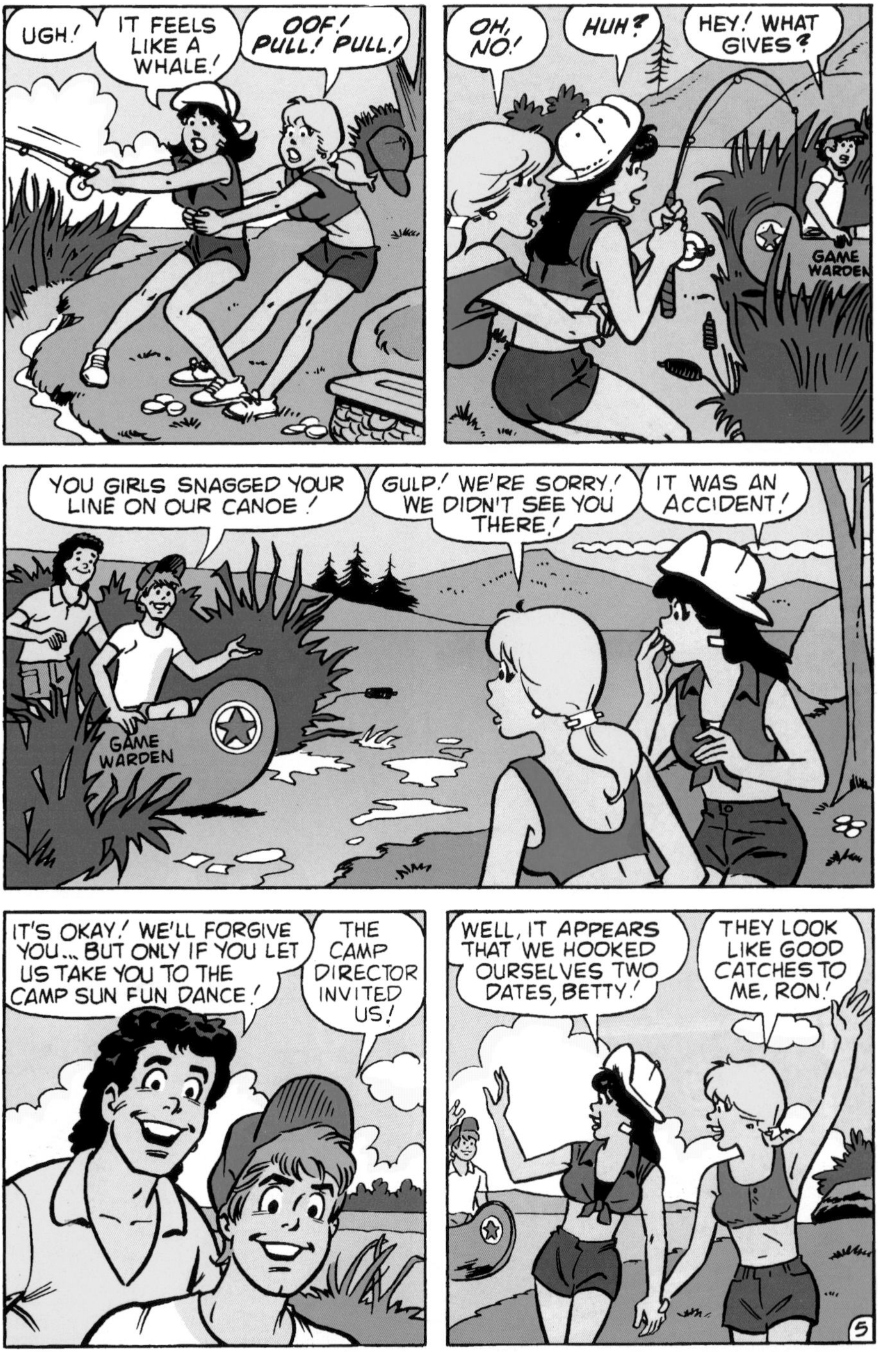
UGH!
IT FEELS LIKE A WHALE!
OOF! PULL! PULL!
OH, NO!
HUH?
HEY! WHAT GIVES?
GAME WARDEN
YOU GIRLS SNAGGED YOUR LINE ON OUR CANOE!
GULP! WE'RE SORRY! WE DIDN'T SEE YOU THERE!
IT WAS AN ACCIDENT!
GAME WARDEN
IT'S OKAY! WE'LL FORGIVE YOU... BUT ONLY IF YOU LET US TAKE YOU TO THE CAMP SUN FUN DANCE!
THE CAMP DIRECTOR INVITED US!
WELL, IT APPEARS THAT WE HOOKED OURSELVES TWO DATES, BETTY!
THEY LOOK LIKE GOOD CATCHES TO ME, RON!
5

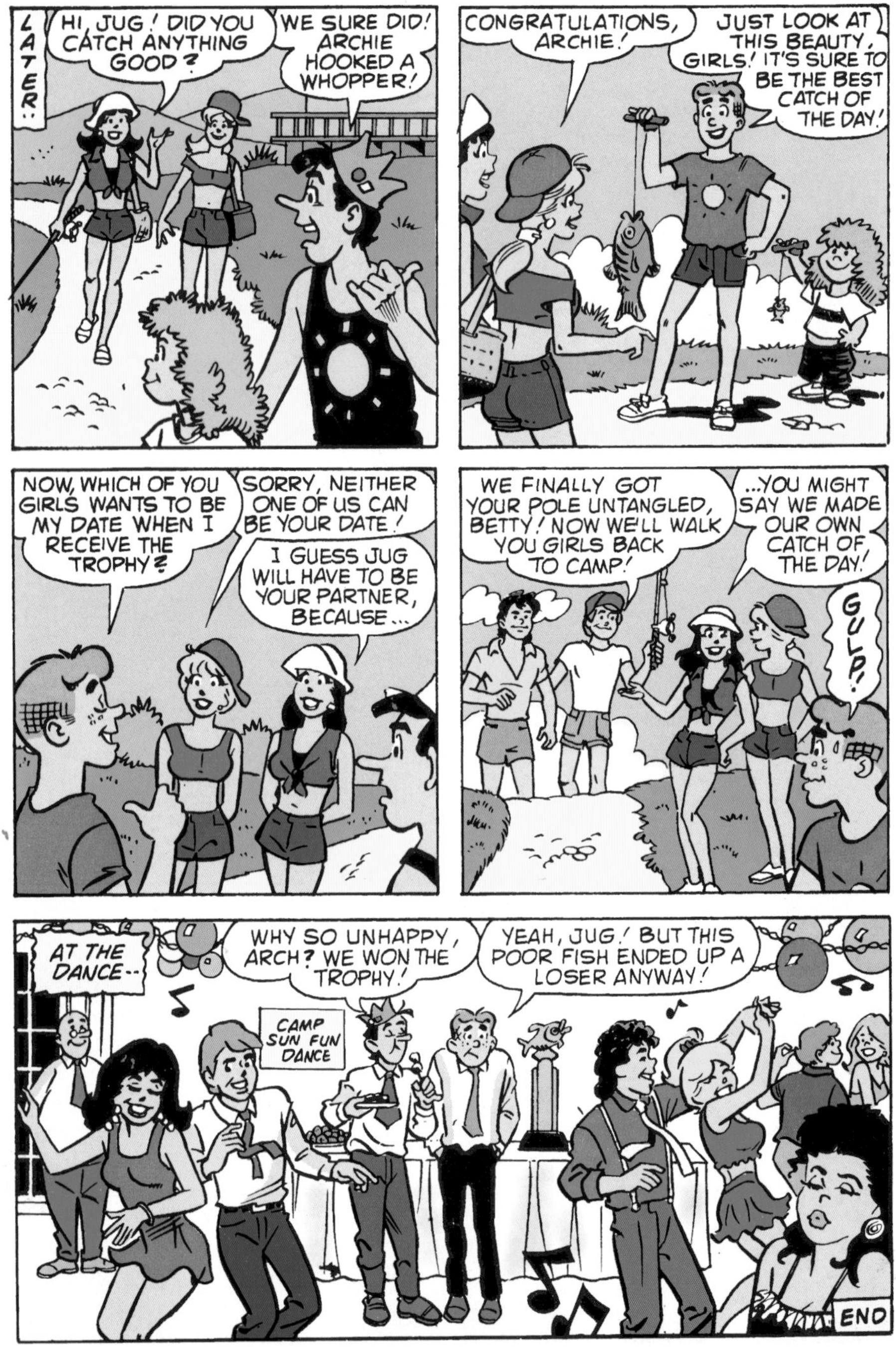
LATER:
HI, JUG! DID YOU CATCH ANYTHING GOOD?
WE SURE DID! ARCHIE HOOKED A WHOPPER!
CONGRATULATIONS, ARCHIE!
JUST LOOK AT THIS BEAUTY, GIRLS! IT'S SURE TO BE THE BEST CATCH OF THE DAY!
NOW, WHICH OF YOU GIRLS WANTS TO BE MY DATE WHEN I RECEIVE THE TROPHY?
SORRY, NEITHER ONE OF US CAN BE YOUR DATE!
I GUESS JUG WILL HAVE TO BE YOUR PARTNER, BECAUSE...
WE FINALLY GOT YOUR POLE UNTANGLED, BETTY! NOW WE'LL WALK YOU GIRLS BACK TO CAMP!
...YOU MIGHT SAY WE MADE OUR OWN CATCH OF THE DAY!
GULP!
AT THE DANCE--
WHY SO UNHAPPY, ARCH? WE WON THE TROPHY!
YEAH, JUG! BUT THIS POOR FISH ENDED UP A LOSER ANYWAY!
CAMP SUN FUN DANCE
END

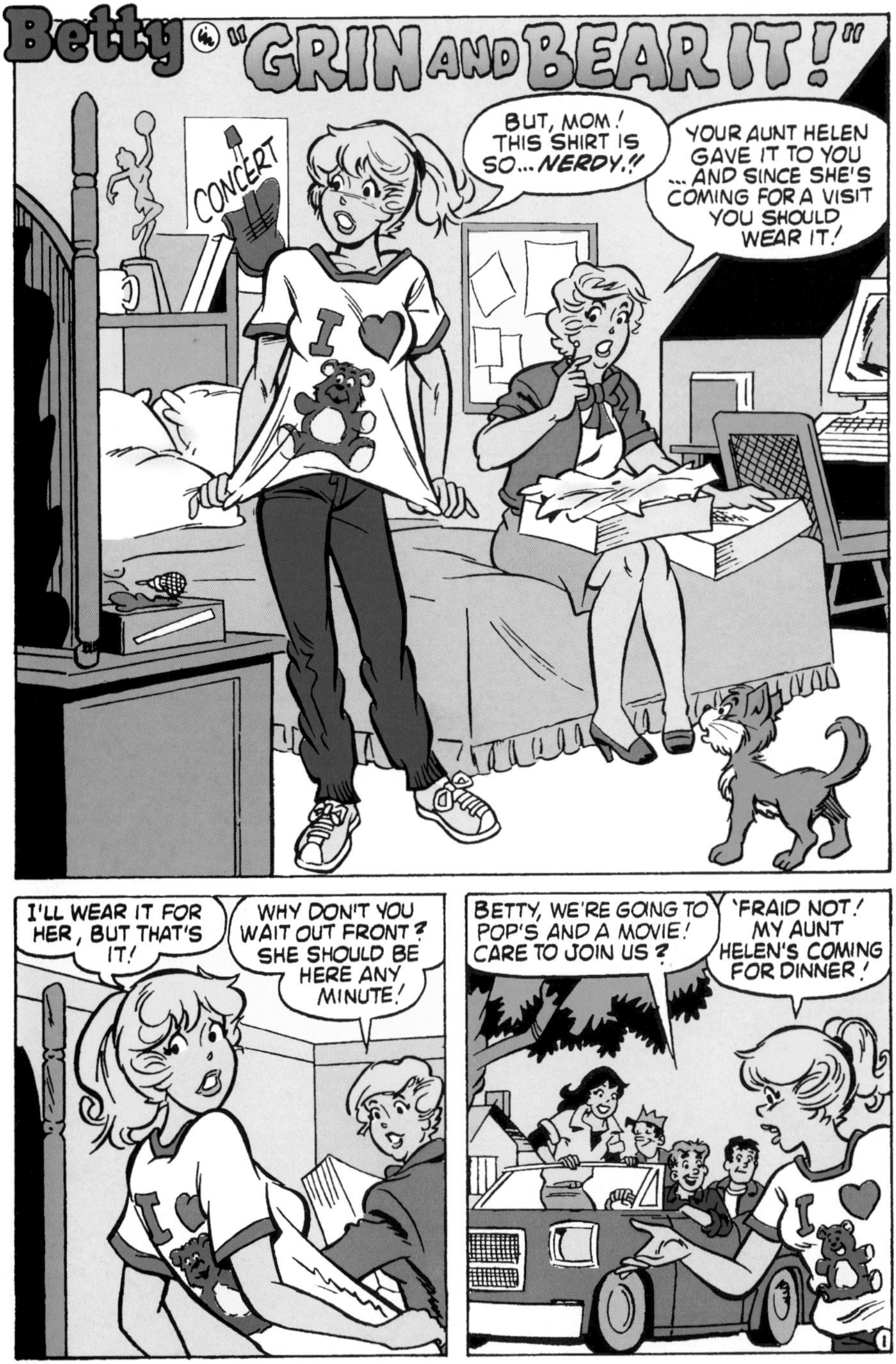
Betty in "GRIN AND BEAR IT!"
CONCERT
BUT, MOM! THIS SHIRT IS SO...NERDY.!!
YOUR AUNT HELEN GAVE IT TO YOU ...AND SINCE SHE'S COMING FOR A VISIT YOU SHOULD WEAR IT!
I'LL WEAR IT FOR HER, BUT THAT'S IT!
WHY DON'T YOU WAIT OUT FRONT? SHE SHOULD BE HERE ANY MINUTE!
BETTY, WE'RE GOING TO POP'S AND A MOVIE! CARE TO JOIN US?
'FRAID NOT! MY AUNT HELEN'S COMING FOR DINNER!
1

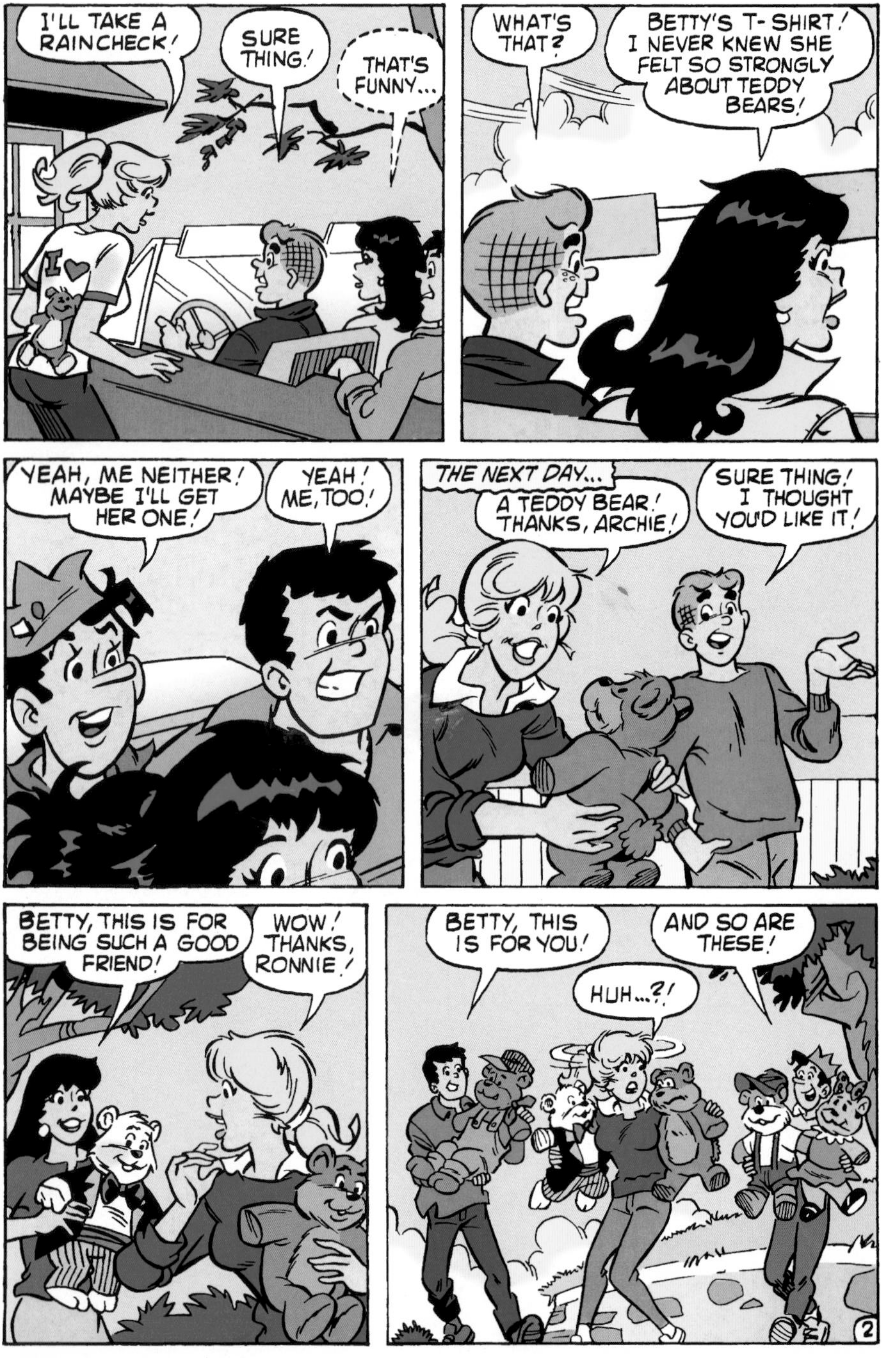
I'LL TAKE A RAINCHECK!
SURE THING!
THAT'S FUNNY...
WHAT'S THAT?
BETTY'S T-SHIRT! I NEVER KNEW SHE FELT SO STRONGLY ABOUT TEDDY BEARS!
YEAH, ME NEITHER! MAYBE I'LL GET HER ONE!
YEAH! ME, TOO!
THE NEXT DAY...
A TEDDY BEAR! THANKS, ARCHIE!
SURE THING! I THOUGHT YOU'D LIKE IT!
BETTY, THIS IS FOR BEING SUCH A GOOD FRIEND!
WOW! THANKS, RONNIE!
BETTY, THIS IS FOR YOU!
AND SO ARE THESE!
HUH...?!
2

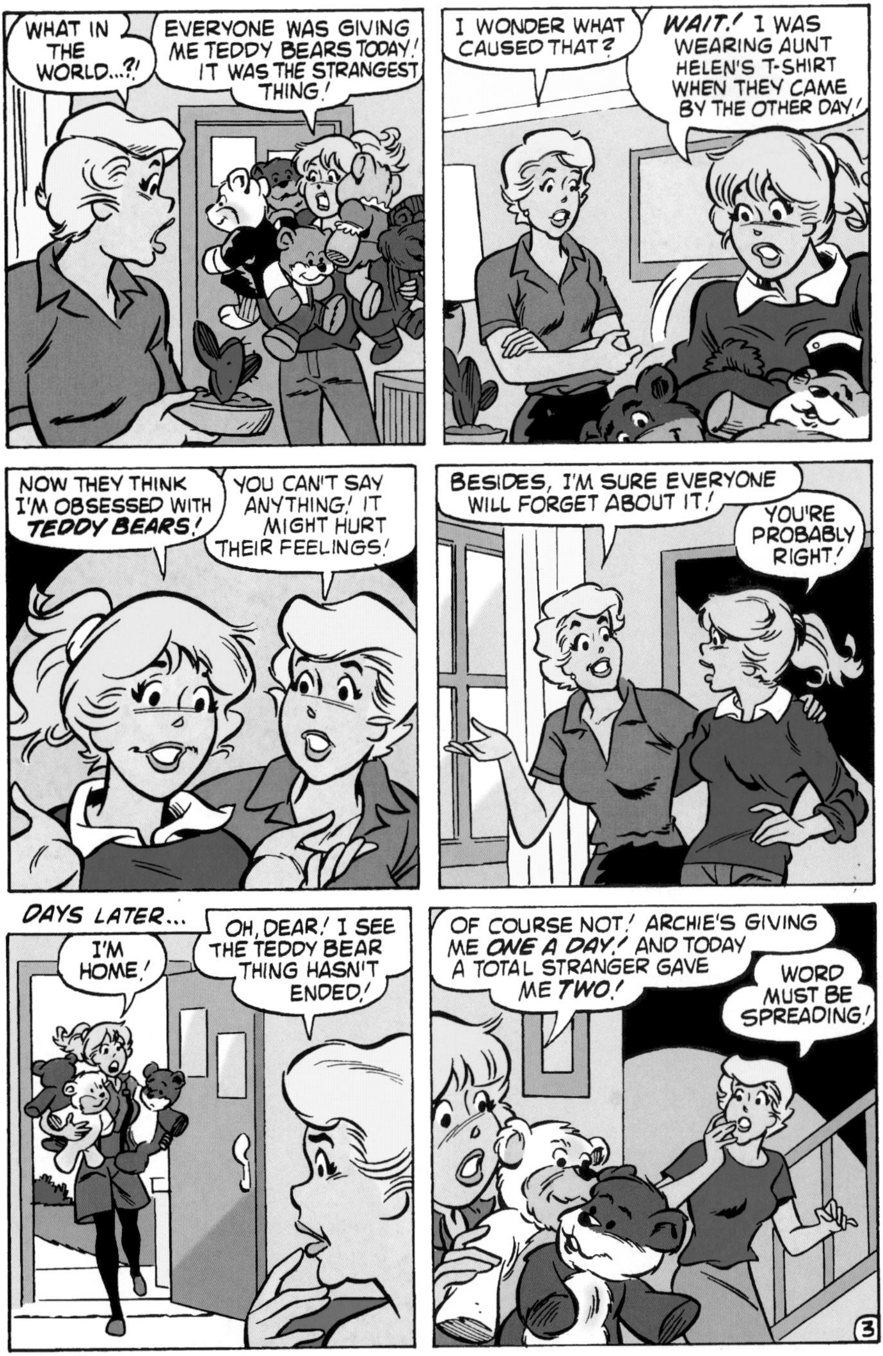
WHAT IN THE WORLD...?!
EVERYONE WAS GIVING ME TEDDY BEARS TODAY! IT WAS THE STRANGEST THING!
I WONDER WHAT CAUSED THAT?
WAIT! I WAS WEARING AUNT HELEN'S T-SHIRT WHEN THEY CAME BY THE OTHER DAY!
NOW THEY THINK I'M OBSESSED WITH TEDDY BEARS!
YOU CAN'T SAY ANYTHING! IT MIGHT HURT THEIR FEELINGS!
BESIDES, I'M SURE EVERYONE WILL FORGET ABOUT IT!
YOU'RE PROBABLY RIGHT!
DAYS LATER...
I'M HOME!
OH, DEAR! I SEE THE TEDDY BEAR THING HASN'T ENDED!
OF COURSE NOT! ARCHIE'S GIVING ME ONE A DAY! AND TODAY A TOTAL STRANGER GAVE ME TWO!
WORD MUST BE SPREADING!
3

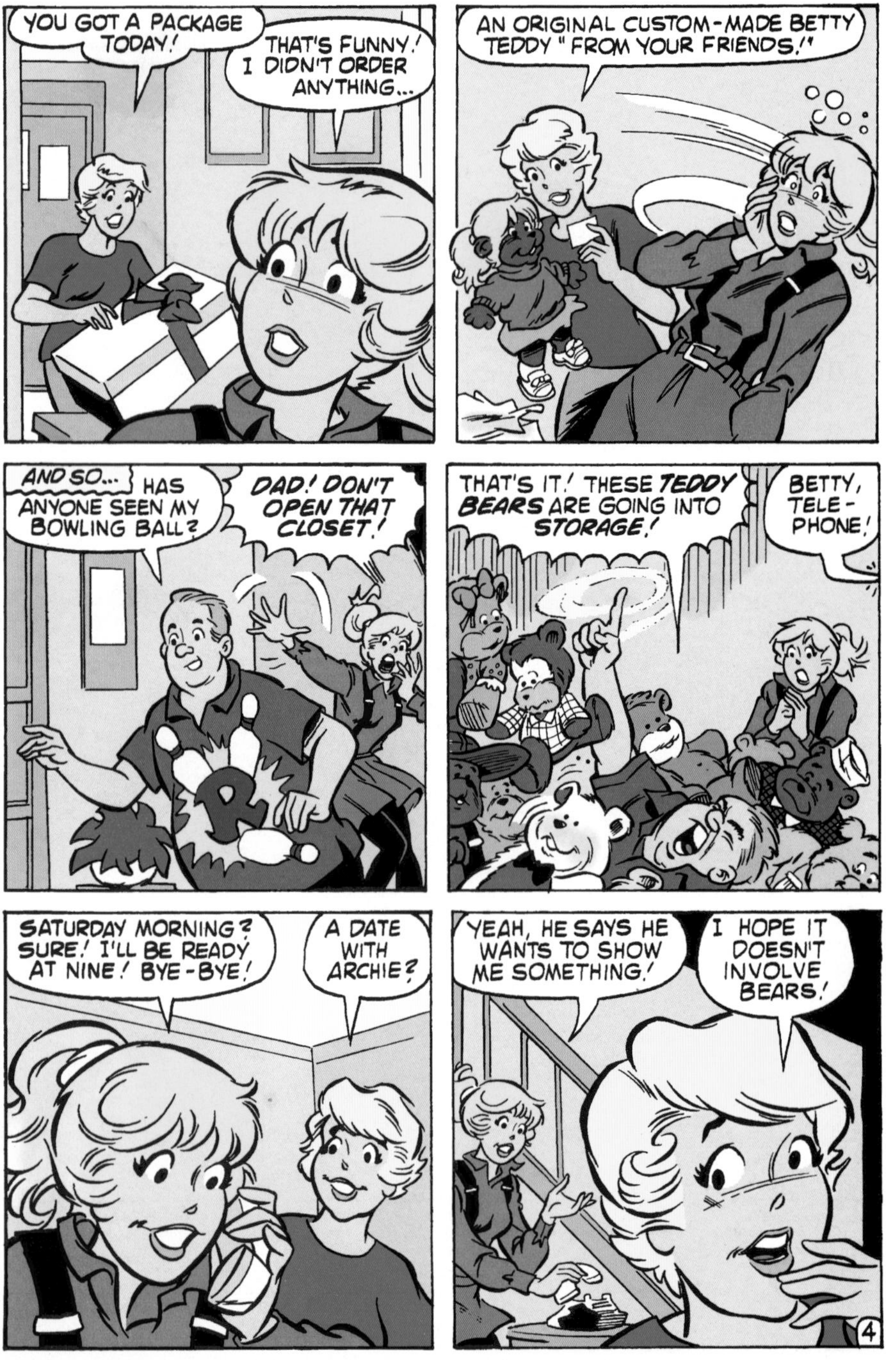

YOU GOT A PACKAGE TODAY!
THAT'S FUNNY! I DIDN'T ORDER ANYTHING...
AN ORIGINAL CUSTOM-MADE BETTY TEDDY " FROM YOUR FRIENDS!"
AND SO...
HAS ANYONE SEEN MY BOWLING BALL?
DAD! DON'T OPEN THAT CLOSET!
THAT'S IT! THESE TEDDY BEARS ARE GOING INTO STORAGE!
BETTY, TELE-PHONE!
SATURDAY MORNING? SURE! I'LL BE READY AT NINE! BYE-BYE!
A DATE WITH ARCHIE?
YEAH, HE SAYS HE WANTS TO SHOW ME SOMETHING!
I HOPE IT DOESN'T INVOLVE BEARS!
4

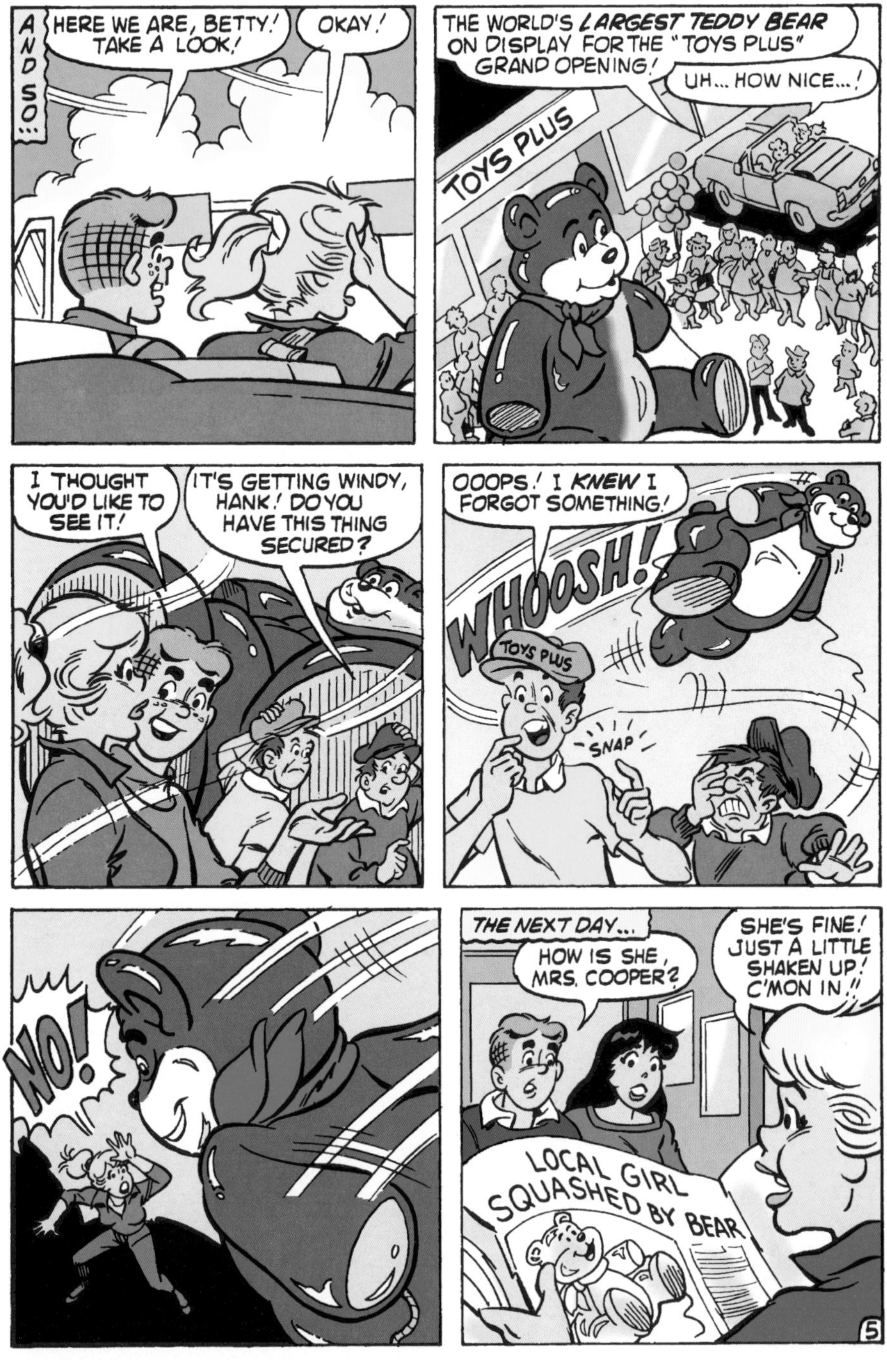
AND SO...
HERE WE ARE, BETTY! TAKE A LOOK!
OKAY!
THE WORLD'S LARGEST TEDDY BEAR ON DISPLAY FOR THE "TOYS PLUS" GRAND OPENING!
UH... HOW NICE...!
TOYS PLUS
I THOUGHT YOU'D LIKE TO SEE IT!
IT'S GETTING WINDY, HANK! DO YOU HAVE THIS THING SECURED?
OOOPS! I KNEW I FORGOT SOMETHING!
WHOOSH!
TOYS PLUS
SNAP
NO!
THE NEXT DAY...
HOW IS SHE, MRS. COOPER?
SHE'S FINE! JUST A LITTLE SHAKEN UP! C'MON IN!!
LOCAL GIRL SQUASHED BY BEAR
5

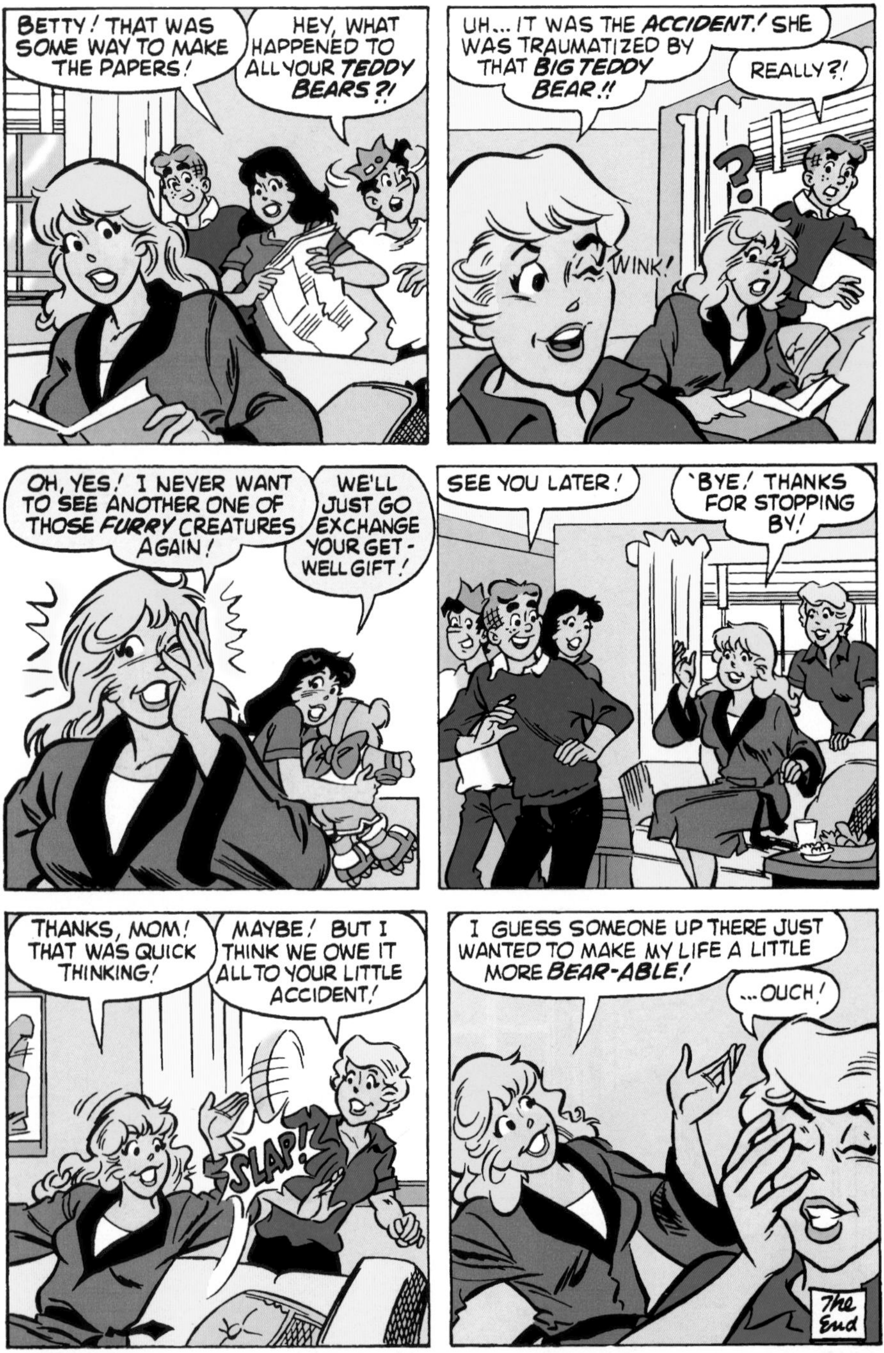
BETTY! THAT WAS SOME WAY TO MAKE THE PAPERS!
HEY, WHAT HAPPENED TO ALL YOUR TEDDY BEARS?!
UH... IT WAS THE ACCIDENT! SHE WAS TRAUMATIZED BY THAT BIG TEDDY BEAR!!
REALLY?!
WINK!
OH, YES! I NEVER WANT TO SEE ANOTHER ONE OF THOSE FURRY CREATURES AGAIN!
WE'LL JUST GO EXCHANGE YOUR GET-WELL GIFT!
SEE YOU LATER!
'BYE! THANKS FOR STOPPING BY!
THANKS, MOM! THAT WAS QUICK THINKING!
MAYBE! BUT I THINK WE OWE IT ALL TO YOUR LITTLE ACCIDENT!
SLAP!?
I GUESS SOMEONE UP THERE JUST WANTED TO MAKE MY LIFE A LITTLE MORE BEAR-ABLE!
...OUCH!
The End